By Andrew Jackson

Text © 2014 Andrew Jackson

Andrew Jackson asserts the moral right to be identified as the author of this work.

Published by Hartlington Press

www.hartlingtonpress.co.uk

A catalogue record for this book is available from the British Library

ISBN: 978-0-9929199-1-7

Typeset in Meridien.

Printed and bound in Great Britain by Hart & Clough Ltd.

To Alex and Matthew

Table Of Contents

Chapter 1

Nobody in his right mind would live in Starlings' Yard.

You had to be mad, bad or broke, that's what the agent had said. He thought I was mad, I could see that. This tall man standing in front of him, with piercing blue eyes, a face submerged beneath a tangle of black hair and beard, wearing a very unfashionable well-worn grey overcoat.

Perhaps he thought I was an unsuccessful criminal on the run, or a tramp wanting to settle down. Or perhaps an artist...

The agent was a fat, pale man who struggled to keep up and kept looking around furtively, all the time trying to persuade me to take somewhere else.

I went up to the first floor to inspect the flat while he stayed in the dark outside the tenement even though the rain was running off his bald head.

It was late November in 1974 and the Edinburgh rain was unrelenting, cascading from cracked gutters onto damp green walls.

He was more relaxed when I pronounced myself happy with the place, and we walked back to his dismal little office to sign the papers. I did so quickly, knowing that if I stopped to think, I would back out and choose somewhere normal, somewhere nice.

I think I felt mildly surprised that he cared. I didn't think letting agents cared very much, and I don't suppose he really did; he just didn't want me to think that he dealt in that sort of property.

My old Anglia took a lot of persuading to drive the short distance to the Yard; it juddered and spat, the car windows were misted up, one windscreen wiper didn't work and the other was making terminal clicking noises. My easel, jammed across the top of plastic bags and cardboard boxes, dug into my neck and had done the whole way up from Yorkshire. I wasn't feeling at my most exuberant (not that 'exuberant' had ever been the word you'd use to describe me). This car load was all I now had in the world.

It was getting dark now, and the streets were full of anonymous dark figures leaning forward against the rain. I drove down the Royal Mile, and parked up in Cant Close, which was as near as I could get a car to my new home. I manhandled the easel out and walked through the narrow archway that led into the Yard.

From above, Edinburgh must look like a vast nebula, with blobs and trails of light reaching out into the darkness. Near the centre, unseen and unknown, was a tiny black hole that broods and sucks darkness into itself. That black hole was Starlings' Yard, a small corner in a great city, passed over by time and the planners, and as sinister as any Doré engraving. The rest of the city was awash with the fads of the seventies: psychedelia, minis and Mary Quant. All that, and the songs of protest that stayed just songs on the lips of the Beautiful People. It was a self-consciously iconic time, and I, as usual, was on the outside, looking in at the whole fabulous party.

Was that perhaps the reason I chose to live here? Maybe. Perversity was not so much a streak in me, more of a wide gash.

I would, ever since I took my first step, always choose the least attractive option and doggedly stick to it; and the more advice was offered, the greater my resolve would grow to stick to the path that I always knew would bring nothing but tears. "I've done it again" I kept thinking as I looked at the dark silhouettes of the buildings, and felt the unease grow until my hands shook. The place seemed blanketed by despair like a fog.

2

I could hear the rumble of traffic, and the screech of a train, and the churn of water along an unseen culvert. But here, these sounds seemed to come from another world. Here, there was nothing. The single cracked street lamp did no more than light up a halo of heavy rain. In the shadows, a shabby man was raking up a smouldering pile of rags; the oily smell filling the Yard. He didn't look up.

As fast as I could, I ferried the bags and boxes from the car into the flat, avoiding any close look at the rooms. Greyness – that's all there was: grey in the room, grey in the Yard, in the city, the sky and in my head. I hate grey.

Once the wet collection of bags had been piled into the centre of the living room, I leant back against the door. It was sticky with other men's grease. It didn't do to think. I hurried off to a bar I'd noticed on the Canongate.

To tell the truth, I'd forgotten just how bad I felt. Twenty-eight, and alone, with a soggy pile of belongings in the worst slum in Edinburgh; and a past that I needed to run away from. Yet I'd chosen it all myself. I had chosen every step of the path. The little boy in the red hat excepted, of course. Every step had been a step down a relentless spiral, always that built-in perversity.

When there was a natural, obvious choice, I had to be different. I had to swim against the current. It amounted to something like a phobia of being ordinary; except that instead of being a man apart, I had become somehow a man non-existent, overlooked by the rest of the world.

It was a great start.

Lights from 'The Three Sisters' spilled out across the street like a beacon. I needed a crowd. Instead, the pub was empty, except for two elderly wispy-headed women sitting on the torn leatherette bench. One of them had removed her teeth and placed them on the table in front of her. They took on a life of their own, as though they were about to join in their

3

disjointed conversation. The thin barman stared into space as he poured my beer. I drank it, and then another, then took my third to a table at the other end of the room from the two women. This didn't deter them.

"No' seen you in here before, love."

The greyer of the two spoke loudly across the room. The barman switched on some music, as if to discourage any conversation in his shrine to despair.

"Night in the city looks pretty to me

Night in the city looks fine."

Her friend made a stab at irony, and wheezed at her cigarette.

"He must have got lost."

"Wet out there, isn't it?"

"He looks like a drowned rat."

The one in the dark green mac had a habit of talking to people in the third person.

"Not the best of days," I tried to smile.

"What's he say?"

"He said, 'Not the best of days'."

"What's that supposed to mean?"

"It's wet."

"That's right."

Silence. Merciful silence. I would finish this pint and move on. But the grey one got up to order another two schooners of sherry, and sat down beside me. Silence. Dreadful silence. Then:

"Whit you dain' here?"

I tried to shrug the question aside. "Having a pint."

"Whit's wrang?"

"Why should there be anything wrong?"

4

"No-one comes roond here if everything's all right."

She turned and shouted across to her friend. The barman turned up the music a little more.

"No-one comes here if things is all right, I said. Isn't that right, Hamish?"

The barman gave no sign of having heard this remark, and just kept wiping glasses with a stained towel. Her friend picked up her teeth, shuffled across to the bar to pick up her sherry, and sat down with us. There was a smell of lily of the valley and broken bladders.

"Trust me, I'm an expert at knowing when thing's ar'nae right. Isn't that right, Winnie?"

"Yer should be by now."

"Nothing's ever been right for me, an' now I got cancer and I'm gain' to dee."

"Don't say that, Bess."

"It's true, though. I got cancer on ma lungs and I'm dee-in'."

"I just don't like to hear you sayin' it, dear. It's no' nice."

"I'm sorry," I said.

"So I ken hard luck when I see it. And I'm looking at it now."

"You could say that."

"I am sayin' that."

"Oh?" I wanted to escape these two.

"Well look at you. Don't you think, Winnie?"

"Wi' all that hair everywhere. He looks like a tramp."

"Oh?"

"Wull ye listen to him? Dinna just say 'Oh' all the time. Am I right?"

Her voice had an edge to it, an anger, almost.

"I suppose so," I said, and walked out. In the next pub, nobody spoke to me and I was glad.

I woke the next morning, fully dressed and in my sleeping bag. I watched a small line of woodlice march across the mattress, a few inches from my face. They paused for a moment, almost as if they were looking in awe at this giant maggot that had usurped their mattress, and then crawled out of vision. The moment hung in the air; I didn't want to move. Me. Here. Now. And no idea of the future.

In a rush I faced the shock of the cold air, fed the meter, and switched on the fire. Two hours later, I'd fed myself, unpacked, and rearranged the miserable sticks of furniture into a semblance of home. I felt better.

It wasn't large, the flat. A narrow hallway, covered in grubby cream glossed anaglypta and brown cracked linoleum, led onto the sitting room which was a reasonable size. In an attempt by some former tenant desperate to cheer the place up it was painted in a tired orange on two walls with a very contradictory yellow on the other two. A doorway with no door led to a small kitchen with a few cupboards, a cracked porcelain sink and a small electric cooker that was caked in black grease. For reasons unknown, the doorway from the hall into the bedroom had been crudely blocked off. Now, the bedroom opened directly into the sitting room, and was painted in the same orange, with the yellow daubed over in migrainous zigzags.

By the end of the week, and a lot of coins fed into the meter for heat, the damp patches on the walls had retreated, and I'd scrubbed as much grease off everything that I could. I decorated the place, trying to cover over the orange and yellow with white paint which, even after four coats, still didn't obliterate them. I picked up some cheap second hand bits of furniture, placed my Lucian Freud and Robert Lenkiewicz prints around the place and established my studio in the sitting room.

I began to get familiar with my surroundings.

The Yard was entered through a narrow archway from Cant Close, which ran at right angles to the Canongate, part of the Royal Mile. Worn, rusty iron pins fixed inside the arch which must have supported gates at one time.

The shabby buildings were arranged around in as random a manner as you could imagine. My flat was on the first floor of the building to the left of the archway. To the right, a similar building stood but some four storeys high as opposed to my three. The other buildings were L-shaped, and abutted onto these. At the far end, between those, a low stone wall supported rusty railings, and an inexplicable stream ran on the other side, emerging from, and disappearing into, a broken stone culvert.

The Yard itself was a mix of gravel and dirt and oily puddles with, here and there, patches of cobbles showing through. It smelt of cinders and rotting cabbages. In the centre was a large square raised stone platform, some two feet high; too large for a mounting block and too small to have been the remains of a dwelling. A filled-in well, perhaps? It was covered in broken stone flags and some not-quite-defeated tufts of brown grass.

More than that, I'd got on nodding acquaintance with a few neighbours in the Yard. The flat above me was empty, except for the rats I could hear scampering across my ceiling at night. Below me lived Sadie, a blousy bleached blonde with large breasts which she displayed to their best advantage, and which wobbled alarmingly when she coughed on her cigarettes. She was probably about thirty, but looked older. She was friendly enough, though.

"I'm just downstairs, lover. Anything you want, you just ask, know what I mean?" and she thrust her breasts forward to make sure I knew what she meant.

The man I'd first seen tending his pile of smouldering rags emerged every evening from the house opposite and repeated the ritual, staring mutely into space even when I smiled at him.

Then there was a young couple, who regularly walked out with a pram. They lived two doors away, on a ground floor flat, and seemed like ghosts from the forties. They both looked very young. He was sharp-nosed and pale with hair parted in the middle and plastered down, wearing a worn-down suit that gave him the air of a Dickensian bank clerk or a Jehovah's Witness. The girl wore a long and demure dress, neat and scrubbed.

They looked out of place in this grimy, scruffy place; but each morning, when they passed, I'd smile and they'd incline their heads and smile back like a pair of robots and say "Good morning." Then, look away and carry on pushing the pram out of the Yard and down the Mile towards Holyrood. I'd watch them; he looking fixedly to the front, she with her gaze always riveted on the pram, and no word spoken.

Then there was the ponytail man, with an Afghan coat, who lived below them, on the ground floor. He was forty-five, fifty perhaps, with a crooked nose and a scarred, stubbled face that said, 'don't meddle!' His hair was long and unkempt, like mine, but a deep chestnut colour, which made him look like some Highland warrior.

Most of the time he'd be alone, sometimes he'd be with the hippy-looking girl. I met him after I'd been there a few days. I'd wandered over to the far side of the Yard, where, below a stone parapet, the turbulent water flowed and muttered in the dark gash below. I leant on the wall, staring at the water, trying to conjure up the idea for a new painting. The current one in progress, Orion, was a non-starter: I'd been smearing layer upon layer of paint on a canvas and the whole thing had lost its way completely. He came over to the railings and stood some feet away.

"Fucking spooky," he said, gazing at the water.

"Aye," I answered, not taking my eyes off the water either (It was a Yorkshire Aye rather than the Scottish). He turned to look at me.

"Settling in OK?"

I looked at him, and saw a terrible pair of grey eyes weighing me up. Despite his smile, there was a ruthlessness in his look that made me feel naked.

"Takes a bit of getting used to. It's OK."

"Here for long?" The casual questions seemed to probe and pierce.

"Don't know. 'Til I'm rich and famous."

"What do you do, then?"

"I'm an artist."

"Is that right?"

The way he looked at me didn't change, but I felt as though that was the most ridiculous thing anyone could have said. Here to wallow amongst the low life for a bit, get a bit of inspiration from us miserable sods. Make some profound commentary on The Human Condition, eh? That's what his look said, except it didn't. His look said nothing.

"What about you?" I asked.

"Oh, this and that," he said, and turned to face the water again.

"I'm Mark," I said, "Mark Kemp."

"I'll see you around, Mark," he said, and walked away into his house.

After that, he seemed quite friendly. He'd nod when he passed, and when he was with the hippy girl, they'd both smile and pass on; she leaning on him, or skittering beside him like a wasp at a picnic. He didn't seem to notice she was there. I noticed her, though.

The weeks passed. I watched the coming of December and the inhabitants of the Yard come and go. Hunched and silent in the day, most of them became raucous or aggressive, reeling drunkenly as they returned from the bars at night.

I worked on the sketches for Darkscape: a series I'd planned ages ago but forgotten until I came here. It was meant to contrast the lights of the city and the stars overhead against its dark and sordid details when you got close to. This seemed the perfect place for it, but it wasn't happening; I stared for hours from my window feeling trapped and people below would look up and see my pale face framed in the dark window and look away again.

I was deeply unfashionable as a painter. My choice, again. The whole art scene was revelling in the psychedelia and dazzle of op- or pop-art, and making psuedomystic and unbelievably vacuous pronouncements. Every college graduate was coming up with another –ism, with pages of complete rubbish to substantiate a talent that should have stuck to potato prints.

I had a talent. A well-trained talent that could produce great paintings, but I was turned away from galleries and dealers. Too intense, they said, in a time when superficiality was the new profundity. Too obsessed, they said, with technique and detail and draughtsmanship, when a splatter of paint was meant to convey any idea you wanted. Don't chain yourself to form, they said. Figurative stuff doesn't cut it, they said.

Ellie, now, she could bend with the breeze. She had a great talent, too, that was the bloody tragedy, but she was happy to chatter on about Morphic Chromaticism or whatever, and churn out stuff that the market wanted, the cynical sold-out bitch! And they fell for it, with the consequence that she sold her stuff and I didn't.

She got articles written about her but they never mentioned me, so I became ruder and more sarcastic than ever, watching the poncy critics and dealers drool over her and her stuff. All the time I glowered in the background, and grew my beard and hair long and was horrid to her. It was inevitable I'd drive her away, and I should have seen it coming – her and that smarmy bastard – but I didn't, so it hurt like Hell and it hadn't stopped hurting since. Bitch.

The bitterness was getting in the way. Weeks passed and I hadn't come up with anything, well, anything that possessed the faintest spark of excitement. On the better days, when the sun cut through the cold, I'd go and sit on the stone block that stood at the centre of the Yard and sketch some of the details of the buildings. Those that walked past gave me suspicious sideways glances or would try and see what I was doing over my shoulder then turn away quickly when I spoke to them. Then I met O'Hanlon.

I'd seen him a few times. He was stick thin, about sixty perhaps, with the gaunt air of a faded academic. He moved awkwardly with a stooped staccato lope. He had long lank black hair, with a startling streak of white hair which ran from the vertex of his scalp down to his left temple. It fell about his shoulders, giving him the air of an eighteenth century anatomist, an effect not diminished by his invariable practice of wearing unrelieved black. One of his eyes was green, the other brown, almost black, and across his right cheek was a long ugly scar. He was straight out of a Victorian Penny Dreadful, but he spoke easily, with a cultured soft Irish voice that was surprisingly deep.

"Good morning, neighbour. I thought it was high time I introduced myself. My name's O'Hanlon."

I stood up and shook his hand. "Mark Kemp," I said.

"I must apologise for not making myself known earlier, but you know how it is. People keep themselves to themselves around here. But I couldn't help noticing you out sketching in all weathers. I take it you're an enthusiastic amateur?"

"Unenthusiastic professional, actually."

"Oh, I do apologise – I'm so sorry."

"No need to. Look, I was about to pack it in: my hands are getting too cold. I was going up for a coffee. Do you want one?"

It was most unlike me, I thought, as he loped up the stairs behind me. I'm not given to acting all hearty to strangers, but I suppose there's a limit to how much solitude you can stand. Anyway, he intrigued me.

He craned his neck, looking around the flat before stooping like a heron over a few of the pictures. I was pleased that he seemed genuinely enthusiastic, more so because he seemed to know what he was talking about, and I really was grateful to talk to someone at last. I told him so, and he grabbed my wrist and pulled me over to the window, spilling his coffee as he went.

"Look. Look out there. There's the Devil of it. All of us here, we come and we go and there's never a word spoken. There's too much you can't say. Look at Grace there. That old biddy beats the hell out of that carpet every day, and I know just why she beats it like that, and I pass her by and she says 'Hello Father' and I say 'Hello Grace, and how are you?' But she never answers, just grinds her false teeth and beats the owd carpet again and again."

"You're a priest, then?"

"Retired. Put out to pasture a bit early. A bit of stress. Nothing at all. But now I spend my time reading and with my bible group and doing my little bit of historical research."

"Oh?"

"Just on the local history side of things. All very amateur-ish, really."

"But you know everybody in the Yard?"

"Oh yes. We may not say a lot, but we see plenty and people think they've got secrets but mostly everyone knows, and nobody says anything. I don't think anybody cares. All too wrapped up in themselves. You'll have felt it." He put his cup down.

"What?"

"The terrible atmosphere of this place. Dear God, listen to me. Three in the afternoon and I'm a philosopher already. Tell you what, come round to my place tonight and we can have a drink and a gossip, if you like."

"I'd like to."

"Good. Now I've a favour to ask. Do you mind if I take one of your paintings away to study for an hour or two?"

"Sure, but –"

"I won't sell it, I promise!"

"You couldn't. I've tried, believe me."

"This one, I think. I'm very obliged to you. Tonight, then. Number three with the black door and on the ground floor."

And with his skinny fingers clutching my Orion ll, he gangled out of the room.

I watched as he crossed the Yard with it. I also noticed her. She was walking into the Yard, arm in arm with another girl in hippie clothes, laughing. Laughing, that is, until she saw O'Hanlon. Had they been cats I'm sure there would have been an arching of backs and a hissing at each other. As it was, there was a just perceptible pause as they momentarily skirted each other, then moved on. Interesting.

I watched her and her friend sit on the stone block and she looked up at my window. I put my fingertips on the glass and, at the same time, she unconsciously ran her hand over her breast, and then looked away, talking to her friend. From time to time, though, she would look up again. I was still there, staring.

13

I turned to my notebook and began to doodle. She was a beauty, with a Pre-Raphaelite mane of long softly-curled auburn hair that framed a pale face with large eyes and high cheekbones. Quickly, the pencil strokes became stronger, with a sense of purpose, and I knew just what I'd been looking for. A feeling had become a form. I would need her as a model, of course, and I didn't think her boyfriend with the ponytail would be having any of that. No harm in asking. No harm? It had to be her; that look was everything!

I was fired up when I called round to O'Hanlon's that evening. I'd been reluctant to stop the scribbling and planning of what was going to be a big series of canvases, but at the same time I was eager to ask O'Hanlon about her, and find out how I might get her to model. Then I remembered that spark that I'd seen between them. Tread carefully, it said.

O'Hanlon's place was a bit of a shock. I knocked at the door, and, hearing no answer, opened the door and shouted, "Hello?"

"Come in."

His voice came from a room to the right, so I crossed the lino-covered hall and into a warm, dark room, full of cigarette smoke. The only light came from a lamp on a small table between two high backed armchairs where smoke from his cigarette curled up from a heavy glass ashtray into the glow. In the darkness beyond I could make out shelves and tables that seemed to be stacked with books and objects. The whole large room in fact seemed to be completely filled apart from this small clearing in the middle. O'Hanlon got up slowly, his face deformed by shadows, accentuating the scar on his cheek. His manner too, seemed to have changed.

"Mark, isn't it?"

"Yes. I'm sorry, I thought you'd –"

"I did, I did, indeed. Come in and sit down. Forgive me, I must have been sunk in a bit of thought, and it doesn't do to think too much, does it! Such men are dangerous, eh? Now, what are you drinking?"

"Do you have any beer?"

"Do you like whisky?"

"Whisky's fine."

He'd had a good head start on the stuff. I felt I'd made a mistake; I wanted to leave. We sat in silence for a few minutes while he watched the tendrils of smoke disappear into darkness. Finally:

"You're a fine painter."

"Thank you. I – "

"You've got technique, and skill. Know the craft of it. I like that painting very much."

"Try telling the dealers that. Technique isn't fashionable anymore."

He leaned forward, slopping a little whisky over his fingers.

"Don't you be guided by that load of monkeys. That's a world gone mad out there – fool's bloody paradise! It's as though we've let everything go to be run by children and idiots. All they see is instant gratification: instant fame, instant knowledge, instant money. Skip read a book: you're an expert. Tell everyone loudly how wonderful you are and you're the toast of the town. Posers and pimps, the lot of them."

His hand was shaking and I was getting uncomfortable, even though it could be me talking. He was angry and the drink was letting it show through. Then the mood evaporated. He talked enthusiastically about my picture, and then art in general. As time went on we rambled a pleasantly winding path around a range of topics; he seemed remarkably well read in many things. Eventually, though, I felt we weren't getting anywhere.

"Thanks for the whisky. I'd better be going, I think."

"No!" It was a command. "A while, please. Have one more. Please."

He poured me another whisky, and for himself, too. He smiled and made an attempt to look relaxed. We sat in silence a while, and I began to make out forms in the surrounding darkness. A broken record deck, a warped picture frame, a plaster statue of the virgin, its head missing. A room full of broken things.

"You've lived here a while?"

"Too long. Twenty years nearly. It's not a good thing: you get sucked down into this place and you can't get out again. Take my tip, do what you have to do in this place and move on quickly. What do you want with living here, anyway?"

"Just some ideas," I said, "I like atmospheres."

"Atmospheres! Now, there's a bloody word! I warn you now: there's a bit too much atmosphere here. Not a good place at all. Dear God, not a good place."

"I imagine it's seen a bit of history."

"It's quite remarkable," he said.

"While the rest of the city's been demolished and rebuilt countless times, they've never bothered with this place. It's been patched and patched again, but the basic fabric of these houses goes back a long way. I've got a load of research written down somewhere."

He waved a hand at the heaps of books and papers in the gloom around us.

"The Yard goes back to before the fourteenth century, at least. Difficult to get beyond that without calling in the archaeologists. Do you know why it's called Starlings' Yard?"

"Not because of the birds?" The sheer din of the starlings had struck me the evening before; they seemed to descend on the Yard like locusts.

"Ah, no! That's what everyone thinks, but if you look at some of the old maps it's marked differently. They used to call it Starvelings' Yard, and that's from the 1700s at least. I'll drop my notebooks round if you're interested."

"Starvelings?"

"Beggars and paupers. In such straits that they were starving. It's been a pretty grim place all along, by the looks of things. Another thing, have you wondered why it's called a yard and not a close or a wynd like all the others round here?"

"I had wondered."

"So did I, it's because these buildings were once little more than a prison. The archway into here was the gates and the poor wretches inside were allowed out once or twice a day to take the outside air in what was basically a prison yard. The better off folk of the town would sometimes take pity or preen their consciences by leaving food outside the gates. Not so long ago, either. Fascinating, fascinating..." he trailed off.

Then he swooped in a way I would find out was characteristic of the man, straight for the throat.

"Why do you hate yourself so much?"

"What?"

"You don't have to live here, you don't have to paint pictures that won't sell, you don't even have to look as maungy as you do. So I say to myself he's not doing it because he has to, so he's doing it because he chooses to, and no one in his right mind would choose your course. So there's a madness in you. We're all bloody mad here, but with you I'd say your insanity was hate. I'm right; I've seen your pictures. I'm also right when I say that hate's turned in on itself, aren't I?"

I tried to deflect his unsettling frankness.

"Takes one to know one, eh?"

"We're talking about you."

Under his lizard stare I told him the lot. I'd only met him that day, but here was I spilling out grudges and hurts like entrails from a half hanged man. I told him about Ellie, about all the twists and turns I'd never told to anybody. I even told him about the little boy in the red hat and cried as I did. I must have had a lot of whisky.

I woke late in the morning with a sore head, a sense of embarrassment and a gap in my memory about getting back. I looked out of the window to see the Yard covered in a thin layer of snow. The girl was there, too, in a purple Afghan coat and a brown and orange hat that must have started life in Tibet. She was by herself, pirouetting like a child, vibrant against the white. I saw O'Hanlon at his window looking at her and drew away quickly.

I dressed in a hurry and went downstairs in to the Yard, but she'd gone. A set of footprints lead away from the trampled patch where she'd been dancing and mingled with the other footprints that ruffled the snow. I became aware that O'Hanlon was still at his window, still staring. I waved at him, but he drew back, and disappeared. I felt the cold seeping through my sweater, but walked over to the railings over the culvert. The stream churned on, the noise louder in the icy air. A splash of colour at the edge of my vision made me turn my head. Purple.

"Hi."

She'd been standing in the shadow of one of the buildings. I had the wishful thought that perhaps she'd been waiting for me. She stayed motionless, her head on one side and a slight smile giving her a questioning look. I stared at her. She had such a beautiful, innocent face, with large eyes and high cheekbones framed by the auburn hair that tumbled round her face and shoulders. Her face was porcelain pale in the snow bright light; her mouth a slash of dark scarlet.

"I saw you dancing."

The words came out unannounced. I cringed inside. Good morning is the standard reply. She still didn't move, nor could I.

"I like to dance." She pushed herself off the wall and was walking, slowly, holding her arms out like a tightrope walker, making every step count.

"I can be Salome...or Mata Hari....or Sheherazade."

She was in front of me now, and I could smell the patchouli oil. I knew I was still staring at her, but her eyes were like magnets. It's rare that you see real beauty. It was my turn to speak, and I couldn't.

"So what sort of pictures do you paint?"

"How do you know I paint?"

"Someone comes here carrying easels and lots of big flat things, then spends his days sketching like crazy? C'mon! You any good?"

"Yes."

"Cool. Do you paint women?"

"Landscapes usually. And buildings."

"Oh."

She gave a little shrug and started to walk away. I let her go, then remembered, and caught up with her.

"I'm Mark."

"I know. Hello, Mark Kemp."

That made my heart leap, or whatever bits leap when you're happy. I asked her what her name was; again she turned and did that slow walk thing.

"I'm Salome...or Mata Hari...or Sheherazade."

"Right."

"Sometimes I'm Cassie. Sometimes I'm not." She touched a mittened hand on my arm, and danced back to her house, singing:

"Girls and boys come out to play,

The moon doth shine as bright as day

Leave your supper and leave your sleep

And come with your playfellows into the street."

I felt something inside I hadn't felt for years, and went to get some sketches down before the feeling evaporated: like so many others before, in that crazy time when I was brim-full of ideas and colours and aware of so many small pathways through my subconscious that I couldn't wait to explore. Feelings that you can't pin down just because they're feelings, and when you try to get hold of them logically, they've vanished, like a dream.

That was before the little boy in the red hat.

I must have worked through most of the night. I woke up in the old arm chair with a small sea of sketches around me on the carpet. I picked a few up and tried to focus on what I'd felt last night. It was there, visible in the morning light, in those sketches. I tried to define 'it', but I couldn't: something vulnerable, but something else, too. Something scary. Cassie held the key to something; a lock that would open a trapdoor in the grimy mess of Starlings' Yard into something beyond.

It wasn't long, of course, before O'Hanlon showed up on the very good pretext of returning my picture, which I'd forgotten to reclaim when I visited him. He said what a pleasant night he'd had and I said I hoped I'd not bored him with my ramblings, he said not at all and that it had been so good to talk as old friends.

"And talking of friends," he said, and I knew why he'd come round, "can I give you a bit of advice? As a friend."

"Go on."

"It's about that girl, Cassie Bowman." He paused awkwardly, but at least I'd found out her second name. "Be very careful, friend, she's not one to get mixed up with."

"Oh, and why's that?"

"Just let it rest there. Don't fall for her ways. I'm telling you this as someone who likes you and would like to see you whole and happy again."

"I only said good morning to her."

"Is that all? Well, that's just fine then. So am I to suppose you stay up all night drawing pictures of everyone you say good morning to? Do you think I'm stupid?"

"What do you mean?"

"I mean that your light was on 'til four o'clock this morning and if all these," he picked up a bundle of the sketches, "aren't of her then I'm blind as well as daft."

"I think these are my private business," I said, probably rather too stiffly, but I didn't like to think of him there last night watching my window, and besides, I was beginning to feel like a schoolboy caught with a girlie magazine. But his anger was welling up, and it broke loose now.

"She's...disturbed. She has misused God's gifts and will come to a bad end. She will hurt you if you continue with her. I do not wish to see you hurt, do you understand? She will lie to you. She will lead you into the darkness, and you will be sucked down into the pit! She is possessed by the Devil himself. And the Devil will destroy her!"

He held up the sheaf of sketches he was holding – my sketches! – and tore them in half, scattering the pieces on the floor as he ranted. Then, silence. He was breathing heavily.

"Why did you do that?" I said, as calmly as I could.

"Sorry," he mumbled, "but please, listen to me. That girl – there's something wrong with her. She's a psychopath, I tell you. It's in her eyes. The things she's said.... I'm just warning

21

you. Just look at your own sketches." He turned and walked out of the room.

What was that about? I wondered, as I retrieved the pieces of the sketches. What could fill a man so full of hate? Jealousy? Lust? A warped sense of values? Or perhaps he was right, and she was wicked. I began to think there were sides to O'Hanlon that were best hidden in the shadows. I wasn't going to let him put me off course. I just wanted her to model for me, dammit, I wasn't going to have a relationship with her other than a professional one. She was someone else's – and I didn't think Mr Ponytail was a man to upset. He'd probably refuse to allow her to sit for me, anyway.

The rhythm of life in Starlings' Yard went on sparse and slow in those days leading up to Christmas. The drunks got a little drunker, that was all.

The young couple came and went and appeared one day with a small Christmas tree. She looked gaunt and miserable; his hair was plastered down firmer than ever. Otherwise nobody there seemed to take any notice of the festivities in the city outside. Tired cassettes played tired carols; tinsel, cotton wool snow and cheap bright lights were everywhere. I saw a man dressed as Santa slip in the snow and cry, "Fuck!" That made me smile because that was real and the rest wasn't and all the time it was like I was outside and the world was just something on the other side of a shop window and I couldn't afford to have it. Anyway there'd been no sign of O'Hanlon apart from glimpses of him at his window.

I'd go out into the streets sometimes, just to remind myself of a greater world beyond the Yard and my thoughts. I'd wander down to the Scottish National Gallery at the foot of the Mound and look at the pictures, out of place amongst the rest of the gallery gawpers. They were out to be seen and to demonstrate their artistic sensitivity, spouting facts out of the catalogues like they'd known them all along and looking at me condescendingly; a tramp getting some warmth where he could. They headed mainly for the gallery bookshop after that, to buy slim but expensive books with obscure titles to grace their coffee tables. They'd never read them. Quite right too, they were unreadable. Turner never had to explain his paintings.

By Christmas Eve I'd become so lonely that I went out and spent the little cash I had on getting drunk, and succeeded. 'The Three Sisters' was a little more crowded than when I'd last been in and there, in the corner, was one of the women I'd spoken to on my first night. She was alone, her teeth grinning beside her schooner of sherry on the table in front of her. She threw me an empty look as I walked past and didn't smile when I spoke to her,

"How's it going?" I asked. She looked blank. "How's your–"

"Passed on," she said, and lowered her eyes to her glass.

"Sorry."

She didn't want to speak, so we left the volumes of grief unopened.

I stood at the bar and drank while the place filled up with grim faced customers. I remember taking a bet with a man with a red face full of broken veins that I couldn't dance a hornpipe and falling heavily. The shock of the cold pavement and trying to balance while the buildings I needed for support lurched and writhed around me, made me cry out because I wanted to stand up but I couldn't.

I woke on a strange bed, like an old hospital bed, fully clothed and feeling like I badly wanted to vomit. Bright sunlight was shining though some thin curtains. The nausea was getting the better of me. I levered myself off the bed and clutching the wall tried to find out where I was, and a toilet. A hand grabbed me by the shoulder. I turned to look – a mistake – as the floor rose up to meet me. The hand propelled me to a toilet and heaved up the whole sorry night into the bowl.

When the sweating and faintness had subsided, and I'd wiped around a bit, I went out into the hallway. It wasn't my flat, but it wasn't far off. From the kitchen door came a smell of bacon frying.

"Fuckin' idiot."

Mr Ponytail was leaning against the sink. I shook my head in a gesture of remorse and wished I hadn't. I recoiled as he handed me a glass of Scotch.

"Take it, for God's sake. It'll steady you up a bit. And there's a bacon bap on the way."

I tried to say something but it just came out as a belch. I took the glass and drank it like some vile medicine.

"And Happy Christmas."

"Oh, shit," I'd forgotten. "Thanks. Happy Christmas. Yeah." I sat at the kitchen table and ate the sandwich he'd put in front of me in silence. I began to feel better.

"God, this is so embarrassing," I said, "what happened?"

He chewed on his sandwich. "You got drunk. Fuckin' idiot."

"Yeah."

"Picked you up in a puddle in the entrance to the Yard. You were out cold. Thought you'd died. I tried to get you to your flat but I couldn't find your key. I was going to dump you in your hallway, then I thought it's fuckin' Christmas so I've done my good deed for the year. Next time I'm leaving you where you drop, OK?"

"Thanks," I managed a bread-filled smile at him. "I'm sorry, I don't know your name yet."

"Rosso."

"Rosso what?"

"Just Rosso. I haven't got another name."

"Look, I feel really stupid about all this. Thanks for what you did. I'd better be off."

He shrugged. I made my way to the door and heard him swear softly. He came into the hall.

"Come back here if you like. You can't spend Christmas on your own."

"That's really kind, but I'd better nurse this hangover."

"Fuck off then."

So two hours later, after a bath and a change of clothes, I stepped out of my front door with a carrier bag and a large package wrapped in newspaper and made my way across to his.

It was a transforming morning – the Yard was coated with ice that sparkled in the frosty sunlight far more than the lights of Princes Street ever could. I'd gathered a few offerings in a plastic bag and knocked on the door of his flat, wondering if his invitation had been genuine, or whether I was just going to make even more of a fool of myself.

His expression gave nothing away, but he didn't seem surprised. I was though, when I saw a small tinsel Christmas tree on the table, and even more surprised to see Cassie sprawled on the brown leatherette settee dressed in an ethnic take on a medieval dress. She was the loveliest thing I'd ever seen. Her beautiful auburn hair covered much of her face. Eat your heart out Dante Gabriel, I thought. She got up lazily and kissed me on the cheek demurely.

"Happy Christmas, Mark Kemp."

"Happy Christmas."

I emptied the bag of its contents: a bottle of cheap red wine, a Camembert, half a bottle of Scotch, and a packet of sausages. Then I thrust the package at Rosso.

"Happy Christmas," I said. "And sorry and thanks."

"We don't do presents here," he said. Tearing eagerly at the wrappings nevertheless. For an instant I saw a child behind that pocked facade. Cassie came round to look at the picture. It was Darkscape II.

"Hey, no, I can't take this, man."

"Please. Happy Christmas."

It felt good. Here was this stone-faced hard case, so obviously happy to get the picture. Cassie looked at me with her head on one side, and smiled at me as though we were friends sharing a moment.

Rosso declared that it was going up on the wall that instant and after hammering a nail in (there were no other pictures up, I noticed) hung it proudly. We then all had to stand in front of it and toast the first piece in his art collection. He spoke with mockery in his voice and I wondered if he was making fun of me. He wasn't - I was to learn that he never spoke in any other way. Rosso mocked the whole world, especially himself.

We put together a makeshift meal and I tried to get to know them, but neither of them wanted to give much away. Rosso answered most questions with a shrug, while Cassie talked in New Age clichés most of the time. The talk circled aimlessly around a silent centre. Eventually, when the talk had drifted to other inhabitants of the Yard, I tried to get an answer to a riddle.

"Do you know much about Father O'Hanlon?" I asked as innocently as I could.

There was a disappointing lack of response.

"Keeps himself to himself. Bit too good for the rest of us," Rosso said.

Cassie snorted. "Yeah, right."

And that was all I could get out of them. Cassie seemed to get increasingly agitated after that and I began to think of going home but of course there was something more I wanted first.

"I'm working on a new series of paintings."

"I'll knock the nails in now," said Rosso. "They'd better be done by next Christmas."

"Oh, they'll be done a long time before that, except..."

I'd rehearsed the approach in my mind during the day, as Rosso became increasingly relaxed by his cans of Double Diamond.

"'cept what?" Cassie said.

"Except I'm short of a model."

"Like a model aeroplane?" Rosso was mocking again.

"Like someone to sit for a portrait," I replied, and left a weighty pause. "A nude portrait."

Rosso played the same game with pauses.

"My appendix scar's too big."

"You mean your cock's too small," said Cassie.

"Actually I meant a woman." I couldn't get past this arm's length cat-and-mouse game they played.

"Actually, Cass, he means you." Rosso swigged his beer.

"He wants to get you into his flat, take all your clothes off and have his artistic way with you. How about that for an offer?"

Cassie wasn't really listening by now. "Whatever," she said, got up and went to the kitchen. Rosso shot her a glance.

"I know it's a bit of a cheek to ask, but Cassie's got just the right face I'm looking for, and it's all above board, but obviously if you're not keen."

"It's nothing to do with me, chum."

"Well, she is your girlfriend."

"Oh?"

"Isn't she?"

"Fuckin' hell."

At that moment there was crash from the kitchen. Rosso disappeared. I heard voices raised in loud whispers, words I couldn't make out, but the atmosphere had become tense, and I knew I was in the way. There was a slap and Cassie's cry from the kitchen. I let myself out into the dark.

Around me the Yard was deserted but for the lights shining though faded curtains and the sound of canned laughter from tinny cheap televisions.

Chapter 2

The next day she came to me.

More snow had fallen on that Christmas night, but the morning sparkled and shone in the sunshine. She stood at the door, swathed in an old Afghan coat and bright red and blue knitted hat, her long hair trailing below it. This was a different Cassie from the one I'd seen yesterday, or the one I'd met first: I was to learn that that was the one constant thing about her; she changed, or appeared to, constantly.

She seemed tense, her thoughts elsewhere as she peered listlessly here and there around the flat. My small talk went ignored, bouncing back at me until the words seemed so meaningless, and the one-way conversation so awkward, that I shut up. I assumed she was nervous about modelling, but then could you assume anything about Cassie.

We sipped coffee out of chipped cups at the kitchen table, whose size at least brought us into a kind of intimacy.

"What about Rosso?" I asked eventually.

"What about him?" she replied.

"Does he mind you doing this?"

"Drinking coffee?"

I was beginning to feel like shaking her. "You know what I mean. Modelling."

She shrugged. "Why should he?"

"He's your boyfriend. Sometimes they don't understand."

I'd learnt the painful way on a number of occasions that some men find it hard to believe the pure appreciation of line and form that motivates artists. They are, of course, right.

"He's not my boyfriend, OK? We're mates, we help each other out. He's got a sort of girlfriend. I do what I want; whatever I want, when I want -"

"Fine, then."

"- and I'm not sure I want to do this."

That felt like a kick in the stomach. She'd seemed up for it before. I felt all my plans going out of the window.

"That's fine," I lied. "It's up to you. I just thought you were OK with the idea."

She shrugged, and for a moment I thought she might be struggling with tears. I leant forward and touched her arm. She withdrew it. I really had to tell her how important it was.

"Listen, I want you to do it. You particularly. You've got just the right face, the look, I want. It's uncanny. I came here because I want to paint this sort of place, but when I get here and start to paint, I realise something's missing. I sit and stare into space and try to see what it was and then out of the mist comes this idea, this picture in my head of a girl that's like something good and beautiful in all the grime. I can see her so clearly then one day I look out of my window and I see her sitting on the block and I can't believe it. I can't explain it, but it's true."

She was looking at me intently now, wide-eyed but expressionless. I was surprised to see a tear roll down her face. Turning away quickly, she got up and headed for the door, trembling. Another tack, quickly.

"Then there's always the money," I tried to joke. "I can't afford to pay you a thing, but when I'm..."

But she was off with a muttered, "I'll see you," leaving the front door swinging open and a hint of patchouli in the air. I watched her go across the Yard to her flat, only to emerge a few moments later and make her way to Rosso's place.

In amongst the disappointment and jealousy the penny finally dropped, sickeningly. That was why her moods were so volatile, that was why she kept skulking off to Rosso.

Now I was angry, and kicked a hole in a perfectly competent canvas that was propped against the wall, hating myself for being teased and fascinated by nothing more mysterious than her drug fuelled moods. I heard her words: "We help each other out." I bet they did. He provided her with drugs, while she provided him with – what? I could hardly imagine her cleaning his flat or ironing his shirts. Sex, then. But she said he's got a girlfriend, so...?

I flung myself on the sofa. Apart from Sadie downstairs I'd never met a prostitute before and it surprised me how much the idea revolted me. Drugs and prostitution hadn't been part of my middle class upbringing. I felt more of an outsider than ever, out of my depth in a foreign land, stung by a bit of cheapskate trash.

I went round to O'Hanlon's and knocked on his door. He looked surprised at first, and then his face broke into its lopsided smile.

"Mark! Now there's a thing! A belated Happy Christmas to you! I thought I was *persona non grata* after my unforgivable display of temper the other day. Come in, come in!"

He led the way down the corridor past piles of old papers, a broken pink plastic foot bath, and a set of golf clubs in a mouldy, torn caddy, to the core of the clutter. Even at midday it was dark and confusing. It was some seconds before I realised there was somebody else in the room, a dark figure in the stale air.

"Mark, this is Eddie Keir. Eddie's one of my little bible group. We've just been chewing the fat about this and that. Ecclesiastes five to be precise."

Eddie looked a bit uncomfortable. He was, like O'Hanlon, a wasted figure of a man with a face that I'd expect to see under the arches of Westminster Bridge than at a bible reading. He gave me a gap-toothed, nicotine stained smile.

"And I think we've got it sussed, so you were just on your way, weren't you, Eddie?"

Eddie took a small battered suitcase and left. O'Hanlon was keeping up with my thoughts, as usual.

"Not the sort you'd normally think of as a Bible student," he said. "But none of them are. I'm not what you'd call a stereotypical Sunday school teacher, either. Would you like a little nip?"

He indicated the whisky bottle. I shook my head. He re-filled his glass.

"But when you think, it's the likes of him who get the most benefit from turning to Christ. Eddie's a no-hoper: a nobody, a nothing. No point to his life at all. Then suddenly he finds out that somebody does love him after all, and loves him for what he is. So he turns his face to the blinding light and follows. Then he finds others are walking in the same direction, too, all unloved and unwashed. He's a new man, Mark, and I'm pleased to think I am a signpost for him. Why, he's even got a bit of self-esteem, which is why he sneaks here for a bit of extra tuition, so that he can be one up on the rest of them! You'd not be feeling like joining us one evening, would you? No, well, you've got your own path to travel, I know. Ars longa, vita brevis, eh? And how is the painting going? Don't tell me, you've come to tell me that you've sold one for thousands of pounds! Don't worry, my boy, it'll happen, I know. So why have you got a face on you like you've been stung by a hornet?"

Good old O'Hanlon: witter, witter, then a punch between the eyes. You couldn't help a plain answer.

"I admit I didn't understand your feelings about that girl - Cassie. Now I know."

"Do you now? That's a good thing, then." He lit a Player's Number 6 and watched the smoke rise to the fog of it that floated below the ceiling. "And what is it that you know about our Miss Bowman now?"

"I've twigged that she's a drug addict and a prostitute."

"And that upsets you?"

"It obviously upsets you."

His laugh turned to a wheezy sort of cough.

"My dear boy, you can't be getting yourself upset by that sort of thing around here. It's everywhere. Most of the men in this place are alcoholics or addicts, so are most of the women and while the women round here can earn a bit of cash from their bodies, they do. It's all they've got to sell. Hey, I'll tell you something – you know Maureen Fletcher?"

"No."

"The fat biddy that goes around with wild grey hair and keeps falling over drunk?"

"Oh, yes."

"She used to be a regular on the game. Not a bad business either. Worked the Canongate area, but drunk all her earnings. Too old and ugly now, but she still earns her vodka by sucking the cocks of the old men hereabouts. You have a look at who's calling at her door. That'll be an education for you!"

He laughed again, a laugh with no warmth in it. "I tell you, if you want to live in a sewer, you've got to expect a few turds."

"Then why are you so against Cassie?"

"Because she has embraced the Devil, that's why."

"How?"

But he wouldn't elaborate. I'd find out sooner or later but I should just take her as I found her for now and he shouldn't have said what he did and isn't the weather glorious and so on. Slowly I calmed down.

I left him, and on my way back, sat on the stone mounting block. There was another dimension to this place now. I looked round at all the shabby doors and thought of all the grimy little vices that made this place what it was. And then I became aware of the tiny little dots of sound that thronged the Yard, like the dots of a pointillist painting. And I tried to piece it all together, tried to make it a whole and fit this complex of dots into more little worlds made of still more dots and make it into a whole. But you can't grasp it, or even begin to. Unless you're on drugs, of course.

I must have fallen asleep. When I woke up, there was a brown and orange Tibetan hat on my head.

I thought about it that evening, and when she came the next day, I was clear about my feelings. I was an artist living in a strange land, and the native culture wasn't my own, but that's exactly why I was here. Artists observe and record impressions and feelings – not make moral judgements (all right: Dadaists, Hogarth and countless others excepted). I was the artist, she was my model. She would pose for me and I would paint her. Fine.

Cassie was wearing a tie-dye dress that should have been demure, but wasn't. She was also wearing an expression that looked like puppy-dog contrition.

"Cassie says she's very, very sorry," Cassie said.

"What for?"

"Being a grotbag yesterday. She was feeling a bit off, but she's fine now, see?" She put on an expression of sweetness, then spoilt it by spluttering into a laugh at her own acting. I ignored my pangs of annoyance.

"No problem. You OK about modelling, then?"

"Anytime you're ready. You show me your brush and I'll show you mine. Now, Mr Picasso?"

She pulled a mock innocent face, then broke down into stifled laughter again. I dragged her through into the kitchen and gave her a coffee. I explained that today I was going to do some drawings of her face, that was all, then tried to explain the idea behind the pictures, but she was continually biting her lip trying not to laugh and usually failing. I tried to get her to sit still and look serious; she just made an exaggerated attempt at it before collapsing in a heap of girlish giggles. In the end I threw the sketchbook across the room.

"Forget it. Go home."

"No, I'll be fine in a minute. Sorry, sorry, sorry."

"I'm not wasting my time with you like this."

"Like what?"

"Like you're high on some shit or other. I thought you'd got something about you but you're just a crazy little acidhead who can't cut it and I can do without that shit and you can just go back to your dope and your pimp and your tricks and get out of my hair. Go on!"

She stood up a bit unsteadily and walked to the door with a stagey air of injured pride. Then she turned and put on a smile.

"Mark?"

"Yes?"

She walked back towards me and slapped my face hard.

"Fuck you," she said, genuinely furious. We glared at each other for several seconds, before her jaw began to tremble and she started sobbing like a baby, and walked out of the door.

I caught up with her on the doorstep. I put my hand on her shoulder, but she turned and flailed me aside.

"I didn't mean that, I need you badly," I said, and she gave a cry of frustration. I guided her back up the stairs, and apart from the odd "Bastard!" she offered little resistance. I laid her out on my bed and left her there.

35

"Sleep it off," I said.

"Bastard," she said, but her sobs subsided as I poured myself a beer and looked out through the grubby net curtains. Rosso stood leaning against his doorway, smoking a reefer and looking at peace with the world. He took a last drag, holding the smoke in his lungs while he flicked the stub away. Glancing up at my window he smiled to himself, gathered his long grey coat around his shoulders and strode out of the Yard.

The sun had gone now, hidden by dark clouds, while an uneasy wind had sprung up, stirring up the dust and the ashes. I felt a sudden shiver of foreboding, "Someone's walking on your grave." My mother would have said. I felt suddenly homesick for a home I didn't have. All over Britain the psychedelic euphoria of a new age was in full swing, everyone was galloping down the new roads of youth, fashion, Biba and Glam rock, free love and re-adjusted morals. I despised it, of course, but yet...

I went back to Cassie. She was sleeping soundly, gently curled on her side, her head resting on an outstretched arm and her face half hidden by the other. Squatting down beside her, I gently moved her arm away from her face. Her breath quickened a little, but that was all.

Freed from the drug-fuelled hurricanes of emotion, her face was innocent and lovely. The fading light deepened her natural pallor, purpling her lips and softening the sharpness of her features into something timeless. She was everywoman and yet just a little child. It struck me then that she was someone's daughter, someone's sister maybe. She too must have roots somewhere else. Then why was she here, screwing up her life and making it worthless? Why was I, for that matter? And I thought of the boy in the red woolly hat and wondered why we start off with so much promise and end up so tainted and bruised and sick of it all.

My sketchpad was by the fireplace where I'd thrown it. I took it up and sat cross-legged on the floor beside her. From there I could see her face clearly, and the curves of her body. Tilting my face sideways to see her face properly I rearranged her arms a little, found a pencil, and began sketching. It was a funny way round it, but we'd achieved the object of the day. I drew thumbnail sketches of her mouth, her ears, her hands, everything. For a little light relief I sketched the generous slew of her breasts under her dress, then the side of her neck, the fall of her hair, the shadows across her face until I had it all there, in fragments, wondering if anyone else had ever seen her with such clarity.

Then she opened her eyes and stared at me blankly for many seconds. She sat up quickly.

"What the hell are you doing?"

"Sketching you. You were asleep."

"Don't bloody do that!"

"Why not?"

"Just don't. It's creepy – like you were – oh I don't know! What the hell."

She swung her legs onto the floor, shook her head then looked at me for a long time. Then she smiled the first genuine smile I'd seen on her.

"Hello," she said.

"Want a beer?" I asked.

The evening had turned into night and the clouds had turned into a storm. The rain was battering the windows and the wind shook them. The flat was dark and cheerless, but while I opened two cans of McEwan's, Cassie busied herself turning on the lamp then dug out a few candles and stuck them on saucers and placed them around the studio. I lit the gas fire, which, not having been used for a long time sent up a howl and a sheet of flame making Cassie cry out in alarm before it settled down to a comforting splutter. We sat on the lumpy old settee and drank.

That evening, I found out a little about Cassie and she found out a little about me.

It was a strange, guarded truth-telling, like two portraits propped up on a couch with words swirling somewhere in between. We exchanged facts, and sometimes leapt into flights of fancy, but there was that bit in the middle – the honest this-is-me bit – that was missing. Maybe it was too soon.

She was twenty two, and had lived in Starlings' Yard for six months. She became evasive when she talked about her background, but it seemed she'd come here to escape from a rather rigid middle-class family who lived in the New Town and which stifled her.

She needed to break out of the chrysalis and become a big beautiful butterfly (her words, not mine). On her metamorphosis she'd also managed to pick up her cocaine habit. She admitted it, but swore to me, as if it was any of my business; that she was getting the upper hand of it, that she was cutting down, that it was just a phase before you got somewhere else – some fluffy cloud of self-knowing, she said. And she was hurt that I'd accused her of being a whore, she'd never do that and she didn't need to anyway, because…

She went into the kitchen and got us some more beers, came out and announced she was going to get a small fix, like, now. My attempts at disapproval made me sound like a headmaster, so I shut up and let her get on with it. She's the model and you're the artist, I told myself again, you don't care what she gets up to.

With practised dexterity, she took a small plastic envelope of white powder, a razor blade, and a pink plastic straw from the tie-dye tote bag she always carried with her. She tapped a little of the powder onto the brown stained coffee table, chopped at it with the razor blade, then played it into two neat parallel lines. Through the straw, she sniffed the first line of powder into her left nostril. She held her breath a fraction, then sat back in the chair, and held the straw out to me.

"Your turn."

I shrank back in a panic. It was just the same reaction I'd had when, as a teenager, I'd gone to a nightclub. The stripper had fixed me with a siren's look and headed towards me. NO! I'd got up and dashed out of the building in a trail of raucous laughter, and left my umbrella behind. NO! This was cocaine. This was danger; like an island I'd never seen, ringed with skulls on poles. This belonged to them – another race that I'd come only to observe, because that was what I did: gaze though thick glass at worlds beyond, minutely recording the hazy images I saw. That was all I'd ever done.

...and bid me come along with her
To the land of the Dancing Dead
But it's all right, Lady Eleanor,
All right, Lady Eleanor,
I'm all right where I am...

"Thanks."

The powder made me sneeze, then shiver violently. For a while, nothing, then a warmth and one of those moments that adepts take a lifetime to achieve. Oh, it was like the veil of the temple ripped aside, lighting up the whole universe and I had a handful of letters and I threw them up into the space and they assembled themselves into the Words of Truth and spelt out...

That's the trouble. You can never remember.

Now Cassie was dancing to Black Sabbath and I was waving my arms around out of time and we opened a bottle of wine and Cassie was saying something serious about ghosts but I was looking at her dress which throbbed with colour as the music punched the smoky air and she drew me up to her and we danced and none of it mattered anymore.

I woke up on the sofa, my neck locked and my right arm paralysed. Fragments of the night came and went like owls, and I did nothing that day, although I felt curiously happy, as though something had changed, which, of course, it had. That evening, I went out from Starlings' Yard and wandered down the Tollbooth. I listened to a guy busking on a guitar and dropped a coin in his hat.

"Can't think straight

'Till it's too late

Then I'm down..."

Next day, Cassie posed while I painted and it went well, I thought. There was an easy atmosphere between us. We'd shared something; we were friends.

She took off her clothes and I sat her on a chair near the window, on a rather precarious pile of cushions. I needed her to be the same height as the mounting block in the Yard to get the shadows right.

I arranged her hair, letting the loose auburn curls hang in front of her shoulders. I got her to lean forward a little, looking up, her hands, palms together, between her knees so that her arms squeezed her heavy breasts together slightly, and her legs dangled with her feet an inch off the floor.

After our false starts I was surprised how easily she took to it. I told her waif and she slipped into waif mode naturally. That was Cassie: she was made of a thousand masks and wore them all like her own skin. Her slim body had just the right undernourished look to it.

I chose my colours carefully; I wanted this to be almost monochrome, a study in brown from the lightest ivory to near black, with contrasts of steely greys and flecks of intense blues – Oxford and ultramarine – and put a generous dollop of each on my palette. We worked for half hour stretches, and drank tea in between. Cassie would wrap herself in my dressing gown and come over to inspect work in progress at each break.

"Is that all you've done?"

"I'm not painting walls, you know."

"I'm going to be an old withered woman by the time you're finished!"

"Back to your chair, then, old withered woman."

While she sat there, she said,

"You know what I was saying the other night, about Hannah?"

"No."

She jerked out of her pose.

"You're telling me I poured my heart out to you and you don't sodding remember?"

"Yup."

"Bastard!"

"What about Hannah?"

Cassie settled back into her pose.

"I was going to say, forget what I said."

"I did."

"Bastard again."

"Don't mention it."

But I was intrigued. Sometime later, I asked,

"So who's Hannah?"

She wouldn't tell me, though. Not then.

At the end of the first day's painting I'd done most of the blocking in. We'd put in hours of work and when she came to look I think she was as excited as I was.

"Hey, that's really good!"

"Don't sound so surprised."

She hadn't bothered with the dressing gown and, as she leant over my shoulder, her breast brushed my cheek. It was just a fleeting, unselfconscious moment but my pulse skipped some beats.

After she'd gone, I couldn't leave the picture alone, and I started to fill in the detail of the background. After all the sketches and the time I'd spent staring at the stones in the Yard, I could do that from memory. I should have given up when the daylight faded but I couldn't. Perhaps there was an element of wanting to please Cassie; I was fired up, and I knew this was the best thing I'd ever done.

Chapter 3

We got on well, in both senses. Two more paintings were finished quicker than I'd ever done before. All of them (and I had planned five altogether) were of the same subject: Cassie, naked and vulnerable, against backgrounds of various views of Starlings' Yard, each of them taking a colour theme from the colours in the local granite. Try it. When you see a lump of grey granite, look again. These at least, I thought, should sell, if there's any love of beauty left in this gimmicky world. What's more, they'd sit very nicely together in an exhibition space.

I wasn't the only one feeling better disposed to the world. Cassie seemed to be making an effort to slow down her habit. Of course, some days she'd turn up so scratchy and tearful, or giggly and jumpy, that I'd have to send her back home - or to Rosso's - and she still took the odd fix when she was with me. But I noticed that the amount of powder was getting smaller.

Most days she was just, well, you could never say herself, because Cassie was as multifaceted as the granite; dreamy, or giddy, or argumentative, tidy and domesticated one minute, chaos the next. Some days she'd flaunt her nakedness shamelessly, others she was demure, reluctant.

We teased and chatted, and I loved her presence in the studio. Even in the dull February days she'd light it up. Strange though, we never went out together on a date, or out anywhere, and we never brought the outside world into the studio. I knew nothing of her life; she knew nothing of mine. I think that's how we both wanted it.

I did notice, however, that Rosso seemed colder, more hostile, even though, as usual, his face gave away nothing. He

43

was like a standing stone: all you got was a resonance inside you. He went about whatever hidden business he had with scarcely a nod. I'd see him in the company of others, all grey, expressionless men, and know them for the pimps and drug dealers they must have been. I felt good about that: I was giving Cassie a purpose, and she was getting off the cocaine, and that was hitting his pocket. No wonder he was turning sour.

We finished the third picture. I say we: Cassie was as wrapped up in the pictures as I was. She talked of our pictures, the pose we liked best, and so on, becoming as excited as a child. Sometimes her suggestions would annoy me, sometimes they'd amuse me, and sometimes they were right.

Before we started the next picture, we took a week's break. Cassie disappeared off for a few days and I did little apart from some sketching up and down the Royal Mile. When she turned up again, I showed them to her, just to prove I hadn't been completely idle. She was skittish, excitable; I suspected she'd just gone and got stoned for the last few days. But she gave me a hug and told me I was a genius, then grabbed my hand and didn't let go of it until we'd reached the art shop in Murchieson Place. She dragged me in, pointed to a pile of small art boards, and asked the assistant in a loud and commanding voice,

"Twenty of those please."

"Cassie, no!" I whispered as loudly as you can whisper.

"Are those the things you do oils and stuff on?" she demanded of the assistant and me at the same time.

The assistant raised his eyebrows ever so slightly and looked at me. I turned red and sweated, and drew her to one side.

"Cassie, I've no money. I'm broke."

"I'm not, see!" and she pulled out a wad of notes from her bag. There must have been thirty pounds there. I gawped, then coloured up even deeper. God only knew where she'd come by that. Had she been out stealing or even...

"Where the hell did that come from?" I forgot to whisper, and the exchange was attracting some tight-lipped smiles from the staff.

"Never mind. But we're going to buy some stuff and you are going to paint some of those pictures and I'm going to sell them and then you can bloody well pay me for all that hanging around with no clothes on!"

I wished the ground would open up, but, as she had me by the ear and was marching me to the desk, I had little option but to buy some small canvas boards and some acrylics while Cassie paid the man with a supercilious flourish.

It made sense, though. I was broke. In line with our un-spoken agreement, I didn't ask again where the money came from. She bought steak and wine and a tape of *Dark Side of the Moon* and while she went home to change, I cooked the meal.

I'd never been happier. I saw her from the kitchen win-dow, skipping over to me, in her purple Afghan coat. Then I saw Rosso, leaning against his doorway, push himself upright and take a step towards her. She turned and I could see out of the misted up window there were some words between them. Rosso didn't look happy, and Cassie looked defiant, especially when she took a five-pound note from her bag and hurled it down in front of him. He waited until she'd walked off into my doorway, then stooped and picked it up, dangling it between his finger and thumb while his eyes turned up to my window.

Cassie came in still trailing an air of defiance, but said nothing about the encounter. She shrugged off the coat; the dress she wore underneath was frankly indecent and surely meant to go over or under something else.

We ate, crowded over the small kitchen table that I'd moved into the studio, lit by candles, drinking wine and listening to more Pink Floyd. When we'd finished eating, we shared a scrap of her powder, and toasted one another in cheap red wine. She rummaged in her bag again and handed me a package, wrapped in cloth.

"What's this?"

"Find out." It was a photograph of her, set in a plain wooden frame. I knew what it meant before she told me.

"Oh wow, Cassie!"

"It's me."

"Never!"

"It's me. I'm giving myself to you."

"I know." There were tears in my eyes.

We stood up simultaneously and she came simply and quietly into my arms. That night, on the same bed I'd explored her body with my pencil, I explored it with my hands.

It was so good.

For the next week, we were never out of each other's company. During the day I'd knock off half a dozen small paintings, while she went out on the Mile to sell them. We started off at five pounds a time, but after the first hour, when Cassie came back with empty hands and a full purse, this was increased to seven, then ten pounds. I don't know what particular sales technique she used, but I suspect it involved a lot of eye contact. We even sold my original sketches and after a week had amassed what seemed like a fortune to us.

The hippie clichés gave way to honesty. We'd talk and cook, and I'd paint, and she'd strum an old guitar she'd brought over from Rosso's and sing bits of Joan Baez. At night, we'd drink and plan wild scenarios for the future and talk of Kathmandu and Marrakech then make love and sleep. It was a beautiful butterfly of a relationship. It couldn't last, of course.

We started on the fourth painting. I altered the plan for this one. Instead of a huddled crouching figure at the base of the mounting block, I posed her squatting, one leg stretched out sideways, arms outstretched on the top of the block and looking altogether more aggressive than the cowering figure I'd seen previously.

It was a hell of a pose to keep up for any time, and Cassie complained volubly and often. I had equal cause to grumble, as I wanted the figure painted from above, and had to erect a rickety arrangement of table atop four chairs above her. And keep painting with a constant feeling that the whole lot would topple down at any minute.

It did once, on the last day of the painting but, by a miracle, the canvas and both our bones were spared. I was putting in some last details to her hair, and glanced back at her face, except it wasn't her face any more. For a split second, I saw the *other*. It had the form of her, but it was as though an image of another, dreadful face had been projected onto it. A face twisted by ugliness and pain, with eyes that stared out of the head and looked straight at me with such loathing.

I knew in that instant that they would haunt me for the rest of my life. Then it vanished. I dropped my brush and jumped down from my perch as Cassie gave a cry and went into some sort of fit. The table and chairs – everything – came crashing down. The whole thing was over in seconds, but I cradled her head while she sobbed and wailed.

"It's all right, Cass, it's OK, it's OK."

"Take it away! Take it away!"

"What is it, Cass? What do you want me to take away?"

"Just take it away!"

47

"I'll take it away. Course I will. Oh, baby, baby."

But a wild fury came over her. Hysteria distorted her features. She pulled at my hair and hit out at my face time and time again, before flinging herself away into a corner, where she lay prostrate and quiet. I covered her with my dressing gown and sat silently beside her, my face bleeding from her nails. Eventually she spoke, her voice muffled by the carpet.

"Go away. Please."

"I'm not leaving you, Cass. Tell me what happened."

"It's her," she said eventually.

"Who?"

But there was no answer.

"Who, Cassie?"

"Hannah," she said it with a sigh.

It was the last word she spoke to me. I'd seen Cassie's torment – the pain she'd never reveal. Like the dark side of the moon. I wanted her to talk now like I'd never wanted anything before. I knew she wouldn't so I knelt on the floor beside her, and said nothing. At last, she pulled herself off the floor, got into her clothes and walked out of the flat, planting a soft sad little kiss on my head as she went.

I'd see her over the next week, in a sorry state. She was often at Rosso's door, and when she wasn't, she'd be sitting on the ground, stoned. I couldn't stand it any longer; I missed her too much. One afternoon, as a damp day turned into a wet night, I saw her, sprawled out against the far wall, her legs stretched out in front of her, like a tossed-aside rag doll in the mud and the drizzle. She wore the same dress, and her skin was smudged with dirt. It looked as though she hadn't eaten for days. I stood in front of her, and spoke her name. She didn't respond, but I talked to her anyway.

"Cassie, I know you can hear me. It's Mark. Stop this, please. You're killing yourself. You're killing me. Whatever it is that's wrong; can't we sort it out? Just running away from it like this isn't helping. Come home with me. Cassie, speak to me, please!"

And I kept on and on, and was by now squatting in front of her, but she wouldn't lift her head. I tried to pick her up: she stirred and looked up at me.

What I saw turned my stomach over. Stamped on her face was that other hideous thing. Its mouth was formed into a gaping, twitching 'O', and its nostril two black gashes, like a pig's snout. But it was the eyes that held me in a sickening embrace. They spoke of suffering beyond pain, older than anyone could imagine, sunken into their sockets, yet burning like iron brands. This time the image wasn't the fleeting nightmare of the time before; it was there, etched over her poor face, seeking me out.

"I love you, Cassie," I said.

I dropped her back onto the ground and ran to get an ambulance. Rosso had a telephone, so I hammered on his door. I sensed O'Hanlon, standing by the entrance to the Yard, watching.

Rosso's flat was in darkness, and there was no response to my hammering. There was a 'phone box not far away in the Canongate, so I ran towards that.

O'Hanlon cried, "The Devil takes care of his own!" as I sped past him.

I dialled 999, with my hands shaking and stumbling over the words. The voice at the other end sounded unflustered, almost bored. I swore under my breath as they asked so many questions, so slowly, until they read out all the details back to me, and I could slam the phone down and get back to Cassie.

The Yard was deserted. There was no Cassie. O'Hanlon had gone, too, and in their place just darkness and silence. I walked over to where she had been lying and shouted her name, but my voice echoed off the walls unanswered, and the rain fell softly where she had been.

I hurried around the Yard, looking in all the nooks and crannies she might have found. I thought she might have tried to get to my flat, and rushed back upstairs, but the place was empty. Baffled and upset, I sat down on the edge of the bed with my head in my hands. I couldn't puzzle this one out.

The sound of an ambulance siren startled me back onto my feet, and down to White Horse Close to tell the crew that I'd lost the patient. They gave me a sarcastic lecture on wasting their valuable time, and shaking their heads with withering looks, backed out of the Cants Close and were gone.

I spent a miserable night looking for her up and down the Mile. Then I remembered something: I hadn't been the only one out in the Yard when I'd gone for the ambulance. Although by that time it was late into the night, I knew O'Hanlon would be up still, among the fumes of smoke and whisky. The light was on, sure enough, and when he opened the door his manner told me he was expecting me.

"Did you find her?" he asked as I stood at his door, struggling to keep the tears at bay.

"No."

"My poor Mark, you look exhausted. Come in, boy," I nodded silently, following him into his room. He poured me half a tumbler of neat Scotch, and I took it willingly.

"What's happened to her? She can't just have vanished," I said.

He shrugged but waited for me to ask the question.

"You were the last one to see her. Where did she go? Why didn't you go to help her?"

"Oh, but I did. When you ran off, I went over to her. You know there was no love lost between us latterly, but you can't see another fellow human suffer like that. Even in her state, though, she would have none of it. She pushed me aside, and screamed for me to go away. Believe me, I tried, Mark, really."

"And what about her face, did you see her face?"

"Yes, of course."

"What did you see?"

"Just a poor, worn-out face."

"Her face?"

"Of course. What are you getting at?"

"When I saw her, I thought...I thought I saw another face....awful... Doesn't make sense. Sorry, it's just..."

"It makes sense to me, Mark. Oh yes. I think you've looked into the face of the Devil himself, and that's a terrible thing for any man. I'm going to have to tell you a few things, boy, things I'd rather I didn't have to tell you, but things I think you'd be better off knowing. I've seen that face, too, and been changed by it forever." He gazed towards the ceiling.

"I've always been an old-fashioned sort of priest. I've seen so much good, but I've also seen so much evil, and if you believe in a God of the good, I've just as sincerely believed in a Devil, and I've always known in my heart that life's a battle between the two. To me, the Devil's as real as God. I used to be such a tiger! A fighter for God, seeking out evil in order to destroy it. You could even say I became obsessed by it, and the obsession gave me the strength to fight it. You know what I found, boy? Most so-called evil is nothing: just weakness or selfishness. Human foibles, that's all. But there is pure evil, thick as the bloody smog in here, which exists outside us. I can smell it. The stench of souls taken by the Devil, and turned rotten by him."

He jabbed the air for emphasis, then leant forward, and looked directly at me.

"Cassie was a troubled girl when she came here. Her poor head was full of occult nonsense and drugs. Sure, she was an innocent Little Red Riding Hood in a wood full of wolves. I tried to warn her, but she wouldn't listen. I had to watch as the darkness swallowed her. We'll have a little more of that Haig, shall we?"

As he shuffled off to get another bottle, I stared at his stained carpet. Cassie and I had taken such pains to keep our past lives out of that cosy studio of mine, both wanting to hide in the present, yet here was O'Hanlon, always three moves ahead of the game, holding up her past in front of me. Why?

He refilled our glasses and gave me a cigarette. He'd never offered me one before; he knew I didn't smoke, and yet he knew I needed one now.

"Now straightforward white witchery I can take; it's a bit of a fad and harmless enough, and if it knocks a bit of spirituality into kids, then why not? But later she got mixed up with darker arts altogether. Edinburgh's full of it: all these hidden away wynds and closes, labyrinths of underground chambers and obscure doorways leading to forgotten rooms. Dark souls of pure evil lured her away. I tried to fight them - God, I tried! But they drugged her and abused her and spat her out. Not before they'd infected her with the seed of Satan himself. Did you not smell it on her? Oh, Mark, did you not smell it on her?"

Perhaps I had. The strange, heady scent she gave off, a mixture of gunmetal and lilies and patchouli that aroused me when we made love. Was that what he was talking about? Was that what evil smelt like?

"Was Rosso part of that?" I couldn't help asking.

"No, I don't think he was. The man's a rogue, I think, but he's not evil in that way. I think he just wanted to help her when these others had finished with her. She'd become hopelessly dependent on drugs by then, and her poor head full of twisted notions. She was convinced she'd been possessed by an evil spirit, but it was more than an old ghost, I believe it was the Devil himself."

"How come you know all this?"

"Believe it or not, we used to be quite friendly. She told me these things, and I tried hard to save her poor soul, but the Devil fought back, and she hated me for trying to tear the heart out of her, and I hated her for the creature she'd become. I hate myself, too, for not being able to save her."

I took my leave of him and went back home, troubled. It didn't add up.

Chapter 4

I must have fallen asleep eventually, for I woke the next day in the armchair to a hammering on my door. It was still very dark outside, and the wind was buffeting the windows. I leapt up, hoping wildly that it was Cassie; she'd be standing there, washed out, but ready to come back and get better. Instead, it was Percy, the grey, cadaverous man who stood silently burning his pile of rags in the Yard every evening.

He'd never spoken to me before, or even looked up when I said hello in passing. Now his face was agitated, and he hopped from one foot to the other as he stood in my doorway. He grabbed my sleeve and indicated that I should go with him. I asked what was wrong (although a panic in the pit of my stomach told me I already knew), but he just kept tugging and pointing, and I realised that he must be deaf and mute. I followed him out of the house and into the Yard. The rain was coming down heavily. He pulled me to the wall that over-looked the steps, and watched me, worried, as I saw what he was pointing to.

It was Cassie. No, it was a soaked and matted tangle of cloth and hair and limbs. But the clothes were her clothes. I could make out gashes on her wrists. A cold sweat broke out on my head, and the nausea rose up in me. I leant over the wall to be sick and felt faint. I turned to Percy, but he'd gone over to Rosso's door and was banging hard on it. Rosso came, and looked over the parapet.

"Oh fuck," was all he said. Then he let out a loud howl and kicked the wall very hard.

We stood there, side by side, for a few minutes, utterly helpless, staring at her body.

Rosso sighed and turned back to his flat.

"Where do you think you're going?" I cried after him.

"I'm phoning the fuzz," he sounded annoyed, but then stepped back to me, looking almost friendly and shrugged, "and they're going to nail me, but I never did that."

He jabbed the air in the direction of her body, and went.

Soon the Yard was crawling with policemen. They were no strangers to the Yard, and were as much in evidence as the inhabitants; but it was for the humdrum misdemeanours that they usually appeared, in twos, with knowing smiles and a willingness to tolerate the eccentricities of the place.

When you're poor, you don't think big as far as crime goes; some petty pilfering, some dope, the odd Saturday night fisticuffs to relieve the frustration. But today, as the grey dawn light struggled into the Yard, they were grim-faced and business-like. They taped off the far end of the Yard, and their cameras flashed without mercy or respect.

They told what was by then a big crowd of onlookers to go back inside. I felt powerless and angry, with the police for pushing me out of what was my tragedy, and with the other residents for turning their backs on her. They could see the state she'd been in, but chose to watch her despair from behind their net curtains. Now those curtains were all drawn unashamedly aside, and their pale faces stared impassively out of the grimy windows onto the scene below. I tried to stay, to get to her, but they insisted, not unkindly, that I was to go back home and wait. A policewoman with a hard face took Rosso back to his place to question him.

It wasn't long before there was a knock on my door. I was crying as I showed the policeman in, and flushed red as his eyes flickered quickly over my surroundings and me.

He was middle aged, and his face was deeply etched with kindly creases.

"Mr Kemp?" His voice was soft, and his accent belonged more to the West Highlands than the city. I nodded; the lump in my throat stopped me speaking. We shook hands.

"I'm Detective Chief Inspector McLeod, Mr Kemp, Colin McLeod. I really am most sorry; it's a terrible thing indeed. You understand that she's dead, don't you?"

I nodded.

"This is a wretched business. I'm not going to keep you long – I just need some basic details from you. Shall we sit down? Thank you. Now, just to keep the record straight, you are Mr Mark Kemp and this is your flat, number four, Starlings' Yard, yes?"

"Yes"

"Do you rent it?"

"Yes."

"So how long have you lived here?"

"Four months."

He waved around the room. "I take it this is what you do for a living?"

"I'm a painter, yes."

He got up from the sofa and crossed over to the pictures of Cassie. He stared at them in silence for some minutes, as though he was reading them, then said,

"I understand from Mr Ross that you were a close friend of Miss Bowman."

"Yes." It came out as a croak; the lump in my throat made it hard to speak. All this Mr Kemp and Miss Bowman: it didn't sound like us at all, but it was. He turned to me.

"I know what you must be going through, and I'm not in the business of making this any harder for you. There'll be more questions later, but for now I just want to get a few facts sorted in my head. Miss Bowman modelled for you did she?"

"That was how I got to know her."

"But it went further than that?"

"Yes."

"Were you in love with her?"

"I suppose so."

"You suppose so?"

"Yes, I loved her. I needed her."

"As a model?"

"As a friend. We needed each other."

"Oh? So why did she need you, do you think?"

How could I tell him? Haunted, evil, possession: not words that policemen want to hear.

"She was trying to get her life back. I think she saw me as the way forward." He looked at me, and scribbled in his book.

"Oh, and what was wrong with her previous life?"

"I don't know. She didn't like talking about it."

"You loved each other but never talked about your past?"

I didn't answer.

"That wasn't fair of me," he said, "I must learn to stick to the facts. Facts like, was she taking drugs?"

There was no point in denying it and very soon he had a pretty good idea, not just about her drug habit, but nearly everything I knew of her. He was a clever man, the inspector, and had a lot of the pieces of the puzzle. But it wasn't the whole truth.

He asked about her family and I had to admit I knew nothing about them. But they'd already been contacted and told, he said. The idea startled me: here was I in this state, but probably just a few moments earlier, her family had been given the news. I had no idea who they were, and they were oblivious of me, but we were sharing a single grief about the same person.

Inspector McLeod left after more expressions of sympathy. I watched him walk out into the Yard and talk to another officer. They both stopped to watch the black body bag being loaded into an unmarked van. The whole scene was being dismantled. Very soon, it would be as though nothing had happened.

I went to bed and stayed there for the next two days.

Poor Cassie. Her face stays with me, papered onto the inside of my skull, along with perhaps ten or so other images that will never disappear. I see her, naked, the light falling sideways over her face, her eyes looking up, vulnerable. At the same time, I see that other, and my stomach turns over, still. I remember the times we had together, healing one another, and when I do think about them, I still cry for the damn waste of it all. Those memories drive me, even now.

When I finally roused myself from my bed and went out I found for once the place was buzzing with life and rumour. The inhabitants were speaking to one another; drawn out of their homes and private miseries by something larger, conjecturing and passing opinions.

By and large they left me alone, and I was thankful. The word was that the police had questioned Rosso and found a large amount of hard drugs on his premises. I called to see him, he didn't look in a good shape either, and he didn't want to talk much.

Some of the others in the Yard had been accusing him of being her dealer, and the police had taken him in for questioning. No, they hadn't found a large stash of cocaine in his flat, and yes, they accepted his story that he'd been trying to limit her habit. No, he wasn't or ever had been her lover, and yes, he'd taken an interest in her because they'd become friends, no more. Then no, he didn't want to talk about it, and yes, he'd like me to leave him alone a while or, to use his words: "Fuck off out of here." So I left him; I still didn't quite trust him, but I knew grief when I saw it (and God knows I'd seen a lot of it) and knew he hadn't killed her.

I went out into the streets of the city where I felt anonymous and where the jostling crowds soothed my sadness.

I've always liked Edinburgh, ever since I studied art there. I like the light and dark of it: the cosmopolitan elegance of the New Town side by side with the gritty chaos of the Old.

Usually I was more attracted to the old parts of the city, whose maze of streets hid so many terrible stories and towering tenement blocks shut out the sky. Now though, after Cassie's death, I wanted something else, something clean and open. So in the next two days, I walked the Gardens, and climbed Carlton Hill, trudged anywhere, anything to get the bad taste out of my mouth.

In the cold bright air of those March days it was good just to stroll down Princes Street, rubbing shoulders with the crowds. From the money I was still making from my sketches and small acrylics I treated myself to some clothes from Binns, and gradually the image of the thing that was once Cassie would fade.

But in the evenings, when I went back and sat and painted, her face would come back to me. I could smell the scent of her in the room, I swear. I felt more alone than I ever had, and that, from someone who'd spent his life feeling lonely, was saying something.

I looked at the paintings we'd done. She seemed alive again: at least I'd given her some sort of immortality. I shut out that other face. I even convinced myself it was a trick of the senses, brought on by staring so hard at something that the eye starts superimposing other images onto it. It wasn't true, but I tried hard to believe it.

McLeod called again, with further, more piercing questions this time. She'd died of a drug overdose, he said. Cocaine, injected intravenously into her arm. Not only that, she'd bled to death after slashing her wrist. Both the hypodermic and the knife had been discovered by her body.

He believed me when I told him that she never took it that way, she always snorted it. There had been no other needle marks on her body, I knew that for a fact. Had someone else injected her? McLeod shrugged.

"Possibly. No apparent motive, though, unless you know something I don't?"

"Nothing I've not told you. I don't think I'm the one to ask, though. I really didn't know much about her."

"But you were in a relationship with her."

"Only for a few weeks. I told you; we didn't ask each other much about the past. We preferred it that way."

"I see. So you knew nothing about her dabblings in the occult?"

I hesitated. "Not from her. O'Hanlon told me something about her having become involved in some satanic sect. He gets a bit obsessed by them. I've never thought they were anything but a bunch of nutters."

"Yes, I've spoken to him. He's quite a character. Did Cassie believe in those sorts of things?"

A silence hung there for a moment.

"I think she believed that she was possessed."

"Oh? And do you believe she was possessed?"

"I think she needed something to blame for her....confusion."

I didn't mention the other face I'd seen, or how Cassie seemed to despair when it became apparent. It would have sounded stupid, and I didn't think police officers would believe in that sort of thing, whatever that sort of thing was. They'd probably suspect I was on drugs too, so it surprised me when McLeod leant back in his chair and stroked his chin.

"I see a lot in this job, and not all of it makes sense. We like to think we live in a logical world, and maybe what's out there abides by the rules of science, but our minds are not rational, Mr Kemp. There is a strange world inside us all; where thought and perception never become conscious. It can perceive things the rational mind never could. I believe there are real forces that only the subconscious mind can detect. It's not a popular idea these days though, not unless you're a flower child. I'm a Highlander, you'll have guessed, and maybe we're a bit closer to such things. You'll be thinking I'm ranting."

"No, I don't. In fact –" I stopped. "Don't get into that."

"What?"

"Only, I wouldn't normally agree, except I did see something," I said, and told him about the 'other' I had seen superimposed on Cassie's face. McLeod listened, not writing any of it in his notebook.

"I can't make sense of it," I said at last. "It just doesn't make any logical sense."

"No, it doesn't, does it?" That was all he said.

He told me the time and place of the funeral, then left. I stared after him. After he'd gone, something struck me. Why should a Detective Chief Inspector bother himself with a dead junkie? There was something uncanny about McLeod.

Three days later, I turned up at the cemetery, feeling alone and nervous. The rain was coming down in a steady drizzle and black umbrellas hid the faces of the mourners who had gathered there. I recognised one or two people from the Yard: Percy was there with his grey, frightened wife, and the couple with the pram had turned up. It was the first time I'd seen them without the pram, and they seemed unable to look at each other. I noticed Rosso's absence, perhaps he knew there would be too many fingers pointing at him. O'Hanlon appeared, and I found myself thinking about the mixture of feelings he could be having. I moved towards him, but he quite deliberately turned away. He probably thought, like me, that this was a private time for all of us.

I felt my stomach tighten as the hearse appeared, and what I presumed were Cassie's family got out from three black cars that had followed it in. They were dressed in unmitigated black. Scottish religion isn't about the spirit of the thing, it's about the rigid observance of the ritual; the grim pleasures of self-denial.

The churchyard, a Victorian triumph of hopeless misery, was now thronged with pinched white faces and black overcoats, giving it the air of a gothic fantasy. I stared at the family as they alighted. A tall, upright woman nearing fifty, who I supposed to be Cassie's mother, walked slowly towards the church, her arm supported by a younger, attractive woman; Cassie's sister, perhaps? The older woman had her head held high, not looking at the other people around them. Despite her greying hair and pinched expression, I saw Cassie's features written on her face, and less so on the younger woman, who was looking impassively around the small crowd. She stared at me for a moment, and then looked away. I felt a hard lump stop my throat, and, as I looked at the coffin, I stifled a sob. I wanted to weep out loud, but here, amongst all this stern-faced company, I couldn't.

We shuffled silently into the church, and I went through the motions of the unfamiliar service, keeping my eyes all the while on the coffin, with my head unbearably full of images of the emaciated corpse within. I saw Cassie as she lay asleep, as she rushed out with me to buy the paints, as she challenged me to take the cocaine with her, as she pirouetted in the snow, and these pictures didn't fit the scene before me.

The minister dragged the service through its prescribed course, with the congregation staring gloomily at him all the while. Near the end, he invited Cassie's sister up to give an address. She was introduced as Penny Knox, so I assumed she was married, but there was no sign of a husband nearby, and no ring on her finger. She was red-eyed, and spoke falteringly, often unable to hold back tears.

"Cassie was a strange and lovely mix of different people," she was saying.

"She could be confident and carefree, then turn and become vulnerable, or angry. Practical or giddy, adventurous or timid; Cassie's company was always stimulating and often left you feeling battered and bewildered. I think that's how we all feel today: bewildered. How could such a beautiful butterfly be taken from us like this? What strange happening led to this tragedy?"

"I probably knew Cassie better than anyone, and she knew me inside out as well. We'd been so close all through our growing up and I've seen a lot of her in the past few years, and I've watched with such sadness to see her turn her back on us, and set off on paths unknown. But I think she had to, and she told me that herself. She also told me there was no malice in it: she needed the time and space to find which of her selves was the real her, and like any voyage of discovery, it was a voyage full of danger."

"I can tell you all today that the greatest tragedy was she had nearly reached the place she wanted to be." She threw a quick glance in my direction. "She was coming out of a time of trouble. She knew the chrysalis was about to become a butterfly. Let's think of her as she was: a brave and lovely person who, in such a short life, explored the world with greater honesty and innocent wonder than anybody else I know. Let us give thanks for her life."

There was a muttered "Amen" from the congregation. I looked round the church: there, standing at the back, was Rosso, but, shortly afterwards, as we filed out of the church I looked round for him, but he was gone.

We stood in a quiet group around the grave, and watched as her coffin was lowered into the ground. It was too much for me. Trying to contain my sobs only made them louder. Through my tears, I saw that Cassie's mother and sister were weeping openly, too. Suddenly, a swirl of wind shook the trees, and a raven flapped from a branch and flew upwards, up into a wild sky, buffeted by the winds. I knew it was her, and I smiled through the tears and bid her farewell.

There was a lunch laid on at the Craigmillar hotel, but I was not inclined to go. It's hard enough for me to make small talk at the best of times. I clutched my coat around me and set off to leave the churchyard, but a voice called out behind me.

"Mr Kemp?" It was Cassie's sister, Penny. I turned to her as she walked up to me. We shook hands. "Are you joining us at the hotel?"

"No, I'm sorry. I'm not really –"

"That's a shame. I've been wanting to meet you. Let me buy you a drink, at least."

"I'd feel very out of place."

"OK, I won't push you. Thanks for coming, anyway."

"Thanks for saying what you did. It was just right."

"Thanks."

"Nice to meet you anyway."

We shook hands and I set off down the drive. Then I realised what a fool I was being, and ran back to her. She was standing in the same spot, as though she was waiting for me.

"I need to see you," I said, "just not at the hotel."

"Good."

"I need to know, about Cassie, I mean. We need to talk."

"Yes, we do," she said. "Are you in on Wednesday?"

"I will be," I promised. She shook my hand, and chewed her lower lip as she did so. She smiled and disappeared into a waiting car.

For the next few days, time hung like a fret, an awkward time when it doesn't feel right to launch into everyday routines again. This was coupled with a feeling that everybody in the Yard knew something, and that none of them was saying anything.

There was little in the papers, either. Another junkie down the tubes, another hopeless life sacrificed to drugs. Mistake or murder? It didn't really matter to the police, or the world at large. These things happened these days; give youth its head and it'll go off the rails.

There were casualties everywhere. Rock stars were making drug deaths almost fashionable. You want freedom? Fine: you pay the price. People shrug their shoulders and, looking smug, walk away. But for every one of these told-you-so deaths there's a broken heart somewhere, and I thought of Cassie's funeral and my eyes would fill; perhaps for Cassie, perhaps for me or perhaps for her family that I didn't even know left bewildered and in tears.

Two days later, on Wednesday, Penny Knox came to see me. My stomach did a little flip as I opened the door to her. She looked so like Cassie, with the same pretty, angular features softened by full lips. But Penny was dressed in an expensive trouser suit and her hair was darker, and slightly shorter, reaching just to her shoulders and neatly groomed.

We shook hands and I invited her in, the place, much like myself had become badly neglected since Cassie's death and I was ashamed of the poor state we were in. She sat gingerly on the sofa, waiting for me to make the coffee.

"How are you?" I seemed to be good at lame starts where these sisters were concerned.

"Oh, you know..." A silence, then, suddenly, "I need to know a lot of things," she said.

"I want to find out everything that led up to her death. I need to understand what the hell's been happening."

There was anger just below the surface. We shared that, at least.

I told her everything as honestly and in as much detail as I could, while she listened quietly, nodding or asking questions from time to time. She had a habit of brushing a lock of her hair against her lips when she was concentrating. When I had told her nearly everything, I stopped. There were runs of tears on her cheeks.

"Thank you," she managed to say.

I got up from my chair crossed over and sat beside her on the couch.

"There's something else," I said. "Something I don't under-stand. It might have all been in my head, but when she was here, posing for the last picture, her face – sort of changed. It was like there was another face superimposed on it. It was all over in a moment so I suppose I wasn't imagining it, but it really shook me up. That was when she ran off in such a state."

Penny was staring at me. "What did it look like?"

I didn't really want to remember it, but I did.

"Ugly. A dirty face that was all twisted and with an open mouth like it was screaming. Nose like a pig's, eyes that shone hate out of them. I can't forget it."

But then I remembered something else that I had forgot-ten. "Hannah! She even gave the bloody thing a name."

Penny looked up at the ceiling. "Oh shit."

And we sat in silence.

At last she said, "Cass was obsessed by this Hannah – thing. I don't think she knew what it was, but she was convinced that the spirit of something bad had entered her. She tried to tell me about it, but I don't hold much truck with that sort of thing. I thought it was just another of her fanciful notions."

"She never mentioned it to me. Just that last time, when it appeared, she called it by name."

She looked steadily at me. "No, she wouldn't. I think she saw you as a chance to escape from a life that was getting unhappier all the time. She really liked you, you know. She wanted a fresh beginning with you – and to forget all the crap that was happening to her."

"Tell me about her."

"Got some more coffee?"

"Sure. Or there's a bottle of Hirondelle?"

"Oh well, any port in a storm. Let's open that, then."

I could see she was used to better and noticed as we drank that her eyes were fixed on the photograph of her sister while she spoke.

"You saw my mother at the funeral. She's a very proud lady, who's seen a lot of the world, and very determined to get her own way. Well, Cass and I both inherited bits of that. I was three years older than her, so I suppose I came out as the responsible, dull one, with mother's ambition and sense of rightness, but Cass had her wilful streak and sense of adventure. Mother and she would fight like stags: great rows and silences. I sometimes thought they enjoyed it, but I hated those rows. They'd both try to inveigle me onto their side."

"What about your father?"

"Och, mother saw him off many years ago. That's why I'm called Knox, though she was the one with the money, and he was a bit of a ne'er-do-well. God knows why they got married in the first place, she was quite young, and I think she was attracted to the carefree life, after a repressed upbringing. I don't remember him at all – he was hardly ever there, and left as soon as I was born. She went back to her maiden name, Bowman.

"Later, she had a fling with some sailor, and Cassie came along. She won't talk about him, though, and I think he buggered off to another war somewhere, and died. There's quite a bit of him in Cass, I think: the headstrong bit. But without him, I suppose the house was a bit of an intense pot of female hormones. Sorry, I'm making it sound worse than it was. It used to be pretty happy most of the time."

I refilled her glass, and mine.

"Cass and I went to the school together: Mary Erskine's – you know it? You don't? You need a guided tour of this city sometime. I'd be the one with my head in the books, while Cass seemed to just play around, but she still got better grades than me. She was really good degree material, but really wasn't interested in all that, so she left school when she was sixteen, with a string of good O-levels.

"What a row that caused! Mother didn't like it at all, as you can imagine. They never really stopped rowing after that, until Cassie just announced she was leaving one day. Mother made all sorts of threats and promises, but she still left – took a bedsit on Dalkeith Road and never came back again.

"She had a series of dead-end jobs: shops, bars - that sort of thing, and gradually the smart clothes became second hand hippy stuff, and she fell in with a crowd of the most pretentious hippies you ever saw. They were full of gobbledegook about New Age things and Paganism and all that.

"I'd meet them when I went to see her. Mostly kids who thought they'd found all the answers and were just smug and still dependent on hand-outs from daddy. After a bit, she moved into a house with them. She grew more and more absorbed into the group, and less interested in the outside world. I used to come away feeling really hurt – she was so distant. I could see that her brains and wilfulness were turning

68

her into one of the leaders, but I worried that she talked more and more of witchcraft and was leading them, or maybe being led, into some strange ways.

"Eventually I wasn't allowed to see her at all. I'd go to this large house in Morningside, and a couple of lads would come out and tell me she didn't want to see me. I used to argue, but they just stared at me, and wouldn't let me see her. Have you got a tissue?"

I gave her the box. She shot me a snooty look.

"One's fine, thank you." She dabbed her eyes, and continued:

"That was a bad time: we'd always been so close, like two sides of the same coin. I felt so lost without her. Perhaps she felt lost too, but lost was always her thing.

"One day, about a year ago, two of the group died. It was all a bit mysterious and tragic. Nothing was ever solved, and the group just seemed to peter out. That's when Cass moved here, and I started seeing her again. She was a mess. She'd obviously picked up a drug habit, and I think she had got mixed up in some nasty sort of cult, though she never talked about it.

"It was a bit of a shock, seeing her so thin and dirty, and something about her seemed to have changed. I couldn't pin it down, because she seemed quite friendly and chatty, sometimes, anyway, but it just wasn't Cass.

"Then, last summer, she started talking about this Hannah, and at first she seemed quite amused by it. She described it as a sort of dream she kept having, something that was happening in this Yard, like she was seeing something through someone else's eyes a long time ago. But as time went on she became more and more troubled by it, and wouldn't talk about it anymore.

"More often than not she'd be stoned on drugs and wouldn't make much sense, but I saw fear in her eyes. I tried to speak to Rosso – I knew he was supplying her – but he was quite rough with me. Then you came on the scene, and she really changed. I was so glad. Her eyes were brighter; she wasn't so drugged up. She talked of what you'd done and what you were going to do – it was the first time I can remember her ever mentioning a future. She asked if I wanted to come and visit you both one Sunday."

"She never mentioned it to me."

"Ach, she wouldn't. That was Cass. It was all arranged. I came to see her a few days before and she had completely changed, she was like a wild frightened thing. That was obviously after you'd seen this Hannah thing. I tried to get her away, to see someone, but she wouldn't. I came the next day, and the next, but she wouldn't even let me into her flat. The day after …"

Her voice suddenly stopped. She got up, and took Cassie's photograph, pressed it to her cheek and finally let go her grief and sobbed like a small child.

I felt awkward. I stood up and put my hands on her shoulders until they stopped heaving, then turned her round to face me. She flung her arms round my shoulders, the photograph still in her hand, and held me tightly to her. Then, a sudden change, just like Cassie, and she pulled herself away, put down the photo, and picking up her leather bag, took another tissue and blew her nose as delicately as she could.

"I must go," she said, and did.

I finished off the wine, then with a tumble of troubling thoughts, went to bed.

Two days later, the postman delivered a letter; it was from Penny.

The envelope was a quality affair of parchment with the words 'Croesus Gallery' in burgundy letters printed in copperplate along the bottom. The same lettering headed the paper inside. Her handwriting was bold and decisive, written with an italic fountain pen:

Mark,

Sorry I left in such a rush last night – you'll understand, I'm sure. I'd like to see you again soon – there's something I want to suggest re Cassie that I'm hoping you might go along with. Is it OK if I call round again? Ring me here at work when you've a moment. (mid-afternoon's best – boss is usually out!!).

Penny Knox

I'll do better than that, I thought: I'll go round and see her this afternoon. She'd aroused my curiosity.

After lunch, I walked down to the New Town, to the printed address on the letterhead: Hanover Street.

The gallery was discreet, opulent, and not one to countenance the down at heel tramp I was getting to resemble. The windows contained some very competent oils by post war modernists, quite well known artists, too, if you're into that sort of thing. I saw my reflection in the window and behind it I could see Penny. She was sitting at an overly pretentious desk, talking earnestly to a customer, leaning back in her swivel chair and laughing.

I felt suddenly ashamed and ridiculous, and walked away, confused. She may have wanted to see me, but in there I'd be an embarrassment to her. Stick to the first plan, and ring her. There was a 'phone box at the end of the street. I waited until the customer left the gallery, then ran along to the box and dialled the number. Her voice was professionally expressionless, but became warm, excited even, when I spoke.

"I was really hoping you'd ring today. You got my letter, then?"

"Yeah. I'm intrigued. When can you come round?"

"I'm free most nights. When's convenient?"

71

I didn't want to sound too over-enthusiastic. "Any time in the next few days. Don't mind at all."

"Monday any good?" That was days away: I couldn't wait that long.

"Fine. Or sooner, if you like."

"Sooner?" Oh, hell.

"Tonight?" I asked, there was a moment's pause.

"OK. Tonight it is. I'm supposed to be doing some work at the gallery, but it'll wait. I'll be round at eight, if that's OK?"

"Great."

"So what are you doing with yourself today?"

"I should be painting but I'm not. I'm wandering around town. Near a posh art gallery in Hanover Street at the moment."

"What? For God's sake come in."

"You're joking. I'd get thrown out."

"Idiot!" The phone went dead.

I stepped out of the box, and towards the gallery. Penny shot out of the gallery door and watched me approach, her hands on her hips, a look of mock exasperation on her face.

"Why didn't you come in?" she demanded.

I told her. She grabbed my arm and dragged me inside. It wasn't so bad, once you were in there. I looked around the walls, impressed.

"Like it?" she asked.

"Like it? Hey, that's a Fergusson, those are by Bellany, and you've got a pretty decent collection of Maxwell prints. Oh, I like."

"Know your stuff, don't you?"

"It's my job. Anyway, I studied here. You get Scottish artists drummed into you until you've forgotten all about Van Gogh."

We chatted for half an hour, enthusing about painting. I reeled off the names of a few contemporaries of mine at art school. Some she knew, most had obviously, like me, sunk into total obscurity.

A ruddy faced, chubby young man with wavy ginger hair walked through the door. He was self-consciously Scottish, and wore an expensive tweed suit to underline the fact, Penny stiffened immediately. This must be the boss. She introduced me to Ian, who shook my hand cursorily and seemed a little annoyed that she'd allowed such a derelict inside his hallowed domain. Without another glance he started talking business to Penny.

I edged quickly to the door and left with an apologetic wave to Penny, who glanced at me awkwardly.

When she turned up that evening she'd dressed down for the occasion. She was in a heavy white polo sweater and a pair of 'A Smile' denims. She proffered a plastic bag with two bottles of wine; good wine, but not as good as the two bottles I'd beggared myself to get that afternoon. She seemed more relaxed than I'd seen her before.

"You've had a tidy-up," she noted.

She couldn't imagine what a frenetic afternoon I'd spent, just as much for my benefit as hers. The bloody place was gleaming. She apologised for having to ignore me when Ian had come back.

"He's a frightful snob, but he's nice when you get to know him."

"Have you known him a long time?"

"Only since I started working there two years ago."

"So you're pretty good friends, then," I said, casually.

"We work pretty well together, I think."

"Bet he drives a Porsche."

"A vintage Jaguar, actually. Why?"

"Just interested." I was sounding silly. The chip on my shoulder was throbbing like a boil.

She grinned.

"He has a very constant partner, He's taken me out twice to exhibition openings and never made a single pass at me, OK?"

"I didn't mean.." I did mean, really.

We sipped the wine, and listened to Hawkwind and felt comfortable. Then she said:

"Where are your paintings?"

I'd moved them into my bedroom and covered them with a sheet – all of them. They were a bit too poignant just now, and I told her so.

"Can I see them?"

"Are you sure you want to?"

"I think so. Yes, I'd really like to."

So I made her close her eyes while I carried the paintings into the sitting room.

I propped them against the walls around her, then told her to open her eyes. She gave a little gasp when she saw them, then, in silence, gazed at each one in turn. I stood, hands in pockets, looking at each picture in turn with her.

Eventually, she sat down again and took a mouthful of wine. She looked up at me, tears overflowing on to her cheeks.

"It's like she's alive again. Mark, these are special."

"Thank you," I said, although I wasn't sure if she meant sentimentally or artistically.

"You've painted the real Cassie. It's like you'd known her for years. Like you'd..." She tailed off, and rocked herself in her chair, trying to stifle her grief.

"Oh, Christ!"

I could see anger rising inside her; she was shaking with emotion. Now was the time.

"So," I said, softly, "what's the deal?"

She leant forward, and I could sense her struggling to calm herself.

"I want your help, Mark. We both know there's more to Cassie's death than anyone's saying, maybe more than anyone knows, and I'm not going to let it rest. Some bastard's murdered her, I just know it. I have to find out what she was mixed up in, and who dragged her into all this mess, and who the hell's this Hannah, anyway? Well?"

"Well, what?"

"Are you going to help me? Look, Mark, you're the only one who feels like me about her death. The police aren't interested. Mother's sticking to the tragic accident idea and couldn't cope with anything else. I need your help."

I'd anticipated this was what she'd come round about, but now she said it, I realised I hadn't worked out an answer. I wanted to help, of course, but...

"I'm going to have to think about this," I said.

"What's there to think about? We want to know what happened to Cass, don't we?"

"Yeah, of course."

"So let's go hunting."

"It's just..."

"Well?"

What was I trying to say? Part of me wanted to join forces with her, and longed to know what twisted paths had led up to Cass's death. But nothing would bring her back, and for once I didn't want to lacerate myself by going through all the pain again by digging up the past.

Besides, I was finding out there were some very seamy sides to the city. I wanted to observe them, not get mixed up in them. I told Penny this, and though it didn't come out very clearly, she got the message. Small creases appeared round her mouth.

"I thought you'd jump at it. I must say I'm disappointed. I thought you had some passion in you. Seems I was mistaken. My fault, obviously. Right then, I'd better be going."

"Don't be silly…"

"Oh, I don't think I'm being silly. I came asking you for help. You don't want to. Fair enough. I don't think we've much to say to each other."

She marched out through the door, closing it with the same firm slam that Cassie had done. I ran out and shouted down the stairwell after her, but she wouldn't look up and shouted at me to get stuffed. I sat on the top step and sighed.

What the hell. Leave her to her own devices. I wasn't going to get mixed up in her private plans. She just needed me, a stranger, to fight her battle for her. She wanted me to go through all that shit, get mixed up in God knows what nastiness, dive back down dark tunnels of the past when I wanted to forget all that, just get on with things, remembering the good times with Cassie.

She was angry with me. By the time I stood up and went back into the flat, I was just as angry with her. I sat down, turned up the music too loud, and kept drinking.

There was a knock on the door. It was Sadie from downstairs, in a pink quilted dressing gown which had cigarette burns down the front. She still had generous amounts of eyeliner and lipstick on, and her hair was a spiky mess.

"Sorry, dear, but I'm trying to get some sleep. I ken ye've just had a bit of a row, but could ye turn it down a bit?"

"Oh, God, I'm sorry. Of course. I wasn't thinking." I went over and turned the record player off.

"You a' right?" she asked, still at the door.

"Yes, yes. Thanks. Fine."

"Ye don't look it. Look, it's nane of ma business, but I'm really sorry about - you know."

"Yeah, well, thanks for that. Sorry about the noise again."

I was trying to close the door on her, but still she stood there.

"Can I come in a minute?"

She walked in and I poured her a glass of expensive wine and found her an ashtray. She settled herself on the couch beside me.

"It's just that we're neighbours, and I think neighbours should help each other out. Be there for each other, don't you think? 'Specially when you live in a dump like this. I've been used to better, you know."

"Most of us have," I replied with a rueful smile, and found myself telling her my sad little story.

As I did, she gradually leant against me, touching my arm, snuggling in closer, and, when I'd done, she kissed me on the cheek. Her breath smelt of beer and cigarettes and wine. I asked her how she had ended up in Starlings' Yard.

"Usual story. There's always a bloody miserable rotten bastard in it, isn't there? Every pantomime has its dame and every woman's story has a bloody miserable rotten bastard in it, like it's the tradition," she said.

"My family used to have class you know; new Wimpey home off Niddrie Mains and all that, but I wasn't too good at school. I could have been, mind you, because I'm no' stupid. Just too many distractions, like boys.

"I was a stunner then, and I played up to the lads, like I loved them to touch me because you could never get a single fucking hug out of my folks. I needed people to hold me. I thought that was what mattered, you know, and because I failed all my exams, I thought what I really wanted was a good man and loads of kids I could cuddle, and a nice house on a new estate like my folks lived in. So you let them have you, and obviously you get pregnant and your folks say you've got to marry him or it'll look bad, so you do, and turns out he's a bastard but the baby comes along, so what can you do?

"I wis such a good mother, me. It was bloody hard, I'll tell you, and that bastard couldn't be bothered working, and I used to shout at him for that and the bastard hit me so many times until once he broke my skull and then they had to take me away and put me in a hostel, and put the kid in care because of the drugs I was taking then.

"I'm clean now, of course. Then they found me this place, and dumped me here. That was four years ago now, but I'm no' staying here, because I know I've still got class, oh yes, I got class. No, lover, I'm off out of here as soon as I've got some money together."

She stopped to draw breath and swallow some wine. I looked at her. I had thought she was much older than me, but she wasn't. She stubbed out her cigarette and I saw her hand shaking. She stared at her lap.

"There's nothing wrong with what I do. Nothing! It makes men happy for a bit. I earn my money. I'm not scrounging off the state am I? I'm proud of that. Lots of things to be proud of. Like, it's only part-time, anyway. I share a room down West Bow with some other girls - we work a rota. It's all right, really, I don't mind. I'm proud."

There was a silence, then she said, quietly, "Someone's got to be at the bottom of the heap, haven't they?"

I heard the desolation in her voice. I put my arm round her shoulders, then she leant back against me. Her pink gown opened as she kissed me. She took my other hand and moved it to her heavy breasts, which I cupped and fondled and kissed, and before long we were in my bed, heaving and sweating together. Two little specks of dust that no-one cared about in a universe of exploding stars and crashing meteors. We both wanted to be rid of the loneliness for a few hours.

Chapter 5

I saw Rosso a few days later as I was standing by the wall overlooking the stream.

I wasn't doing much: the days were hanging heavy and quite often I'd come to this spot where Cassie had died, and stand, watching the water and listen to the churning sound it made. At other times, I'd seen Rosso there, too, leaning against the railings, like me, and staring at the water. You could listen to the sound and not think of anything.

I became aware of him standing some feet away, looking at the water too. I gave him a little nod.

"Howya doing?" he said, still not taking eyes off the stream.

"OK, I suppose."

"Missing her?"

I nodded.

"Me too," he said. He looked at me and I saw the tears flowing down his cheeks.

"It's shite. I didn't know anything could be this shite."

"Yeah."

"I loved her, too," he said.

This wasn't like the Rosso I'd seen: the silent mockery was gone. Who was he? I'd no idea; he'd just been there at the periphery of things, a just-out-of-sight threat in some way. He'd had a relationship with Cassie, but what?

"Look, I know what you're thinking and it's' wrong – all of it," he said. "There's things you don't know…" He shook his head in frustration.

"Like what?" I asked, "I know you supplied her with drugs and it was drugs that killed her."

"I know, but...", and he wept again, aloud, which set me off. I went up to him and put my arm around his shoulders, and we stayed like that until the grief subsided.

"Fancy a cup of tea?" I said.

We sat over the Formica table in the café just down the Canongate, the one that stunk of stale tobacco. I watched him roll a cigarette, and thought how outwardly similar we must look: both of us in long grubby coats, and long unruly hair, even the same beards. He exhaled a lungful of smoke out through his teeth.

"I'd like to know what happened to Cassie," I said. "You knew her longer than me."

"I don't know. I just tried to help her, that's all. You learn not to ask questions round here."

"But didn't she tell you where she came from?"

"She didn't have to."

"Meaning what?"

"Meaning nothing. Don't ask fucking questions. Right?"

"Rosso, I need to know. It's doing my head in."

"I know, I know."

"Well?"

"I can't say, and I really don't know what happened to her that last week. Not for sure. Maybe sometime, eh? Maybe sometime we'll both know it all, and then we'll be able to sleep. Meantime, don't go asking questions, or you'll end up dead, too. I mean it, OK?"

I started to ask why, but his look shut me up. I tried another tack.

"Did she ever talk about someone called Hannah?"

"Maybe. Load of balls. She could be out of her tree some-times. She'd say all sorts of crap."

"What did she say about her?"

"How the hell should I remember? I'm not as fucking nosey as you."

"But you watch, don't you? You see things." He gave a small chuckle.

"Yeah."

"Did you ever see this Hannah?" I asked. There was the slightest pause.

"It was all in her mind. Like a kid with an imaginary friend."

"I think this Hannah was real."

"Fuck off," he said, and there was no way of getting any-thing else out of him. We talked a bit of this and that, and then I got up to go.

"Thanks for what you told me," I said. He smiled and before I turned away, said, very softly:

"O' Hanlon may be more help to you."

He looked down at his tobacco tin and rolled another cigarette. I walked out of the café and looked at the late afternoon sun strike the setts on the road and saw a tinge of yellow in the light, the first glimpse of spring.

Two days later, another letter, another surprise. This time it was written on Basildon Bond paper from Mrs Bowman:

Dear Mr Kemp,

Please forgive my writing to you in this fashion, but there are obviously concerns that we have in common. I feel it would advantage both of us if these could be aired. Do please call at the above address during the week. Anytime would be suitable, particularly Thursday next week at 2.00 pm. I will of course quite understand if you would rather not, but I would greatly like the opportunity of meeting you.

Yours sincerely,

Cicely Bowman.

It was a summons, and although I was free to ignore it, and my first instincts were to do just that, I was intrigued. I duly presented myself at the address in Drumsheuch Gardens on the appointed hour. The house was typical Edinburgh New Town: a solid sandstone terraced town house in a graceful but bleakly tidy street. I rang the bell: a brass, hand pulled contraption that set off a clanging bell somewhere inside. Cecily Bowman came to the door. At the funeral she looked as though she had never mastered the knack of smiling, so I was surprised by the warmth of her greeting.

"Mr Kemp. How good of you to come. There was no need for such a drastic change of appearance. You don't look a bit like you!"

How did she know that? Oh, yes, the funeral. I wouldn't have thought she'd noticed.

It was true, though, I didn't look like me anymore. Answering some impulse (perhaps it had been that meeting with Rosso: I just didn't want to look like that anymore). I had been to the barber's, and had most of the hair and beard chopped off, and undertaken another trip to Binns to get something smarter, in this case a dark red corded shirt and some (only just slightly flared) white trousers. I was still feeling a bit self-conscious.

She ushered me into the sitting room.

This was more like I expected. The austere elegance that only Edinburgh can create, deeply rooted in the Calvinis and Protestant ethics that shaped the town. The Old Town had contained the entire population, bad and good, in its teeming warrens.

Those overcrowded tenements polarised the wicked and the saintly, and when the New Town had been built, it seemed to me that the saintly had budded off there, leaving the Old Town to stew in its vices.

The New Towners wrapped themselves in a rigid mantle of dogma and self-denying belief. The large amounts of money they made weren't paraded around. Their homes were restrained, full of dark polished wood, never cosy or self-indulgent, never indulging in any individuality. But the wealth was there, quietly but very firmly there.

Cicely Bowman's room was typical. Those paintings weren't cheap, the furniture should have been in a museum, the rose bowl was full of fresh blooms. At each end of the marble mantelpiece, in identical silver frames, were photos of Cassie and Penny, which must have been taken a few years ago. Not a thing out of place, including Cicely Bowman.

She wasted no time in coming to the point, speaking with the precise vowels of Edinburgh gentry.

"I'm grateful to you for coming, Mr Kemp. You must have thought my invitation rather unusual."

"I was pleased you asked."

"The reason is, of course, Cassie."

"Of course." No indulging in pleasantries here, I thought, but then she smiled brightly.

"You'll take some tea, Mr Kemp."

She said the words without a question mark, and strode off, leaving me to look around the room. There was a fortune here in paintings alone, including a very nice portrait of her done probably thirty years ago. It could have been Penny, painted yesterday. But what really impressed me was a small painting beside and behind the door, almost tucked out of sight. It was a Braque, an original. God knows what that would fetch now. I was gazing at it when Mrs Bowman appeared with a tea tray.

"You've found my favourite, I see." She put down the tray and stood beside me, contemplating it. "Georges Braque."

"I know."

"Of course, you're an artist. He gave it to me, you know. Oh yes, I got to know Georges quite well. I was only a young girl then, of course. We were in Normandy. I used to tease him about the shape of his head. What days! I wasn't always a middle aged lady entombed amongst her belongings. Sit down, Mr Kemp."

"Do call me Mark."

"Very well."

"How are – things?" I asked.

"Not at their best, obviously, but we have to put a face on, don't we? To be honest, Mr Kemp – Mark – I did much of my grieving before she died. I have lived with the pain of her waywardness for years. The more I tried to protect her, the more determined she became to go her own way. I'm not going to cry."

But she was. She pressed her lips together, hard.

"She took a road with an inevitable end. When she reached that end I was expecting it. I just didn't expect it to hurt this much. That is why I felt I needed to speak to you."

"Oh?"

"You knew her such a short time, Mr Kemp. I don't know how well you knew her, nor do I want to. However, it's obvious you are not unintelligent, and I'm sure you will have discovered for yourself that Cassie showed you only what she wanted you to see. Such a sweet child, but her father's personality, no question. Tempestuous and single-minded – but I'm telling you what you must know. She destroyed herself, Mr Kemp. By whatever agencies or under whatever circumstances it happened, she destroyed herself. Nothing more needs be said."

"Perhaps not, no."

"That's why I so wanted to meet you. Of course, I am interested to meet any of her companions, but you especially. Penny tells me that you were a great help to Cassie, and I must thank you for that, although it must be said that it was also in your company that she became so ill and died."

"You're not suggesting –"

"No, of course not! Her death was inevitable, your presence was irrelevant. What I'm trying to say, Mr Kemp – sorry, Mark - is that there's no point asking questions. The outcome was a *fait accompli*. I admire your stance on the matter. In the course of what little communication I have with Penny, I gathered that she was perhaps a little at odds with you on letting both Cassie and her recent past rest in peace.

"I've asked you here to say that I am utterly at one with you. Cassie's tragic death was the result of her wretched drug habit. It doesn't matter if she administered the fatal dose or someone else did. There is no purpose served by raking up the past, I think we're agreed."

"Well, yes, I suppose, but –"

"That's settled the matter. I'm so glad we see eye to eye. We will both persuade Penny that her so-called mission is pointless, offensive even."

"Oh, I don't think I'll be seeing Penny again. I don't think she wants anything more to do with me."

"Mr Kemp, you don't know her. You will assuredly be seeing her again. But you must stick to your guns. I need to mourn Cassie's death in my way, and to make an issue of it will only keeps the wounds open."

My thoughts exactly, or they were. But her manner, and her assumption that she knew how I was thinking, were annoying me. I got to my feet.

"I think, Mrs Bowman, that you've just persuaded me otherwise. I'm going to – I have to make my own decisions, and I thought I'd decided to let things rest, but these – things, these questions, won't go away.

"I've tried, but there's something evil going on. Nothing's what it seems, and I'm sorry, I can't bloody well sleep these days feeling like that. I'm happy to keep anything I learn to myself. I don't have to share it with Penny or you, so you can carry on believing what you want to believe."

"You are a wilful young man, Mr Kemp, and if I may say so, rather forthright to the point of rudeness, too."

"Then we don't spoil a pair, do we?"

"Very well, Mr Kemp. I'm sorry you feel as you do. I think you are very foolish if you think you can play around with my daughter's memory. My daughter, Mr Kemp! She may have been your plaything for a short while, but she will be my daughter for ever. Consider that, and, if you have any decency, you will leave her past in peace."

"Her past was anything but peaceful!"

"There's no need to raise your voice."

"Oh, isn't there?"

I was picking up Bowman habits fast, for I turned around and walked out of the front door, hearing my name shouted behind me. I walked up Queensferry Road quickly, angrily. Damn the whole family! Penny wanted me to do one thing, so I reflexively do the other and fall straight into the clutches of her mother who insists I keep doing what I'm doing, so I spin around again…

I'd calmed down a bit by the time I'd reached Princes Street. I walked through the gardens feeling chilly with the drizzle and my lack of hair, but went and sat on a bench in the East Gardens. I looked up at the Mound, and the looming skyline of the Old Town, its rooftops and spires like the spines on the back of a sleeping dragon, black against a blood red sky.

My anger had, true to type, turned in on itself. I had to make my own mind up. My perversity was just a weakness: the result would have been the same if I'd just said "yes" to everyone. Saying "no" all the time was no different.

The answer came like a small flower opening up inside me. Cassie had given me something: a kind of commitment. She trusted me. I couldn't stay out of this one; I couldn't be the observer any more. Simple, really.

The rain had become heavier. My clothes were wet, and it was beginning to get dark again.

Chapter 6

I thought about ringing Penny again, but the idea of getting embroiled in the Bowman's forceful ways dissuaded me. They were both using me, and I didn't like that. Instead, remembering Rosso's parting words, I called round to O'Hanlon.

He fussed kindly around me, and talked easily and sadly of Cassie's death.

"I think we're all a little lost since her death," he admitted.

"I thought you hated her."

"No, Mark. I hated the evil inside her. That was a worm, a serpent of the Devil that had taken the poor girl over. To lose a beautiful butterfly like her is a tragedy that affects us all.

"Don't you feel it?

"The Yard seems to tick over in its grey, sad way like it always has, but something has changed, and do you know, I can't put words to it. Now, for me, that's saying something, eh? There's shock, but there's also a kind of relief, as though something's been exorcised: you must have felt it."

"I think I've been too wrapped up in my own feelings to notice anything."

"Maybe, but perhaps you don't want to admit there was something evil inside her."

"I never saw it."

The ash dropped from the end of his cigarette onto his threadbare trousers as he leaned forward.

"Didn't you? Didn't you?"

His smile was gone, and his eyes glared into mine, so that I had to turn away. It took me a while to whisper the answer.

"Yes."

"Who was it, Mark, who?"

"Hannah," I barely managed to croak out.

"Yes! Now, you're going to sit there, young fellow, and I'm going to tell you a nasty, terrible tale. And I'm going to need a stiff drink to tell you, and you're going to need one to hear it."

With that, he rose from his chair, a thin black heron of a man who seemed to tower high above me before swooping down into a nearby cupboard to produce the whisky and glasses. He filled the glasses despite my protesting that I'd never drink that much, and raised his.

"To happier days, my friend, eh?" He folded himself into his chair again, and savoured his first mouthful in silence, thoughtfully.

"You're an artist," he said eventually. "You sense the atmosphere of a place. You see colours that I can't, shapes I'd never notice, but I have a different eye, I see shadows of the spirit, places where God's light can't shine. We're both here for that reason: the darkness.

"That darkness began about a hundred and fifty years ago, 1824 it was. At that time the Yard would be like the others, teeming with all sorts; some better off, some so poor they would starve to death.

"The conditions would have been intolerable to us: no sewers and overcrowding meant cholera and typhoid were always present. It was just a few years before Burke and Hare reared their heads, and in the year of this tale, a massive fire had swept through the Old Town, destroying the Tron Kirk and a lot of the buildings. So there's homeless families trying to muscle in on crowded tenements.

"Oh, life was cheap, then, but it went on. Starlings' Yard might have been the poor relation of other Closes, but life everywhere was much the same. There'd be chatter and arguments and laughter and shouting echoing round these walls; the whole place would be teeming with life.

"In that ant heap lived a young girl. That's right, Hannah. She was a strange girl, rather simple, and I rather think, reading between the lines, she must have suffered from epilepsy. Her parents looked after her, as much as they could, for in this poor place, they were the poorest. I keep wondering which one their room was.

"Having Hannah as their only child must have been just one more cruel joke in a life full of them. Then one winter, they both died within a few days of each other. Starvation and pneumonia, I suppose. I think about it sometimes; two stiff cold corpses and that girl, who must have been fifteen when they died, huddled in a corner, looking at them with eyes that couldn't understand.

"Afterwards, Hannah's life was a misery. She lived alone in the room, friendless and scared. She must have survived on scraps of food she found and sometimes perhaps the kindlier women would leave bowls of food out for her. The others were too poor and stupid to care; they wouldn't have known what to make of her. Perhaps, when you're that poor, you can't feel pity for anyone except yourself. But they treated her as different.

"They would tease her and the children would call out names to her back. The men would laugh at her, but that didn't stop them pulling her down into the shadows and forcing themselves into her when they pleased. So the women made an outcast of her, for they thought she'd led their men on when she hadn't, she hadn't understood at all.

"She had four children by four unknown fathers. She must have delivered them herself, like an animal in that bare room and God knows how she fed them. Two of them died in infancy, but the others, against all odds, lived. But she became more unhinged, her fits more frequent. The rest of the Yard grew scared of her and her unnatural ways as she would prowl the Yard in all weathers, trailing her children behind her and yowling like a dog. The men stopped teasing her or raping her, now that she was haunting all their lives and making them afraid, and they began blaming her for everything that was wrong with their lives. Their fear turned to hate.

"One summer's evening she was singing to her children. Most of the other families were out in the Yard talking and trying to ignore poor mad Hannah. Then one of the men, finishing his cider bottle and tired of her noise, threw it at her. It hit her on the head, cutting her forehead and making the blood run. Instead of getting angry or crying out, she started to laugh at him, and laughed and laughed until they couldn't stand it and another man picked up a stone and threw it, too.

"Some primeval instinct took hold of them, everyone screamed all their hate and frustration on poor Hannah. Throwing stones, pushing her down. She howled as they broke her body, and beat her face to a mass of blood and splintered bone. Her scalp hung in tatters off her shattered skull while some dark cavity still screamed out a curse at them. And she kept screaming until the last breath had been knocked out of her and her silence went on for ever. But her children were screaming too, so the crowd, having killed the mother, lifted them up and threw them into one of the cellars with their mother's corpse. They piled stones over the trapdoor, then drifted away, ignoring the cries that grew fainter, and after a few days, stopped altogether. That day, the Devil took over this place, and the silence began.

"No one said anything. They were all guilty. It was only many years later that the story was told and written down. But that act of evil taints this place; for evil begets evil, and that girl's ghost haunts us all, literally so, in Cassie's case. For now, Hannah's spirit will be satisfied. Then it will rise again, and seek a fresh victim, over and over. God have mercy."

He leant back and shut his eyes. I reached out to the whisky bottle and filled my glass.

Still with his eyes shut, he said, "The Devil lives here. He and I are old acquaintances. I am ready."

I said nothing, for the image of Hannah surrounded by the maddened crowd was too clear, so we sat in silence.

At last, at his request, we recited the Lord's Prayer together. I thanked him, and left.

Outside, it was bright. The April air held a promise of warmth, I leant against the door to my house and looked around at the Yard.

I could almost see Hannah crouching on the mounting block while the stones broke her. Her face was the face I'd seen on Cassie's, distorted in pure animal pain.

When I went in at last, I tried to scribble a few sketches, but my mind was elsewhere. Another story was forming, I sensed it. There was more than this ghostly connection between Hannah and Cassie.

There was a web of links from the past to the present; a net that we were all caught up in. We're all trapped in the cobwebs of the past, but the spider in the centre of this web had eaten Cassie. Was that what O'Hanlon meant, when he said the Devil lived here? Was Starlings' Yard the centre of some great unseen web? The spider, the Devil? I'd had too much whisky for that time of day perhaps, and my mind was tumbling ideas around.

It was no good, I had to ring Penny. She sounded a bit aloof; perhaps because she was at work, perhaps because she was still angry with me, perhaps because she just was, but she agreed to see me after work.

We met in a chic-looking café in Rose Street. It was a strange reunion; rather formal, guarded almost. She was dressed in a very business-like black two piece, which made me feel I was being interviewed.

"How's work?" I asked.

"Fine."

"And what about other things?"

"What other things?"

"You know…"

"OK. Early days. I gather you've seen mother."

"Yes."

"And she told me you quite agreed with her about hushing everything up."

Then the tension broke.

"Oh, did she?" I said. "Well, she's lying to you. I wasn't having her dictate to me any more than you. I do things my way, not to order, right?"

She raised her eyebrows. "Go on."

"I think you Bowmans or Knoxes, or whoever you are, are a bit too used to getting your own way, and if we don't snap to attention when you call, you get all uppity."

Her eyebrows lifted another notch. "True."

"Well, here's something you should know about me. You push me one way, I'll go in the opposite direction, so we're not exactly made for each other."

"I was hardly asking for a lifelong partnership."

"It doesn't matter if you're just asking me to buy you a drink, that's the way I am, and I'm not intimidated by your high-handed way, or your mother's. So, I've said it."

I suddenly lost the wind from my sails.

"I just thought you should know."

"And will you?"

"Will I what?"

"Buy me a drink?"

She smiled such a smile that I had to laugh. She linked her arm through mine as we stepped next door to Paddy's Bar. She paid for the drinks, and sat opposite me.

"It wasn't meant to come out like that," she said. "But I was counting on your help, and yes, I suppose if I get blown off course I get into a stew about it. In fact, I've been mentally sticking pins into your effigy since then."

"I think I've been mentally feeling them," I said. "Especially after talking to your mother. Yes, of course I want to find out more, but at my own pace, and I'm backing off when I think it's getting to heavy, right? Oh and not a word to your mother about what I'm up to."

"Now who's the forceful one? OK, it's a deal: you go your way and I'll go mine, but we share anything we learn, yes?"

"Right."

She held out a hand, and I shook it. I told her about my encounter with Rosso, and as I did, our heads grew conspiratorially closer.

"I had him down as the villain of the piece, but now I'm not sure. I thought he was all sorts – her lover, her pimp, her supplier. He kept her in heroin, right enough, but I believe him when he says he was trying to get her off it. But he wouldn't say anything more, he's a bit of the jigsaw that you just have to keep picking up and putting down again."

"Strange. Cassie refused to talk about him. I'd assumed they were lovers, but he's got a girlfriend hasn't he?"

"Yes," I said. "So perhaps he was just her supplier."

"Maybe. I still think there's more of a connection, otherwise why would they both be so cagey about it?"

"Christ knows. So that gets us nowhere. But that's not all, I think I've sussed out the Hannah thing."

And as the evening grew into the night, I told her the tale that O'Hanlon had told me earlier that day. She listened like a little girl being told a bedtime ghost story, all wide eyed and fearful. When I'd finished, she sat in silence, just like I had. I went and got us another drink.

"Do you think Cassie knew all that?" she asked when I returned.

"No idea. I'm sure she felt it, though. No, someone must have told her, otherwise how would she know her name was Hannah? Was she really haunted by her spirit?"

"That depends on whether you believe in ghosts or not. Do you?"

"I didn't, but that thing I saw, like something coming out of her..."

"Well, I don't. I think somebody had filled her head with a load of stuff. You know how impressionable she was."

"But what about that thing I saw?"

"Trick of the light. You've got an artist's imagination."

"I saw it twice, it was no trick of the light, and how do you explain her having that sort of fit thing when I first saw it?"

"I don't know. I don't want to know. I'll just stick to my comfy preconceptions, thanks."

"But never mind ghosts. Suppose some event, some suffering like that, caused a really strong emotion to get sort of imprinted on a place, in the walls or something; and then it could get played back through someone else's mind like a tape recorder, or ..."

I was struggling. "I don't really believe in ghosts either. But I've seen one," I added lamely.

Our discussion was interesting, but I'd found out nothing that helped us. As an artist, I suppose I could claim that filling in the background is just as important.

Penny, however, had done a bit of ferreting through some old newspaper reports and come up with the names of two members of Cassie's commune when the two deaths had occurred. Their names had been reported as witnesses at the coroner's inquest. She produced a photocopy of the account.

The coroner today recorded a verdict of suicide on two men who had been found hanged at a house in DalkeithRoad. They were James Rossiter, 22 and Vernon McKenzie, 21.

They were discovered by one of the members of the socialist commune to which they both belonged. Alan Trapp, aged 19, had found the bodies hanging from a beam in the garage attached to the property.

Another resident, Fiona Gilchrist, 24, stated that the pair had talked previously about a suicide pact, and seemed obsessed with death. Her testimony led the coroner to record his verdict, and he expressed his sorrow to the families of both men.

"They seemed to be pretty perfunctory about the whole thing. I'm not sure they got anywhere near the truth. Socialist commune, indeed! Anyway, there's a couple of names to be going on with. I'll write them down for you."

"Hang on, why me?"

"Because you've got the time, and anyway, I wouldn't have the first clue how to go about it."

"Neither have I. You're doing it again."

"What?"

"Bossing me about."

"I know. Sorry. Forget it, then."

Of course. I took the names, Alan Trapp and Fiona Gilchrist but I'd no idea where to start looking. The phone book, presumably.

Penny thanked me like she really meant it, and then changed the subject. She'd been talking to Ian (he of the Jaguar and the tweeds) about my pictures. He'd been rather non-committal, but, yes, he'd have a look at some of them.

I couldn't help the big grin that spread across my face. I could have hugged her. I think it was the first time I'd seen her smile like that, too: just pure warmth and pleasure lighting up her features. Our meetings so far hadn't been about the happiest of subjects. Then she became earnest again.

"Please don't get your hopes up too high. Ian's notoriously picky. He usually likes his artists to be famous or dead, preferably both. Have you had exhibitions before?"

"One or two. My stuff's not very fashionable, though, is it? Figurative doesn't cut these days. I usually get pissed off with gallery owners: they're just out to make a buck by flogging what's fashionable."

"You can't blame them," she said. "They've a living to make but Ian's actually a cut above the majority; he really tries to sell quality rather than fashion. Ian's taken pains to train my eye, and you've got quality, Mark, I can tell when something's special. You're a risk, though, because you're unknown, so he may well not be interested. You'll have to be nice to him."

"Oh, God. Really?"

"Really."

When I got back home that night, I found a note that had been pushed through my letterbox. It simply said,

Please remember what I said. Don't ask questions round here. Rosso.

I felt a sudden unease. What had he seen, what did he know? Why had he felt it necessary to write this note?

I looked out across the dark Yard. Dimly lit windows curtained in drab fabrics only heightened the blackness of the buildings and behind each window, small lives eked out their time. Somewhere in the night, a dog was barking, pointlessly. Rosso's flat was in darkness. I closed the curtains and went to bed.

Penny drove round in the morning to pick up my paintings. We'd – no, she'd – decided that the Anglia didn't give the right impression. I'd said to hell with that, but she'd insisted. "I told you so," I said as we struggled to fit the paintings in the back of her mini.

I was wearing my best clothes. All right, I know there were principles at stake, but I needed a lucky break, so sod the principles for now.

I was surprised how nervous I was. Ian was sitting at the desk, minding the shop, but stood up to shake my hand and greet me cheerfully. Perhaps he wasn't as bad as all that. He helped us in with the paintings, before we sat round the desk, drinking proper coffee.

He seemed in no hurry to see the paintings, but asked me about my training, experience, previous exhibitions, all that. The answers weren't impressive. I saw him glance at Penny while she, in turn, looked at the floor. He told me how he'd set up the gallery, his rather illustrious training in fine arts, and the type of pictures he was interested in, none of which sounded in the least encouraging as far as I was concerned.

Eventually he gestured to the paintings.

One by one, I unwrapped them, and held them up for him to see. Two from the Darkscape series, two from the Cassie lot, and a few cityscapes I'd done. I started talking about them, but he waved me to silence with a gesture of his hand. One by one, he stared at them, not showing any flicker of expression. One by one, he nodded to see the next. When he'd seen them all, he looked at me, still without emotion, as though I was just another painting. Then he turned to Penny.

"You're getting a good eye, lass."

He turned to me then, and smiled. "You're a remarkable artist, Mark. Quite remarkable. These have the stuff of greatness in them. I like them a lot. It's a shame they're not really suitable for my gallery."

"No, I can see that. Thanks for the complimentary remarks, though." I made to pack them away, but he said,

"Mind if I keep these a day or so?"

"Go ahead."

"I'd just like to have another look at them. Pick them up in a day or so, eh?"

So I left them there while Penny drove me home in silence. We only spoke when I'd got out.

"Thanks anyway."

"Sorry. I told you he was picky. At least he liked them."

"Yeah."

She drove off, leaving me feeling deflated. There wasn't a dealer in the land who wanted to handle my pictures. What the hell, I was used to getting turned down.

I couldn't face the thought of getting stuck into a painting, although I'd done quite a few sketches for the Hannah series and the thought of them excited me, even if they weren't ever going to fire up a dealer. In fact, I couldn't settle to anything except successive cups of coffee.

Eventually, I walked to the telephone box just up the Mile. I opened one of the directories. There were hundreds of Gilchrists, and a lot of F.Gilchrists, too. Anyway she might not have a phone, or she could have married, moved away, anything. This was a silly idea. However, there were just two A.Trapps listed. I noted down both addresses, and, more out of idleness than any burning curiosity, went back to my car and drove to Morningside to check out the first address.

The house was a very substantial one off the main road. It didn't look as though it could belong to a recent commune dweller.

I parked the car opposite and watched. After a while a very elegant-looking lady of about seventy appeared in the living room, picked up a book, and sat down. I turned on the ignition, and drove off, to the next destination: Bryants Road, off Leith Walk, to the north of the city.

The address was a flat in a rather dilapidated street. I parked nearby, and then wandered to the door. There it was, on the name card above flat 3: Trapp. Now what? This was silly, too. If I hung about inside, I'd get reported for loitering, if I waited outside I'd have no idea which of the occupants this Trapp was. I could think of no possible excuse to knock on the door either.

I was about to drive off again when I saw a thin young man, with a wiry shock of straw-coloured hair sticking up almost vertically from a very angular head. He walked up to the door, paused to get out a set of keys and let himself in. It had to be him: he was the right age, and looked fairly eccentric.

I sat in the car, and waited. I started to feel foolish again. It was half past five. He was probably in for the evening. Was I supposed to sit there all night? No way. He'd probably come out again tomorrow. If he got home at five thirty, the chances were he worked nine to five in town (one amongst a hundred possibilities, I admit), so the likeliest time to catch him would be when he left the house at, say, eight thirty.

At eight the next morning I was parked up with a good view of his front door. At eight fifteen he came out, put his keys in his pocket, and walked to the bus stop.

The traffic was building up: following him was going to be difficult. A bus drew up; I drove off, but as I drove behind the bus and stopped behind it, I saw him hanging back. Wrong bus! I had to keep driving, but parked again a hundred yards further on.

I got out of the car and could see him getting on the next bus, a number ten. I let it pass, and then followed behind as best I could. I knew the route, but I needed to see where he got off. While the bus passed slowly through Leith Walk,

Princes Street, and then swung up the Lothian Road, I was finding my efforts at sleuthing were causing other cars to sound their horns, and twice I thought a policeman was coming up to me.

I was sweating with anxiety, but it paid off. I saw him get off at Bread Street, so I turned rather abruptly down there, and found a place to park. I looked anxiously behind; there he was, coming down the street, a small leather briefcase and a long black coat. It was a warm morning, but I just felt he wore that coat the whole year through.

I let him pass me, and then, when he was safely ahead, got out of the car to follow him. Down into West Port he went, and to my joy, stopped at a shop, got his keys out of his pocket, and let himself in. It was five to nine. I walked nonchalantly past the shop, with but a glance at the window. *Worlds Apart – Second Hand Books*, the begrimed sign over the window said. It seemed to specialise in the occult.

I went down into the Grassmarket to treat myself to a coffee. This was going to be a good day, I thought. I wish I hadn't.

I was rather proud of myself for tracking him down. Even as an exercise in itself, even if I didn't really want to know anything more about him, it was a new achievement, a bit of action in what was the rather contemplative life I led.

Over the rather tasteless coffee, I wondered about what to do next. What did I want from him? I pulled out my sketch-book and began to make a list:

Right Alan Trapp?

Did he know Cassie?

What went on in Dalkeith Road?

What was C's part in it?

Why did she leave?

Who else involved?

I realised then it was a futile quest. The man wasn't going to tumble all his murky past out to a stranger. What's more, Rosso's warning came to me: Don't ask questions! If there was some sort of network, something unpleasant behind Cassie's death, then they'd soon get wind of someone grubbing about trying to find out the truth.

Still, there was no harm in seeing him, having a chat. I finished my coffee, vowing not to go into that café again, and returned to the shop. I lingered outside for a few moments, looking at the books in the window, then went in.

He was sitting behind an untidy counter, reading a book, and there was a half-eaten apple in front of him. He glanced up as I entered, and we exchanged good mornings. I walked along the shelves; they contained the books you'd expect, certainly nothing overly sinister, apart from the odd piece of Crowleyana. He asked if there was anything in particular I was looking for (oh, yes!) and I replied that I was just browsing but was interested in writing a piece for a magazine on Satanism in Scotland.

"Oh," he said. "We don't have a lot in that line. There's a few books behind you there, up on the top. Is it the history you're after, or modern practice?"

"Oh, historical stuff really." I didn't want to display too much of interest.

"That's probably all there is."

I looked, and for the sake of realism, picked out a cheap-looking volume.

"It must be fascinating, working in this sort of shop," I said chattily.

He shrugged, his skinny shoulders rising above his ears.

"It's a bit too quiet most of the time. Still it gives me a chance to get on with some reading."

"You've plenty of books to go at."

"Not really my sort of thing."

I placed my book on the counter. He stood up. I glanced at what he'd been reading: *Bleak House*. He carefully wrapped mine, which for something so cheap-looking, cost a fortune. I noticed his unnaturally long skinny fingers and thin wrists. He laboriously wrote out a receipt.

"Why have you been following me?" he asked, not looking up.

My heart started pounding.

"Sorry?"

"I asked: why have you been following me?" He looked up for the first time, and stared at me. Above a large, angular nose, his eyes were a startling watery blue. The skin was stretched over his cheekbones, like a cadaver.

"I haven't!" I was flushing bright red and sweating.

"You were parked near my house last night, and then again this morning. You blundered about following me on the bus, and down here to the shop. Why?"

I really couldn't think of any reply except the truth.

"I think you knew Cassie Bowman."

"Ah."

"I'm a friend of hers, I mean, I was a friend. She died."

"I know, and you think because I was in the same commune as her, I could tell you more about her past?"

"Well, yes."

"Take a warning. Don't try to get any information out of me or anyone else. Now, just leave the shop, and don't come back. Go."

I turned and opened the door.

"Excuse me!" he called out, holding out the wrapped package like Marley's ghost.

"Your book, Mr Kemp."

Chapter 7

That was not the end of the nightmare that day.

I knew something was wrong as I climbed the stairs to my flat. The door was open. I cautiously went inside, in case an intruder might have got in. They certainly had, for the place, though deserted, was a mess. The sofas had been ripped with a knife, there was stuff strewn all over the floor, everything breakable was broken. I went into the bedroom, and my worst fears were realised: the pictures of Cassie had been slashed down the middle of each one. On the wall, daubed in ultramarine blue paint, was scrawled in large letters:

NEXT TIME IT'S YOU

I sat down on the bed and started to cry, holding one of the slashed portraits to me like a broken doll.

I couldn't think what to do, where to go. I wanted someone to hold me like a kid, to cuddle me and make it all right.

I made my way up to the 'phone box, still clutching the ruined picture, and rang the gallery. It was Ian who answered, and cheerily began asking how I was, but I broke in:

"I must speak to Penny!"

He must have heard my desperation, for he said no more but put Penny on. I don't think I made sense – I just kept saying *"Please!"* over and over again. I put the phone down and returned to the wreckage, numbly picking stuff up and putting it down again.

She came round very quickly, and gasped as she saw the flat. She didn't need asking, she just came over and sat beside me on the gutted sofa, put her arms round me, and held me. I could feel her sobs, too, her tears mingling with mine as our faces pressed together.

"You fucking idiots! Sitting there like fucking babes in the wood."

Rosso's loud and angry voice made us both start. He strode into the room in a fury.

"I warned you, didn't I? Well, didn't I? What a fucking fool you are! Now they're on to you. They'd have cheerfully ripped you open like this lot. For God's sake!"

He stamped around, kicking the debris furiously. Penny's arm was across my chest, almost protectively, as if she were afraid he'd start attacking me. But he took a few deep breaths and calmed down.

"I saw you rushing off like a madman just now. I feared something like this had happened. Well, you can't stay here, can you? Come to my place now, both of you."

We followed him meekly across the Yard. I was talking of calling the police, but Rosso snorted and told me not to be a fucking idiot. He picked up a pebble from the ground and hurled it against a wall to relieve his feelings. It shattered into fragments.

He sat us down like two guilty children, and I told them both of my attempts to track down Alan Trapp, of his words to me, and of my shock when I heard him call me by name.

"And you put him up to this?" Rosso asked unbelievingly of Penny. She nodded.

"Trust a fucking woman."

That needled her into sitting up.

"What do you expect me to do? It's my sister who's dead and I'm certain she was killed. Do you think I'm just going to stand back and say, well never mind? I need to know the truth." She paused, and sighed. "But I never expected this."

"No, it's this idiot. I warned him, there's some nasty people out there," Rosso laughed, but there was no mirth in it. He got up and went over to the window. He looked out as he spoke; slowly, carefully.

"Cassie's death was the end of something and a beginning. Like her death cleared the way for another phase to start. Like I said: there's some scum out there. People distorted by evil. You think I'm one of them; that I pushed drugs onto Cassie until they broke her. Well, that's not the way it was.

"When I met her she was far gone: a crazy butterfly on two bags of dope a day. I cut her down over the months to a point where you could see the real Cassie again. Then you came on the scene, and gave her a reason to get straight. She loved you, you know? I think it was the first time she'd loved anyone.

"I'm on your side, believe me. When I tell you to drop the questions, I mean drop the bloody questions, for your sakes. Things are going to start getting rough."

"What things?" I asked.

Rosso shrugged his shoulders and came back to the settee. Whenever there was something difficult to explain, Rosso always just shrugged his shoulders.

"Don't ask," he said. "You're a pair of innocent wee lambs. Keep it that way."

"What about you? Are you involved in these 'things' whatever they are?" Penny asked.

He didn't speak for a while, just kept looking at the wall, then.

"Aye. I wish I wasn't, but I am."

"In what way?"

Another shrug.

For the second time, I slept on Rosso's spare bed. Penny had gone back to her flat, thoughtful and quiet.

In the morning Rosso and I salvaged what we could from the flat and piled the ruined settees in the Yard and burnt them. From the doors of the tenements, people came down to watch. Percy was there, grey and mute, watching the flames licking around the remains of my furniture.

Then the young couple came with their pram and stood, hand in hand, eyes staring and unblinking. I noticed for the first time that the pram was empty. Angus from over Rosso's flat came with a concertina, and played a slow mournful tune as the flames rose and curled in the frosty morning air.

Others came: O'Hanlon, Jeannie, the fat lady who was always pegging out and taking in her washing, Murdo, Percy, all of them, the whole Yard must have been there. Sadie came out in an outfit that must have been her working clothes and held my hand.

They stood in silence, each in his own thoughts, until Angus started to play *Will Ye Go, Lassie, Go*? And then, the whole lot of them sang along, quietly; quavering at first, then gathering momentum, until the final chorus ended like a choir at a requiem mass. Then I realised this is what it was for them, this bonfire was Cassie's funeral pyre. This was their farewell, and as the flames died down, I knew I had to say something.

"Thank you," I said.

"Cassie was a ray of hope for me, and I think for all of us. Once again, this place has tried to kill that hope but I promise you, I won't let it. I hope her spirit stays with you."

There was silence.

Just as I was beginning to think I'd got the wrong idea and made a fool of myself, O'Hanlon came up and shook my hand in silence, and Rosso's, then Murdo followed suit, and then everyone queued up to shake our hands, all in silence. Some had tears in their eyes.

I had been right, this was their farewell. Angus started to play *The Parting Glass.*

"...But since it falls unto my lot

That I should rise and you should not.

I'll gently go, and softly call:

Goodnight, and joy be with you all."

Every one of them sang it as though it was their own requiem and for those minutes there was a magic which floated up from Starlings' Yard into the air and up into the heaven which had eluded us all until now. Now it seemed to all of us that someone might be listening.

Afterwards, everyone melted back into their own flats and into their own sadness. Rosso and I stayed out there and looked at one another: both of us were crying.

I wanted to leave this place as soon as I could, and close yet another chapter of my life which had gone hideously wrong. It didn't even cause me much upset: this was the pattern and I was getting used to it. I had taken Rosso's warnings gladly to heart, and wanted only to extricate myself from the tentacles of whatever sordid thing was going on.

There is a romance to the underworld, a fascination with evil and other people's tragedy, and nowhere is this nearer the surface than in the Old Town of Edinburgh. A dark heart beats here; you can feel it and breathe it. Layer upon grimy layer of human tragedy rises from the jumble of dark buildings that lean oppressively over the streets. So much of it is history, wrapped up in ghoulish stories for the tourists and placed safely in the past. It becomes grimly picturesque.

But that heart still beats even today, feeding off the souls of the dead, generating a deathly pulse that grips the present tenants of this place. No wonder they built the New Town. The planners deliberately turned their back on that darkness, knowing they could never eradicate it they built their shrine to enlightenment and rationality in a different place. But it's still here, still very much alive.

Penny too seemed to have taken Rosso's message on board. We didn't talk about it much, it wasn't her style to back down, nor mine, so we just tacitly pretended to each other that this was a tactical retreat. Neither of us would admit how scared and shaken we'd been.

Cassie's flat needed emptying; so while I was still staying at Rosso's, Penny and I went up to her place on the second floor of the building on the far corner of the Yard to mine.

It struck me that I'd never seen it. Nothing odd about that, she just always came round to me. The police had been in, to take photographs and look for evidence, then given Penny the key.

As we climbed the stairs, I felt anxiety knot my stomach. Penny's hand, I noticed, was shaking as she put the key in the lock.

I don't really know what I expected to find. Chaos and clutter, I suppose.

Instead, the flat was clean and tidy, apart from the mess from the last week of her life. The kitchen had been cleaned, although there were the congealed and rotting remains of the food she'd grazed on in the last few disintegrating days of her life. Talking in whispers, we found a plastic bag and threw all the food we could find into it, and moved on.

The living room was bare, apart from some Habitat furniture and a few books. I noticed the one that lay open on the settee – Gombrich's *The Story of Art*. Bless you, darling Cassie, I thought, you never told me. Penny was struggling to keep up her usual efficiency, I could tell. We moved silently into the bedroom.

The single bed was made, her clothes ironed and hanging on a rail. On her counterpane was a large old teddy bear, and beside the bed, a photograph of Cicely, Penny and she, which must have been taken four or five years ago. They were all laughing. Next to the photograph lay a bible.

The room was like a nun's cell; simple and stark. I couldn't make sense of it at first, but, as we stared at the scene, I shut my eyes, and imagined her in this room, and my heart reached out to this poor girl who had ventured forth after an innocent upbringing into a world full of wolves and wicked things. She had so wanted to get out of that world, and took refuge in a teddy bear, a photograph, the comfort of a bible and me as well... and I'd failed her.

Penny was clutching the teddy bear, and her eyes were wet.

"Mark, meet Simon. He was my teddy bear for years, but Cassie fell in love with him when she was six and I was ten. We fought like cats over him, but in the end she won. I had to pretend I was too grown up for teddy bears. She carried him off and never stopped loving him. I used to hear her in her bedroom at home talking to him, telling him her little girl's secrets. And here he is still. Well, Simon, you're coming home with me now."

I took the books, and Penny, the bear. The rest we left to a house clearance firm who came a week later and removed the last traces of her life.

When Penny suggested it some days later, I moved out of Rosso's and in with her, as a lodger. I wasn't going back to the flat in Starlings' Yard for a while and she had a spare room or two in her large apartment in Dean Village.

Like Penny, her flat wasn't giving in to the current trend in décor. Off white throughout, and expensively furnished, with some good pictures on the wall. It might have had the same choking sterile effect of her mother's house, except the severity was relieved by a bit of untidiness, which made the place welcoming. I felt at home there, it was like taking a lungful of fresh air after walking through a sewer.

Things definitely took a turn for the better when Penny came back from work one day covered in smiles and with the news that Ian had showed my canvases to Patrick Burn. The man was a well-respected art dealer, and was just setting up a new gallery in town dealing mainly with the 20th Century Scottish masters, but also seeking to promote contemporary Scottish work in the mainstream tradition (according to Penny). He'd been impressed, and wanted to meet me to discuss hanging one or two pieces as a trial.

When I met him, he was not as I expected.

Instead of the self-confident and overfed look of the dealers I'd known, this man was lean, with tense, bright eyes that radiated a serious passion for his work. He was craggily handsome, with distinguished sweeping grey hair. He was dressed in a grey mohair suit which radiated formality, and money. My two pictures were leaning against the wall of his office.

He came straight to the point.

"I like these two. I'd like to see others though."

I told him what had happened to the others. He waved a dismissive arm.

"Bring them in anyway."

I did, the next day. He ran his pale hands over the rips. He peered at the Cassie portraits.

"These are very fine. Very fine. It'll be simple enough to re-line these. I've got a man who does that sort of thing like a magician and then we can leave you to do any re-touching. It'll reduce their value somewhat, and as there'll be the cost of restoration and given that you're not known, I don't think we should overestimate their worth."

He mentioned a sum that was wildly over any price I'd have asked and I felt my heart beating wildly in my chest as I walked out and went round to the Croesus Gallery as fast as I could.

I could have hugged Ian; in fact, I think I did. I was pouring out thanks and grinning dementedly. Ian produced a whisky bottle and a few glasses, Penny wiped a happy tear from her eye, and we drank a toast. It was good, as good as it could get but being me, I couldn't get a small knot of uneasiness out from inside. I tried explaining it to Penny that evening, only to be met with a snort of derision:

"Honestly, can't you ever just be unconditionally happy for once?"

"Me? Nah."

"What on earth's bugging you, then?"

"It's like I'm scared of succeeding, you know? Like I'm going to get all middle class and something's going to disappear."

"God, you haven't even sold a picture yet and you're all lathered up about being spoilt by success. What's the matter with you?"

I told her what was wrong with me. I was an outsider. A Steppenwolf destined to prowl around the fringes of society, unable or unwilling to enter the fold.

I explained the shock of recognition I'd felt when I'd read Colin Wilson's *The Outsider* for the first time. His analysis of those talented, gloomy existentialists fitted me exactly; so exactly that I felt an almost numinous elation as I read about the thinkers and artists who felt a constant preoccupation with the meaninglessness of everything. And then found redemption in the odd small thing, a snatch of music, an everyday scene, something in the everyday that acquired a significance beyond itself and gave meaning to everything else.

Like the Yard's farewell to Cassie. These few, like me, had to exist beyond the bubble of the here and now, watching and recording, seeking the spiritual in the stews of daily life.

That's what guided every line and dab of paint on my canvases and dictated my preference for the forgotten backwaters of life, like Starlings' Yard. It was the fear of getting sucked into the bubble that made me uneasy.

To my surprise, Penny came over, sat beside me, put her arms around me and kissed me gently. I looked at her. The lamplight softened the angles of her face and her eyes were wide open, looking back up at me. Cassie's green eyes.

"That was nice," I smiled.

"There's more where that came from."

"Why?"

"Because I know just what you mean. It explains you - some of you, anyway, and it tells me a lot about myself, too. I just got a feeling of being incredibly close to you." She kissed me again and I kissed her back.

That night, we slept together for the first time. We held on to each other like babes in a storm, and I felt new warmth seep into my frozen emotions again.

Chapter 8

In the morning, when the sun filled the room with a green-gold light and I could feel its warmth on my face, we lay side by side in her bed, I told her that I was going back to Starlings' Yard. I wanted to paint and the place still held its strange attraction for me. There were still rich seams to be mined there.

Penny propped herself up on one elbow. She had beautiful, full breasts.

"Are you sure that's wise?" She frowned. "I really want to get the place out of my system. I don't think it's safe to go back."

"I'm just going back during the day to use the flat as a studio. I'll sketch and paint there and I won't get mixed up with anything else. I'll be back each day and cook you a meal and let you use me as your sexual slave. Deal?"

"I like the sound of that. OK, but be careful, please. They'll be watching. Whoever 'they' are."

"I've a feeling friend Trapp isn't too low down the list, but our fingers have been duly burned, and if I'm seen to be there just painting happily away, I think they'll lose interest."

"I'm not so sure," she said, "I just don't trust that place."

"Anyway," I said, "have you gone off the idea of finding out what happened to Cassie?"

"Yes, I have. Well, no I haven't, but we brushed with something very nasty, something that even the police won't touch. We wouldn't stand a chance."

"I know. Don't worry, I'm not going down that road again. Now, give us a cuddle."

"I'll be late for work!"

"So?"

"Ach, you're right. Come here...."

The Yard was almost welcoming. Spring sun lit up the courtyard, throwing a cast of colour over the stones and the rubbish, picking out the details of peeling painted doors. There too, was the familiar smell of the place, something I'd grown not to notice when I lived there, but which now drew me into it like the arms of an old friend.

There was no-one about, but the twitch of a curtain or two told me my return had been noted.

I set up a makeshift studio in the flat, and started some sketches for another series. An evolution from the Cassie series, still placing the human figure against the textures of the nooks and crannies of the Yard, but this was to be a dark, nocturnal set of pictures with a single source of light illuminating the picture. That way, I was concentrating on the shadows, making the absence of light sculpt the shape and texture of the stones and the figure.

Who that figure was going to be, I didn't know yet, but I'd have a look through the directories. Whoever it was, she would never have the passive intensity that Cassie radiated.

My thoughts strayed to her: flitting like a fairy between innocent happiness and terror, trapped in the black web that lay invisible over the Old Town. I remembered the warmth of her body, then her cold crumpled corpse, and her laughter, and the thing that had possessed her, until the images swam in and out through my mind like a shoal of strange fish.

I looked down at my sketchpad: I'd drawn her, the very essence of her, with spindly arms that stretched out along the stones like the Grünewald crucifixion, while her naked body crouched in quarter profile among the debris on the ground. I looked up at the sky and thanked her, and then she must have heard me and given me the answer. It was obvious!

I went round to Sadie's and knocked at her door. I was taken aback when she let me in, for it was spotless, and expensively furnished. I told her so.

"Wages of sin, dear, that's all. Told you: I'm not staying here. This lot's coming with me when I move. Cup of tea?"

As we sipped, I asked her if she would model for me. You see, the idea (that I'm still convinced Cassie sent to me) was blindingly simple. The strength of my pictures lay in placing figures against their natural background. They were all here! I was living amongst the very people that animated the Yard. If I could get them to pose – there was enough material here for a lifetime.

"You want me to lie there naked for you?" said Sadie, "I'm not sure about that."

"But you lie naked in front of strangers all the time!" I blundered.

"That's business, dear, that's different."

"And what about you and me?" I asked.

"That's personal and private. Just us, know what I mean?"

Eventually we worked out a deal. She'd model for the same rates as she got from her clients, as she called them. It was lot more than I paid models normally, but then, I suppose it would be.

She was a good model. She exuded sex, so I placed her in some erotic poses, and laid down the basis for what was to become a series of five pictures, (Crannies, i – v, but these were all taken up into private collections later). After we'd finished, she'd make us a cup of tea and ask me to play with her breasts.

A few weeks later, I went back to the Yard as dusk fell, armed with a camera and a torch, to get some preliminary studies for the stones. Penny wasn't very keen on the idea; the further away Starlings' Yard receded in her mind, the more she feared the place. I laughed it off, told her it had to be done anyway, and arranged to meet her in The Melrose Bar afterwards, as she'd got an exhibition opening to attend in the town anyway.

There was no-one about when I got there in the dark. A pile of embers in a corner spoke of Percy's recent presence, and one or two lit windows cast a dim glow over the Yard.

The spot I had in mind was on the right hand side of the Yard. The houses there had been built on what looked like the levelled off remains of an earlier structure. The dressed stone of the building sat on rough-hewn, darker stone, about three feet high, and it was possible to trace the outline of three stone arches in the stonework, filled in with mortar and rubble.

Nobody really noticed it, for it was half obscured behind a line of dustbins. But in my search for details in the previous series, I'd seen it, and become aware, as I looked harder at it, of the scratches and chips, of the parts worn smooth, or of the anonymous stains that had become part of the fabric of the stones.

I quietly moved the bins, disturbing a cat in the process, then crouched down. I'd sketched them quite a few times before, in daylight; but now, in the dark as I shone the torch on the stone from different angles, the effect of the moving light made the stones seem to come alive and change shape.

That faculty of the brain to make meaning out of random marks created illusions of carved faces and fantastic animals that appeared and faded back into the darkness. At each new position of the torch, I lay on the ground with my camera and took a photograph, as well as a quick sketch of the shapes. On the fourth position, a hand grabbed the collar of my coat and hauled me roughly onto my back. It was Rosso: an angry Rosso, looking the more so as the torchlight lit his face from below.

"What're ye fuckin' doin'?"

"Just some studies for a -"

"Get away! Now!" he whispered and hauled me to my feet, putting my torch out and hastily replacing the bins before pushing me roughly towards his flat. I was too surprised to resist. He bundled me through the door and confronted me in the hall.

"How many times do you need telling? I warned you, didn't I? Keep out of this place!"

"Look, I'm here as an artist, that's all. I'm not poking my nose into anything round here. I just want to paint some bloody pictures!"

"They don't know that, do they? Crawling about at night like a spy with a camera? What are they going to think? Even the walls have got eyes round here."

His face was close to mine, and I could see a change in his appearance since we'd last met. His face was leaner, and showed the signs of strain. He wasn't normally the most elegant of people, but now the signs of self-neglect were obvious.

"You look terrible," I told him.

"Yeah, well. Now please get away from here, and stay away."

I wanted to, badly. Life was getting on a good track.

"I can't," I said.

I thought he was going to hit me: his fists curled and he reddened alarmingly. Then he collapsed on the sofa, and ran his hand through his hair. He looked exhausted. He went to the kitchen and returned with two cans of beer. He passed one to me and we drank in silence. Elbows on knees, he dangled the can in front of him and stared at the floor.

"Then we'll try and sort this out together, but only as long as you know what you're up against. Christ knows, I'm tired."

"Tell me."

"I am telling you. Just listen, will ya?" There was another silence.

"Cassie was murdered. She was repeatedly injected with large doses of heroin in that last week until she died, and then they slit her fuckin' wrist. Jesus!"

"Who would do that? Why?"

"I don't know who. It doesn't really matter. But I know why."

"What do you mean, it doesn't matter?"

"Stop butting in! I'm trying to tell ya! It doesn't matter because whoever it was held her down and mainlined her was a nobody, a bit of scum following someone else's orders. I don't know who gave the orders: that's what we need to find out. Why they wanted her dead is simple. She knew who the leaders were. Look, this town's built on evil, and it doesn't suddenly go away."

I could sense that. Four hundred years ago, the town built a wall to protect itself against English attacks. As it happened, it proved completely useless for its purpose, but had the unforeseen effect of corralling in a rapidly expanding population.

The overcrowding was extreme, forcing the rise of tenements up to fourteen storeys high, with as many as two hundred crammed onto each floor. Rooms and vaults were carved into soft sandstone that lay under the city. Conditions for rich and poor alike were cramped, smelly, and lethal.

Life was cheap, and the struggle to make a living frequently involved theft and murder. Crime became engrained in the place and still today the dark wynds were no places to stray alone. The flocks of tourists and the antics of students still couldn't completely smother the atmosphere of darkness underneath.

Rosso kept talking, in a voice that was trying to be objective:

"There's something big and bad going on round here; there has been for a long time, like some sort of evil mafia and what's happening now has been going on for a hundred years. Once it was diamonds, or whisky, or whatever. Now it's drugs, too. Oh, there are little outfits all over the place doing some dealing, but this is different. It's evolved into a cult, with its own rituals and priestly brotherhood."

"Satanism?"

"Something like. I don't know. All I know is what I've told you and that's what Cassie told me."

"Why should they kill her?"

"She broke ranks. She was part of it once. That commune in Dalkeith Road was where they got their teeth into her. I think they were grooming her for some sort of job. Prostitution, probably. They recruit a lot of people: misfits and petty criminals mostly. The dregs of society who relish the thought of revenge on the society that outcast them."

"Steppenwolves."

"Nah, steppenwolves are freethinkers. This lot are sorry little buggers with grudges that have become organised into a pack. Once in, they're trapped; any backsliding on their part and they know some of their fellow thugs are going to be given orders to knife them. In Cassie's case, inject them. She was part of the network of minions, and when you came along, she was determined to escape all that. I worried myself sick. I was very offhand with you, perhaps you'd noticed?"

"Oh yes, I just assumed it was jealousy."

"Now you know different. Loving you was the best thing she'd ever done, but it signed her death warrant. She knew too much to be allowed to escape. That's why I said it's not worth finding out who did the actual job. The real murderers are the inner core, and they're invisible."

"How about O'Hanlon?"

"I'm sure he's in there somewhere. No proof, apart from seeing him hang out with a few shady sorts, but they're mostly from round here, so he could just be being neighbourly. He's not, of course, but..."

"Why don't we go to the police?"

He gave me a look.

"They're not going to set a foot near that lot. They know about the organisation, but they're not going to stir up the hornets' nest. A few junkies die, but you saw how little attention they gave Cassie's death. Anyone sniffing around is dead meat. That's why I've been telling you to back off."

Something occurred to me then.

"Where do you fit into all this, then? How did you get involved with Cassie? How come they haven't got you nailed? Who the hell are you, Rosso?"

He smiled to himself.

"Don't ask me that – yet. I'm a bit of a wanderer, that's all. I've been at sea, the forces, that sort of thing. I'll tell you everything, but not now. I'm on your side, I swear to you, and I want to find out the whole truth even more than you do, but they're watching us. You've had a warning; I've had several. Now you must go, and not come back here for a while. I'll see you out and then you just act out a little charade with me."

We swapped phone numbers, then he started to shout and manhandled me out of the front door, pushing me and shouting at me to get out and stop getting mixed up in other people's business. I did my best to remonstrate back and made a show of promising to disappear. I realised we were putting on a show for the Yard. Eyes would be watching. Maybe some of those eyes would know we were putting on a charade.

I suddenly felt a sense of being in a dangerous situation.

After a last shove that sent me sprawling, I picked myself up and walked quickly out of the Yard. I walked up Niddry Street, before I remembered, Penny!

I hurried along to the Melrose. It was ten thirty. I was very late.

Penny was there, being propositioned by a man in a beer-stained T-shirt, and looked relieved and annoyed at the same time as I sat beside her and pointedly kissed her. The man in the T-shirt looked surprised and wearily disappointed, and walked off.

She rounded on me, "You'd better learn something: I don't take to being kept waiting in bars on my own. Where have you been?"

I got a beer and another glass of wine for her, and told her what had happened. She held my hand under the table.

"We've got to leave this whole thing alone. It's scary. I'm sorry I ever got you involved. Well, no I'm not, of course, but this is too big. No more sleuthing, no more going back to that horrible place, nothing. You are moving in with me and setting up a studio and you're going to paint some bonny pictures and I'm going to sell them, and –"

"- and we'll drink wine and make love, and be the toast of the town," I cried out.

We both said "Yes!" together and laughed a laugh of relief, and as we drank, I forgot Rosso's drawn face and the menace of that place. Once again, we pushed all that to somewhere far away and went back to her flat.

There was a wildness to that night: a bacchanalia of hope. Penny's stock of good wine took a severe beating. We drank to the sound of Bob Dylan, Van de Graaf Generator, to Emerson, Lake and Palmer, and then, while Deep Purple played through her outrageously large speakers, she stood up in front of me and slowly, provocatively, took off her clothes.

She swayed to the music and the alcohol as she ran her hands over her body, then took my hands, inviting me to explore her. She removed my clothes, then took another record from its sleeve and turned off the lights, leaving only two candles flickering. We made love on the carpet to Fauré's *Requiem*, and to this day I cannot listen to it without getting an erection.

I woke in broad daylight alone. I lay there, with a banging head and a sense of guilt. After a while, I got up and found Penny sprawled in bed, sleeping soundly. I joined her, and together we slept like the Babes in the Wood until it was getting dark again.

A month passed and I was slowly drawn into Penny's world. She was clever about the whole process. A meeting with a few friends, an evening with Ian and surprise, his male partner, a night at the theatre to see one of her friends act the part of Nora in 'A Doll's House'. We even went to see Cicely together. It had to happen, sooner or later, but I was uneasy about it. However, Cicely was not only forgiving, but delightful company. Brushing aside my apology for my behaviour at our previous meeting with a sweep of her hand. She gave me a firm kiss on my cheek and a mischievous grin.

It seemed I was no longer the Steppenwolf, at least on the face of it. I had been invited into the fold and came in like a lamb. I started liking their world.

The week before, at my request, Penny had taken me to Jenner's to get some clothes that might fit in better with this new life. I'd even asked if I might try on a suit. The assistant fussed over us and suggested a dark blue thing. I came out of the changing room; the assistant clasped his hands with approval, but Penny, I saw, was grinning and shaking her head. We tried another and another, until Penny grabbed me by the arm and led me off, laughing. We settled for some grandad shirts and some very skinny jeans.

Penny and her mother were shrewd people, they saw through pretence and mocked the poseurs that they inevitably came across. For the first time, I felt that they and their friends, respected the forces which drove me. Until then I had been dismissed by those in the comfortable middle class world that just got embarrassed by any real emotion, didn't – couldn't – feel it, and mocked it.

I found the evening with Cicely a pleasure.

She'd been quite a girl, it transpired. Having spent her teens in France, she'd got to know (in every sense, it became clear) a lot of artists – famous ones as well. She'd tales to tell that were definitely not included in my art history lectures.

She wasn't the frosted glass dowager that I had supposed. After her time in France she'd been a nurse, then gone on to study for a degree in anthropology. It turned out she was a bit of an authority on myth and shamanistic practices, a lecturer on the subject at the University. I listened, fascinated, as she spoke of a recent expedition to the Mapuche in Patagonia, where women took on the shaman role and were reputed to be able to ward off evil.

"I learnt a good deal from them," she said.

"I suppose we think of native beliefs as simple, or even wrong, but that's not so. Their notion of good and evil is different from ours. They think of the spirit as essentially good, and that any evil comes from outside, in the form of bad spirits. These spirits are very real to them. They can, in trances, see them, and send them packing. What's rather fascinating, well, to me at any rate, you can wake up when I've finished; is that in other cultures, they claim the same thing, and in so many different cultures, the description of these evil spirits is almost identical. Is that diffusionism, or are they seeing something real, I wonder?"

"What do you believe?" asked Penny. This stuff was apparently new to her.

"As an academic, or as me?" she replied.

"Academically, the answer is cross cultural contact, but I can't say there's much evidence of that. The academics would twist any theory around to avoid admitting the reality of spirits, and I wouldn't dare voice it in my work, but here's a thing: I think I do actually believe these things have some sort of reality. Aren't I getting to be a batty old woman?"

I thought of the creature that I had seen infesting Cassie, but said nothing. I caught Penny's glance. Suddenly, Cassie's image came vividly back to me.

As her maid (yes, I wasn't even scoffing), brought in some coffee and a tray of liqueurs, I needed to talk about her. I asked how Cicely was feeling. Penny stiffened a little beside me and looked at the table, but Cicely gave me a long look.

"Thank you for asking, Mark. Someone had to. Poor Cassie, her memory sitting with us like an elephant in the room. To be honest, I'm feeling rather low and lost these days."

"Then let's not spoil the evening," Penny said.

"We won't. It's been too nice to spoil," said Cicely. "But something needs saying. Thank you, Mark. I have some things to say, but first, perhaps a toast to the poor girl's memory?"

So we stood with our Atholl Brose in our hands and together pledged her memory. We stayed there a minute or so, in silence, each one of us with our thoughts.

"God bless her, poor child," Cicely said. A tear ran down her cheek. "I must, however, put the record straight. I was rather abrupt with you, Mark, and I apologise, but I had my reasons, and they were not the reasons I gave you."

"No. I thought not."

"Cassie was killed by a very nasty organisation. She stumbled into it and then tried to stumble out, but they weren't having it. Once in, you can't leave – they've far too much to hide. Cassie was trying to get a grip on her life but the fear

126

had given her innocence another dimension. I don't want Penny or you getting involved, or you'll end up dead too."

I told her that Rosso had said as much, and gave her my word that I was going to heed good advice and not going to even think of trying to tackle something so powerful and ruthless.

"Ah," she said, "Rosso! How is he, these days?"

"What, you know him?"

"Oh, yes. An old family friend. Always took an interest in Cassie. Bit of a rough diamond, but a diamond nevertheless."

"I'd no idea! Let's fix up an evening," Penny said.

"No, dear, I'd rather not, but thank you for the thought. It's best for now that we don't meet."

"Why, for God's sake?" asked Penny.

Cicely raised her hand and refused to be drawn any further. I told her what Rosso had told me.

"You say he told you he didn't know the name of this organisation? I find that rather strange. He knows as well as I do."

Penny and I both stared at her.

"Mother, did I just hear you say you know who these people are?"

"I don't know individual names. But the organisation, yes. I believe you should know the name, then forget all about it. It's called Oculus."

Chapter 9

I rang Rosso to ask him why he hadn't saw fit to tell me about Oculus, or the fact that he knew Cicely Bowman. Christ, he could even shrug down a telephone line.

"How much else are you hiding from me?" I asked, annoyed.

"Not much."

"I don't believe you. I know you don't want me getting into deep water, but you also said you need my help. What's it to be, Rosso?"

"OK, OK, I'm sorry. Look, meet me under Binns' clock tomorrow at two and I'll be straight with you, I promise. Just make sure there's no-one following you. Walk along a few quiet streets and keep your eyes skinned. If someone's tracking you, don't meet me, OK?"

I did as he said, and saw nobody.

I saw him standing under the clock, and when he saw me, he tipped his head to indicate that I should follow him. He led the way into a quiet café. I came and sat down at his table, and we ordered some tea and cakes. He made sure we couldn't be overheard, and started talking in a soft voice.

"Oculus is an evil cult, as I told you. It started as an outcast branch of the Scottish Masonic order at the start of the century. A few of them had tried to corrupt the Order, bringing their own slant to the rituals. Then they formed their own society, highly secret, with their own mumbo-jumbo using Masonic symbols for their own twisted ends.

"It was shortly after a guy called McGregor Mathers had left the Masons and set up something called the Order of the

Golden Dawn, that there suddenly seemed to be all sorts of mystic societies springing up, all dabbling in the occult, and Oculus was one of these.

"Mathers always fancied himself as a Scot and added the McGregor to his name. For a year or two he came to Edinburgh. That was at a time when he was still friends with a rather strange and unpleasant character called Aleister Crowley, who saw himself as a black magician. Mathers later got scared by the direction that Oculus was taking and high-tailed it back to England. Most of these various orders carried on but became watered down into gentlemen's clubs with a bit of an excuse to dress up and recite bits of symbolic mumbo-jumbo."

The waitress brought our teas, and Rosso fell silent while she clattered them onto the table. He bit greedily into his cake, then continued.

"But Oculus evolved differently, feeding off the desperation and poverty of the Old Town. Its secret hierarchy developed their rituals to give a mock credence to their goings on. They were involved in all sorts – assassination, smuggling, prostitution and drug dealing. All this in the name of the Devil, who they convinced themselves, offered a 'left-hand path', an alternative philosophy of life, saying that embracing Evil was every bit as relevant as embracing Good.

"Thanks to all this can't they succeeded in attracting some quite high profile people to their ranks. To this day, they continue to be a cancer in the town. The fucking little rats that work for them are everywhere. There are probably about twenty 'initiates', but hundreds of underlings who get their kicks from being nasty and being connected to a powerful secret brotherhood. They make approaches to potential recruits from the criminal underworld, and kids willing to dabble in occultism. The commune in Dalkeith Road was set up by them to lure people like Cassie: gullible teenagers going though that phase of getting obsessed by occultism and Devil worship.

"Cassie used to tell me about it: all a bit of fun, she called it. But then it must have started getting serious and she wouldn't speak about it anymore. I think that's when she was hooked on drugs, and they were turning her onto the streets to pay for the habit. Two of the lads in the commune got scared they were getting in too deep, panicked, and went to the police who started poking around. Shortly after, they were found hanged, and the cops tried to find out who was behind it, but never pinned it on anyone: a suicide pact, they decided, conveniently.

"The commune closed down after that – that's when I found her a flat in Starlings' Yard, and she moved in. Bad move. I'm convinced it's the centre of Oculus operations, and I led her right into the trap."

"How do you know all this?"

"The early stuff is on the record, until the books go quiet on the subject. Cassie told me about visits from men to the commune who used to lead their rituals, she even told me they'd mentioned the name Oculus during these rituals, making out it was white witchcraft and would give them all occult powers. The rest you hear on the street: I have some rather shifty acquaintances, but not shifty enough to know who any of the leaders are."

"And why do you think Starlings' Yard is connected to it?"

"Because the ritual makes references to Hannah. Cassie told me that much: it's how she learned about the story. The ritual suggests that Hannah's death liberated the evil spirits in Starlings' Yard, and that it's those spirits that are summonsed during the rituals. It's a load of bloody tosh of course, but, well, there's something evil there; I can feel it, and it's getting to me, pal, it's really getting to me. Come on, let's pay up and go."

He stood up abruptly, leaving me to pay as he went quickly outside, as though he needed air. I saw him through the window, anxiously jiggling his hands in the pockets of his coat. I joined him.

"I've said enough," he said, "I'll see you."

"What's wrong?" I cried, as he started to walk away.

"Every fucking thing!"

And he was gone.

I walked back to the flat, the unease as strong as ever.

On the way, I passed the chemist where I'd left the photographs I'd taken of the Yard at night to be processed weeks ago. I'd put the place out of my mind and had been planning another painting.

Penny was still at work. I put the fire on and rifled through the photos while I waited for the kettle to boil. There were some nice ones of Penny and some indifferent ones of me taken while we were larking about on a walk. A few of the Cityscape series, ruined by the reflection of the flashbulb. Then the ones of the stones in the Yard. I glanced through them; they'd come out quite well, with the texture of the stones thrown into dramatic relief by the torchlight. I looked closer, then I felt my stomach turn over.

I was looking at a picture of an area of stone wall about six foot by four, its history written in the worn surface. In the top left hand corner was a light patch – what I assumed was the focus of the torch beam, but the torchlight was coming from the other direction. The patch of light was a ghostly face, one that I knew too well. Hannah!

I closed my eyes, feeling sick. Was there no escape? I looked at the other photographs. That twisted face was there too, but fading. I stared at the wall, and the face was there like a projected slide. As I sat, unmoving, I became aware of Cassie standing behind me. My scalp prickled: I knew it was her.

131

"Cassie?"

There was a feeling of – what? – Calm? Love? A yearning? She was so close behind me now: three feet...two? Suddenly, I felt hands around my throat. I put my own hands to my throat to prise off the tightening grip, before my neck was twisted violently and a sick laugh rang in my ears before I must have passed out.

Penny was shaking me and calling out my name. I remember that. Her voice was urgent, panicking.

"Mark, for God's sake, talk to me!"

"Cassie?"

"Penny, you fool!"

"Oh, yeah. Hello, Penny."

"What the hell's happened to you?"

"I've been spooked – Christ knows."

She helped me to my feet. It was hard to breathe. She walked me round, then marched me to the bathroom, where she pushed me in front of the mirror. My face seemed puffy, and around my neck were some livid bruises.

I tried to tell her what had happened, but she seemed distracted and angry.

"Penny, believe me, I've been attacked by a ghost - Hannah's ghost, or Cassie's."

"It's shit! All this talk of ghosts, it's rubbish! Stop it!"

She'd come against something that wasn't on her map. Penny, the rationalist, had seen something she couldn't explain, and she was angry. Spooks weren't allowed into her flat. I showed her the photographs. At first she refused to see the face, but I was insistent. She saw it, and wept.

"I want it to go away. Why won't it leave us alone?" She kept repeating it. The trauma of the evening put words into my mouth.

"Because I – we've been chosen. I know that now. I've never believed in destiny. I thought that what we do, we do with a free will, but I know differently now: I've been chosen to see this thing through. There's no going back, Penny."

"That's not true!"

"Oh, yes, it is. Sorry, love, but I've had enough of this. I'm going to destroy Oculus and let Cassie rest."

"You're still in love with her, aren't you?"

"What are you getting at?"

"I'm doing what I can for you, Mark. I love you, but you're making it difficult. Forget the past, you've got a future. With me! Cassie's dead!"

"Not properly!"

"Go to her, then! Go on, get out!"

She was screaming at me. I'd never seen her like that. I went out into the warm rain of the July night and paced the street until I was soaking wet and weary. I heard Penny calling my name somewhere behind me, her voice ringing in the street. I stopped, leaning against a lamp post until she was there, at the end of the street, still calling out. She stopped when she saw me.

"Mark? Mark, don't do this. I don't know what's happening." She walked up to me. "I can't bear this. Like we've been infected by some alien thing. Come back, please, Mark. You need nursing, not shouting at. Sorry."

"I'm scared, too."

"I know."

She held out her hand; I took it. When we were back at the flat, I told her about the boy in the red hat. It was right time.

"I told you about Ellie and when we were in Whitby, and I also told you we didn't have children. Well, that wasn't true: we did. One, a boy. Robert, his name was. Brilliant little kid, but when he was three, he got poorly and he wouldn't get better.

"Eventually, they found out that he'd got leukaemia. Poor scrap, what he went through: all sorts of damned treatments, and I suppose he didn't know what it was all about. He just took it as it came. His chemotherapy made his hair drop out; that's when we bought him a red bobble hat. He was so taken with it – even when his hair grew back for a while he wouldn't be separated from it. That's the image I have: a pale boy with a smile and a red woolly hat. Nothing stays, though. Two years ago, this month, he died."

There was a long silence. Penny said nothing, but poured me a Scotch and held my hand while I had a little weep. She was crying, too. I wiped our tears away with the back of my hand.

"And you know why I'm telling you this, now?"

"Because it was high time you did."

"Sure, but also because of what happened afterwards.

"We both tried to cope in our own ways, you see. But they were different ways. Ellie wanted to talk over it, endlessly. I was different, I just ran away. I worked, I drank, anything but face it. So we came to arguments and recriminations. I grew bitter and jealous. My fault - I just couldn't deal with it.

"We parted, and I came up here. I put all the blame on her and ran. I showed my pictures once to O'Hanlon, and do you know what he said straight away? 'Why do you hate yourself?' And he was right, but I've never really seen it. I've been hating myself for a long time, and it's got to stop," I looked up at Penny. "It's got to stop because I love you, and you don't deserve damaged goods."

She wanted to say something, but I waved her to silence.

"I loved your sister too, in a different way. Don't you see? We both hated what we were, and tried to set up some sort of fairy-tale world where we could ignore the outside. But you

134

can't live forever like that. Reality caught up with Cassie and now it's caught up with me. If I run away from what's happening, I'll be angry with myself forever, and I'll take it out on you. You've got to let me go, Penny, just for a while, until I confront this thing and it gets sorted out. It's for you, it's for me, it's for Cassie, and most of all, it's for Robert. I need you to understand."

"I don't know what to say."

"Say something, for God's sake."

"First of all, I love you, too. I love you, even if you are all fucked up. Aren't we all? Secondly, I'd rather a damaged you than a dead you. You can't do this to me. You don't have to be a hero for my sake."

"I don't want to be a hero. I'm the last person on this earth to be a hero. I just want to be free of this evil cloud and be able to look everyone I've loved in the face again."

"I know, I know. I'm just not as strong as you. I'm really scared, Mark."

"So am I. All I know is it's got to be done. You'll be safely out of the equation."

"That's just why I'm scared. I'm coming with you."

"No, you're not. It's my decision."

"And from now on, buddy, your decision is our decision. I've got my own ghosts to lay."

We said nothing more; we just held on to each other.

•

Chapter 10

Daylight didn't alter things. What we'd said, we meant. We locked up Penny's flat, and left the key with Cicely to keep an eye on the place, before loading up Penny's car with some essentials and setting off to Starlings' Yard.

It wasn't long before we had our first visitor.

Rosso bundled through the door, incredulous. He was half cross, half happy. I sat him down and told him everything that had happened, whilst Penny started to tidy and clean like a woman obsessed.

He saw the marks on my neck and showed me similar bruises on his arms. I told him about the photographs and was slightly disappointed when he didn't seem surprised. He'd seen things, unexplained things, things that shouldn't happen but did. More than ever, the place was a focus for "bad vibes", as he put it.

Penny produced some coffee, and the three of us sat down to discuss what we should do. We were all worn down by waiting, passive and helpless, for something to happen. We had to risk kicking the hornets' nest. That meant letting it out that we were back in the game, and taking on Oculus.

We needed to stick together at all times: Rosso would move in with us, and we'd start with O'Hanlon, assuming he was central to the organisation. Any reprisals would then be laid at his door, and he wouldn't risk that. After that, Alan Trapp's bookshop needed watching – he probably had some interesting visitors.

It was a dangerous game of cat and mouse, but there was a sense of relief in the air. Rosso went off to collect some stuff, and returned with a large bag which contained, amongst the clothes, two service revolvers.

Penny was horrified and I can't say I was happy, but Rosso insisted. They were a leftover from his service days and just needed to be hidden around the flat as a precaution. Penny and I handled them, feeling the weight, while Rosso explained a few basics, and after only a few minutes it seemed quite natural to hold one.

I decided it was time to bait the hook, and took my sketchpad out into the Yard. A few of the residents passed and waved or said, "Good morning", as though I'd never been away.

It wasn't long before O'Hanlon appeared.

"Mark! Now I am pleased. I quite thought we'd scared you away." I told him I'd been staying with a friend.

"Oh, quite, quite! You needed to get away, after all the turmoil, but, my word, it is good to see you again. Tell you what, are you busy with the drawing, or have you time for some coffee?"

He'd taken the bait!

We went over to his flat. It hadn't changed. He made me a cup of instant coffee, but poured himself a whisky. We sat in his room, which even at that time on a bright morning was shrouded in darkness and lit by the perpetual glow of his lamp.

He told me the news: Smithy's wife had been taken away in an ambulance with a gastric haemorrhage, and they'd arrested Murdo on suspicion of robbery, but they'd had to let him go. And him? Oh, he'd been on with this and that, nosing into some musty old books, as usual. Then I noticed the old gleam in his eye as he stroked his nose.

"Now you tell me how you are, young man. I've been worried about you, you know. We've been praying for you."

I told him about Penny (he would have already seen we'd moved back together), about the hopeful news about some of my pictures. Then it was my turn to lean forward and take the bull by the horns.

"Now, I've decided to come back and find out what really happened to Cassie. I wish I didn't have to, but I must. I think you can see a long way into people's souls. Tell me you understand why."

"Thank you for the compliment, bless you. You're right, I can. It's not a boast, it's a gift and a curse, like your artistic ability. Are you sure you know what you're taking on?"

"I know about Oculus, if that's what you mean."

"Yes, that's what I mean. Not only them, but something else besides."

"What?"

"You tell me."

"You mean the spirits, the evil or whatever."

"I do. Is that what caused the marks on your neck?"

Damn him. "Yes."

"Then you know what you're taking on and you know the three of you are mad to think you can fight the forces of evil, spiritual and physical, don't you?"

"Yes we do, but we can't walk away from it."

He laughed. "Then you'll do for me! Now, what did you want from me?"

"Nothing. Or maybe you could give me some information."

"Which is why you were dispatched to lure me, eh? Let me ask you directly and answer me honestly, you think I'm involved with Oculus?"

I couldn't find words. I looked helplessly at him, my mind working fast.

"We think that the centre –"

"Yes or no, please."

"Yes."

The playful smile left his face. There was silence as he poured himself another whisky, and waved the bottle at me in question. I shook my head. He drank a large mouthful.

"Now, that's what I knew you were going to say. It makes sense. I presume you've done your homework, and found out my past?"

I was being spun like a top, and shook my head.

"No? Dear me. Well, I'll save you the trouble – you can check it out in the newspaper records; I imagine you've been too busy thinking about your own troubles to do much sleuthing.

"It's a poor little tale, really. I was quite the model priest at first, but I had the fire of the zealot upon me. A little parish priest in County Clare but with such a passion on me that I thought God spoke to me directly, so I would preach like the Devil himself, forgive the phrase. Soon I was attracting a crowd of followers and I believed I was bringing them to God and young fool that I was never saw that I was becoming like a God to them.

"People flocked, especially the women, for you'd not believe it now but I was a handsome strap of a lad with a mane of black hair and fire in his eyes. It wasn't pleasing to the cardinals at all: it's fine to bring the flock to the altar, but they saw what I didn't, that I had a power that wasn't God's, even if I thought it was. They brought pressure to bear, but I wasn't having it. I carried on, feeling God and me were the best of friends and carrying all before us.

"Women were fascinated, and despite resisting at first, the inevitable happened. Once I'd had one, many, many others followed. That gave the Church what it needed, and I was excommunicated – the full *vitandus*, too. It was a real scandal at the time, and wasn't I quite the celebrity. I fled to Edinburgh, and I ended up here, a rather bitter but wiser man. Now you're thinking to yourself, why is he telling me this? Does that make him anti-church and therefore a worshipper of devils, or is he still best friends with his God? Who the hell's O'Hanlon, eh?"

"Um..."

"Now we have a problem here, you and me, Mark. You can't know, can you, whether I'm a devil or an angel? And whatever I say, we're in a fix."

"What do you mean?"

"I could tell you I'm on your side, that I live here to fight Oculus and the Devil, but can you believe me? Am I selling you a tale to trap you? If I said I am part of Oculus and I was raising the Devil, what do you do then? Because either the organisation or the Devil would wipe you three off the face of the earth now you've told me. So you'd better ask me."

"Devil or angel, then?"

"Good boy. Now I'm telling you honestly, but you're not going to believe it. I'm both.

"You can fall out with the Church and for a while you fall out with God, but you get to understand that God and the Church are different, so God is still my friend, in the final reckoning, perhaps my only friend."

He fell silent for a minute, his different coloured eyes glittered and his streak of white hair gave him a demonic air. Taking a long draw of his cigarette and exhaling the smoke, which curled up into the lamplight, he spoke again.

"Now I'm going to tell you something else too. I'm a Devil. I belong to the inner circle of Oculus. I know who they are and everything they're up to. Now, that's raised the stakes a bit, hasn't it?"

"I don't know what to say."

"You don't need to say anything. If you believe me, you don't know if the angel in me is going to fight alongside you or the devil part of me is going to have the three of you destroyed. So you can't trust me and if you don't believe me, then you don't trust me anyway."

"You're playing games with me."

"This is not a game. Look, Mark, you'll just have to trust that I'm telling the truth. You only have the word of an excommunicated priest that I won't be after you, but Oculus will, and I'll tell you something else. Look for the oculus. It's very near. I can't say more, because they'd kill me. You're on your own. I'm supping with the Devil, but I have my reasons. Let's just say I've been waiting for you for a long time."

"How do you mean?"

"I mean you have powers you don't even know about yet, but I can see them. There's only you can destroy Oculus."

"What are you talking about?"

He gave a little smile, but said nothing.

"What do I tell the others?"

"You can tell them what I've told you. No-one else, mind. Now back you go, and be very careful."

As I got to his door, he put a hand on my arm.

"Remember one thing. They use fear as a big weapon, but they're only human."

He placed his bony hand on my forehead. "God be with you."

Then as he opened the door, he gave a little tutting sound and said,

"This damned door! I keep forgetting to get the lock fixed. I remind myself every morning when I go out, then blow me, I forget two minutes after. My head's too full of bookish nonsense, you see."

Back in the flat, I told the others what O'Hanlon had said and swore them to secrecy.

Rosso nodded.

"It fits. Didn't I say that I thought he was tied up in it? He's an oddball, I've never really got on with him, but I've never felt bad vibes when I've spoken to him and I trust my vibes."

"OK, then," said Penny, "Assume we trust him to be telling the truth, what's he telling us?"

I butted in. "I've spoken to him a lot and I don't think he could lie if he wanted to, but he's got a mind like a chess player. He's given us the information and I'll bet he already knows what we're going to do. Scary!"

Penny thought a minute.

"Then suppose we decide what we think he'd want us to decide and then do something else?"

"Like what?" said Rosso. "We don't know what he wants us to do. We can't stay here forever, waiting. We've got to make the first move."

"We have," I said. "We've moved here, that must show them we're up to something. I say wait for them to respond."

Rosso snorted. "How are they going to respond? Do they just watch us, and find out we're toothless or do they just pick off three nice easy targets? I learnt a few things in my navy days and one of them is that you'll never win a fight if you just stay moored in the harbour all day. You need to take the initiative and flush the enemy out."

"So, what do we do?" Penny asked him.

"Like we said, we go and take a look at that bookshop."

The 'Dragonfly Bar' was a grubby affair, but afforded a view of the *Worlds Apart* bookshop. Rosso, of course, knew Davey, the barman, like he seemed to know everybody. Davey didn't want to know the reason why, but was happy to let me sit by the window all day, watching. I arrived at half past eight in the morning and was let in by arrangement with Davey, who lived upstairs.

Penny was at work, and Rosso had his usual imponderable things to do.

I settled down over the first of innumerable cups of coffee, camera and notebook at the ready.

At ten to nine, Alan Trapp opened up the shop. I noted the time.

People passed by: only a few, as the town was still winding up to the day's activities. At ten, a young woman went in, all frizzy hair and tie dye. Hardly a suspect, but I took a photograph and recorded the time. A few others came and went, and I began to get a picture of the sort of person who would call into bookshops. At eleven-fifteen, a dark car drew up, and a well-dressed, thick set man got out. He was dressed in a suit and expensive overcoat, and glanced up and down the street before entering the shop.

My skin tingled.

This wasn't a casual browser, or even, I guessed, another dealer. I took a photograph but as he was a distance away, made a quick sketch in the notebook and noted the registration number.

In the bar, a few regulars were gathering, taking their first drink of the day. I ordered another coffee.

Shortly after, another, smaller man entered the shop with the same purposeful air as the other. I sketched what detail I could of his features.

Immediately afterwards, two more men, scruffily dressed, walked in. They were not the types to be frequenting bookshops. They were there for about 15 minutes then one of them left the shop and headed down towards the Grass-market.

I gasped: as O'Hanlon walked into the shop.

I'd struck gold! This proved it. Oculus must use this place as a rendezvous and if we could identify the other men...

I made more hurried sketches.

O'Hanlon left, as did the man in the overcoat. I jotted down the time, but in doing so, knocked the notebook onto the floor. As I bent over to pick it up, I felt a sharp jab in my side and the weight of someone sitting beside me.

I left the notebook under the seat and straightened slowly.

"That's right, nice and slow. Now you and I are going to take a little stroll together. If you try and run off or raise the alarm, this knife is going to go straight into your spleen. Now start walking."

The voice was soft in my ear. I turned to look at him: it was the man who had left and walked down to the Grass-market. He must have doubled back to enter the pub unnoticed.

He was a nondescript, rather grubby man with a face lined with too many cares and vices. The knifepoint jabbed a bit harder. He took my camera as I stood up, slowly, and went out of the pub with him close beside me. I could smell the stale sweat on him. No-one looked up, or seemed to notice anything wrong.

Outside, he held on to my arm tightly walking me briskly into the bookshop and up to the counter. Alan Trapp looked me up and down with an unpleasant smile.

"Really, Mr Kemp, you won't listen, will you?"

He took the camera opened it with his delicate fingers and pulled out the film, then methodically smashed it with an iron bar from under the counter.

He nodded to the man who steered me towards a door at the rear of the shop marked 'Staff Only'.

144

A lot smarter than the shop, the room was more than a staff cubbyhole. It was big enough to contain a large table and chairs and a desk to the side, piled with files.

I didn't get a chance to take in much more as the knife, now at my throat and painful, coaxed me down onto one of the chairs. The man wound some adhesive tape tightly around my head, covering my eyes.

Blinded, I felt anxiety turn to panic. After all those coffees, my bladder tightened; I needed to urinate badly.

He stuffed a rag into my mouth, then wound more tape around the rest of my face and tied my hands to the back of the chair.

With a mocking, "Comfy?" he left the room and locked the door.

I wanted to shout, but couldn't. I could feel a trickle of blood running down my throat from the knife wound. The tape made breathing difficult and my arms hurt from the awkward position they were trussed in.

I sat there for a long, long time. How long, I don't know. Two hours? I must have passed out once and emptied my bladder and bowels. I'd never known such pain or fear before.

At last the key turned in the lock and the door opened and shut again. I sensed men standing in front of me. My head which had sagged onto my chest, was grabbed by my hair and pulled my back sharply.

The voice that spoke was soft, deep and well spoken. It could have belonged to the man with the car.

"Now, Mr Kemp, I'm sorry if we kept you waiting. Oh, but you don't look very comfortable; untie his hands, will you?"

The rope was removed and I gave a grunt of pain as I bought my arms down by my sides.

"You are becoming tiresome." The voice continued

145

"It's wrong to poke your nose into other people's private business. You haven't learnt the lesson yet, have you?"

The hands grabbed my wrists and held them out in front of me. What was happening?

"One lesson, Mr Kemp. Don't persist with your prying."

I felt the pliers close around a fingernail and then my head exploded with the pain as the nail was slowly torn off. I writhed in the chair and tried to scream.

"The second lesson Mr Kemp, the Dalkeith Road chapter is closed."

As the next nail was torn off, the pain took on the form of colours and sharp shapes in my head. Zigzags, yellow and black pulsed and hung there. One by one they twisted and tore; I heard the voice speaking but I couldn't hear what it was saying.

Then something happened.

The intense pain billowed out like a parachute unfolding, real and physical, flooding my body with a floating sensation.

For an instant, I floated out of my sorry body and saw the men at their work, and the body, my body, with its head grotesquely swaddled in tape. With those moments of detachment came new powers. Synapses were making new connections; connections that have heightened my perception ever since.

I must have passed out but remember being bundled into a car.

Another shriek as they slammed the door on my arm.

A ride, feeling sick, then the door flung open. The pavement met me with a hard crack, and silence.

I woke to a white softness. The pain was there, but woolly. I looked at my arm, covered in plaster and bandages, and saw a hand resting on it. I started instinctively but looked up and tried to focus: it was Penny.

146

"Oh, love," she said.

Chapter 11

I left the Western General Hospital after a couple of days with a good supply of painkillers and a face that looked like the loser in a prize fight. The hospital had wanted to involve the police and took a good deal of persuading not to.

Penny and Rosso took me back to her flat and spoiled me rotten.

My pain subsided and I got used to the plaster on my broken right arm. The other two stopped spoiling me. Things had changed.

Despite the apparent disaster, we'd got somewhere. For a start, I'd remembered the dropped notebook at the Dragonfly. Rosso had gone and reclaimed it and it wasn't long before we'd identified the man in the car.

He was Gerry McCall, the owner of a few nightclubs around Edinburgh. One of those characters specialising in shady deals conducted in back rooms. A drug dealer feeding the lucrative student market. Rosso knew of him: the police had got him to court on one occasion, but he'd got a good advocate. He was nasty, powerful, and clever.

So we'd put a name to one, no, two of Oculus.

Rosso had chuckled when he saw my sketch of the other, smaller man: Nick Gilchrist, a would-be arch criminal who tried to keep up with the big boys but had neither the wit nor the charisma to make much of anything. He might be just an underling for Oculus, but the suit said he was trying to be up there. Rosso couldn't identify the two hoods that I had sketched but immediately we realised that Oculus might have its own hierarchy and internal strife.

Then of course, there was O'Hanlon.

O'Hanlon spoke the truth: he was fighting them from the inside. Ultimately, he was on the side of the angels. I knew this. I could sense the mental agonies that O'Hanlon had been through and his wrestles with God and the Devil.

Thanks to the pain I had endured, my body had grown antennae that could reach into the dark and touch things that previously couldn't be touched. Now I saw things with a terrible clarity.

O'Hanlon had seen and spoken of a power lying dormant in me but like the pain I'd endured this power was not something you can describe.

I hadn't said much to Penny or Rosso about it for fear of being taken discreetly to some psychiatric clinic but it was real. I think it was always there in my pictures.

I knew I had to speak to Cicely. One evening, when Rosso had gone out in search of "a bit of skirt" – his phrase, which made Penny roll her eyes – I brought the subject up.

It was time Cicely came round and even higher time that she met Rosso. There was something connecting them and I needed to put that bit of jigsaw together.

Penny invited her around for a meal explaining that Rosso had gone back to the flat for a few days. Likewise, we persuaded Rosso to stay in for an evening (poor guy, I think he was just trying to give us some space).

Later that week, they met.

We'd suggested to Rosso that we'd celebrate the two hundred and thirty first anniversary of the Treaty of Worms for a laugh, just to celebrate our friendship. Rosso went along with it with a snort and a grin, and even dug out some smart clothes.

I cooked; not easy with a plaster pot on your arm, but I insisted.

We laid the table for three, and Rosso - yes, Rosso - made a table decoration out of candles and flowers. Penny came back from work wreathed in smiles and changed into a black dress that was indecent and had me mauling her playfully. She, equally playfully, responded.

We opened the first of many bottles of wine then stood up and drank a toast to the Treaty of Worms. As though on cue, the doorbell rang.

Rosso looked up, immediately suspicious. Penny went to the door and ushered her mother in.

Time stood still for a while as Cicely walked into the room, she saw Rosso and he saw her. He broke the silence:

"Bastards!"

"Captain Ross. Well, here's a well-engineered surprise," said Cicely. "I should be rather cross with you two."

To my surprise, Rosso went over to her and shook her hand, she responded by wrapping her arms around him and kissing him. When they broke free Rosso rounded on me.

"You and your fucking tricks! Sorry, Cissy, but this is a bit of a shock."

"I see you two have met before," said Penny, with aplomb. It was my cue to say my piece.

"I'm sorry Cicely, and I'm sorry Rosso, but this had to happen and now's the time. We've a fight on our hands and you're both part of it. There's obviously some history between you two and if you don't want to tell us, don't. But I need you both on the same side and well, here we are."

"You might at least pour me a glass of red," said Cicely.

We chatted about this and that. Cicely asked Rosso what he was doing these days. Rosso told her he was running a course for young offenders – taking them into the hills and getting them to work as a team and then trying to get them jobs. Penny and I must have looked astonished.

"You never told us," I said.

That shrug again. "You never asked."

We sat down to a starter of melon and grapefruit. Rosso and Cicely managed to keep the conversation interesting, but irksomely light.

It wasn't until halfway through a slightly overcooked venison stew that Penny placed her hands on the edge of the table and leant forward.

"Don't you think it's time we heard the full story, mother?"

Cicely took a large sip of her wine (she could tuck the stuff away, could Cicely), and said:

"Since you've engineered the evening for that purpose, I suppose we've no choice. I rather hoped that the past could remain in the past, but... It's time, isn't it, Rosso?"

"Yes, I suppose it is."

"You or me?"

"You first."

"Fair do's. Penny, Mark, meet Captain Oliver Ross, RM retired. Ross, O. on the roster lists and ever after called Rosso.

"We met in the infirmary when he was wounded in Korea and I was a nurse on the ward. I'm afraid we got a little carried away. Oh, dear, this is going to be difficult. Your turn, Oliver."

Penny had turned pale. I held her hand. I guessed what was coming.

"We fell in love – no, don't say we didn't, Cissy. It was very good, and I'll be truthful and say that I've never loved anyone so much before or since."

"Don't be daft, Oliver."

"It's true. You were on your own, you'd left Penny's father. It was all rather – oh, dammit, there's no way to put this easily. I'm Cassie's father."

"I don't believe I'm hearing this," said Penny.

"No, well, I've spent most of my life trying to keep it from you," said Cissy. "We were both rather free spirits and we decided that we needed to tread our own paths. Oliver went back to the war and earned himself a fair collection of medals and I went off to study and bring the two of you up. We met a few times, but you'd decided you were bowing out gracefully. Just like a man."

"It wasn't like that!"

"Yes, it was. You could face a storm of bullets but not a wife and daughter."

"Different paths Cissy. But I never left her, or you. I kept an eye on her, didn't I? I paid for her education, I paid the rent on her flat, I tried to look after her, please believe me."

"Oh, I do. You looked after her much better than I did."

This was all getting too much to cope with and something was puzzling me.

"Did Cassie know you were her father?" I asked.

For the first time since I'd known him he was serious, not dodging behind a smokescreen.

"I think she did. I never told her, and she never gave a hint if she suspected. She made advances to other men, but she never came on to me."

"Why didn't you tell her?"

"Christ knows. Shame? If she knew her father was just a slum dosser. Well…that's what beats me up the whole time. It could all have been so different."

"Yes, Ollie, it could," Cicely said, pointedly. Ollie! Christ!

"Yeah, well, we just do what we do."

152

"Not good enough, Ollie. I want to know why you ended up here."

"My business, Cissy, what goes on in my head."

"As you wish."

But the silence after that stretched out uncomfortably.

Eventually, Rosso looked up, a haunted look on his face, then gazed at the table.

"I'd seen too much in action. You get hardened when you're in the thick of it; you almost revel in it. But the day comes when you have to stop fighting and return to the ordinary world."

"When you're back there, you see how it was and you can't square it in your head. It takes everyone a bit differently but you're in a bad place, all alone, because no-one can know how bad it is. So I drank, and kept on drinking, and felt ashamed."

"So I had to give you up, Cissy. I was no good for you. I buried myself here. It seemed right – here, amongst all the other suffering and broken souls. It wasn't until Cassie came onto the scene that I felt anything. I knew she was mine. God, that feeling of love: it all came flooding back. It was like waking up after a twenty year sleep. Shit. I shouldn't –"

He just shrugged.

I looked at him. He was lying. It was a good story, but it wasn't true. Cicely was crying, and it shocked me; loud sobs pent up all those empty years.

"Now you damn well tell me."

Penny, too, was weeping.

"Don't cry. Don't be sad," I said, rather crassly.

"I'm not sad, it's too much at once. That's all. I think I'm very happy."

As the evening wore on, we learnt more of their time together. There'd been such a passion between them, so much so that they'd both got scared and walled themselves off; each pursuing their own paths, and each of them ending up despite what might and should have been, being isolated and alone.

Fellow steppenwolves!

That night, we began to see what we had to do.

Chapter 12

We went our separate ways: Cicely to her house, Penny to her flat, Rosso and I to Starlings' Yard. We were going to ground for a while to let things quieten down.

The days were shortening as October rounded off the summer and the noisy tourists were replaced by noisier students.

There was the exhibition to prepare for and now that my arm was out of plaster and my fingernails were growing back, I needed to get on with my painting.

In addition to the two Cityscapes, Patrick also wanted three new canvases, big ones. That put the pressure on.

I don't think I've ever enjoyed painting so much, before or since. There was a focus now, a feeling of purpose and intensity. The pictures would be called Starlings' Yard, I, II and III.

My big coup was persuading Murdo and Angus to pose for me in the flat. Originally clothed, I eventually persuaded them (separately, with some financial incentive) to pose naked, well almost. Their skinny, grey bodies were the perfect foils for the background I would set them against. We talked as I sketched and painted them and I learnt something of their past lives.

Murdo was seventy six now, with a grey stubble on his head and a straggly grey beard. His face reminded me a little of a bust of Hippocrates I'd seen. Heavily lined and stern, with serious, questioning eyes that seemed fixed on some far horizon. He was lean to the point of being cadaverous, and coughed his way through his cigarettes, which he held curled up in his hand, army style. He had started life off in Portobello, his parents had both died when he was a few years old. He was never told what they'd died of or even who they were.

"That must have made things hard for you," I said as I tried painting in the muscles of his scrawny neck.

"Aye, well, I was a Dean's boy after that."

"What's one of those?" I asked.

"An orphan, ken. From Dean's Orphanage. Big place near Dean village, but it closed doon. Something else noo, a school I think. There wis hundreds of us orphans. Ah didnae like it. Like ye were just a nuisance, like ye didnae have feelings. Then ah was sent aff tae the army. Bluidy great, that was, tae start. Ye had friends there – comrades. For once in ma life, ah mattered. But alang comes the war and we were packed aff tae France. Aw shit, mon, aw shit."

"Bad, eh?"

"Ye fuckin' jokin'? I was in Wipers and Passchendaele. I should have died wi' the rest o' them, but I didnae. They think that's a' history, well it bloody isn't. It's here, mon, in ma heid, every bluidy minute. I got invalidated oot wi' shell shock, an' after four years they said I'm better and they kicked me oot, but they knew I wasna better, but they didna ken whit tae dae wi' me. Bastards. Sae I went on the road, but they didnae like that, either. See, naebody kens whit tae dae wi' me. Naebody ever did."

"What did you want, then?"

"Me? Want? When did I ever dare have a want? Things just happen ta me; I go whaur ah'm put. Ye're folks is deid, pal, ye're aff tae the orphanage, where ye'll dae whit ye're told. Ye're tae auld for the orphanage lad, we've decided ye're joining the airmy. Ye're aff tae France, pal, them's ye're orders. Ye've gone daft, pal, ye're awa' tae the loony bin. We've decided ye're cured, pal, ye're on yer ain.

"Sae I gae oot on the road, like I'm waiting. Waiting for someone tae decide whit tae dae wi' me. Sometimes they put

156

me in a hostel, sometimes they let me oot. Sometimes ah'm well, sometimes ah'm sick, and I was bluidy sick when I got the pneumonee, ah can tell ye. Then ah'm in hospital a while, 'til they decide ah can'nae stay theer, but ah'm nae fit tae be on the road, so they find me ma place here. That wis thirty year ago."

"Do you like it here?"

"Like it? Theer's a question. How should I ken? Ah dinna ken whit it is tae like onything or nae like it. Ah just sit in ma flat and listen tae the wireless and smoke ma fags, and try not tae see the pictures in ma heid."

"What pictures?"

"A' that stuff. They telt me I wis cured from the shell-shock, but they dinae ken. It's theer, a' the time, like ane o' them auld newsreels, black an' white and scratchy. Over an' over. Drives ye bluidy mad, it does."

I didn't pry any further. He fell silent and I carried on painting. At least now I knew what he was seeing with that faraway look. I spent a long time painting his eyes.

Angus was younger, easier to talk to, and his features were more expressive than Murdo's. The lines on his face all converged on a pair of bright blue eyes which still shone and twinkled, and although the corners of his mouth were turned down into a perpetual expression of distaste, there was always an engaging ghost of a smile on his lips.

He spoke of his younger days playing accordion with a band, of the dances he would go to, the good times with the whisky and the women. He'd married a beautiful black-haired Irish girl who was as wild as he was and they'd moved into a small house in the Haymarket.

They led a fine, carefree life, until he discovered her in bed with the double bass player from the band. They rowed and argued until she left him and ran off with her lover. The band broke up, and he was left on his own. With no job and no house, he moved into Starlings' Yard and stayed here ever since.

Drink, which had been such a part of his former life, took over as he tried to smother his grief, and the more he drank, the more he mourned for his lost love. In his head, she became a goddess, and he worshipped her. In his downward spiral as the drink would first console him, then destroy him, the jigs and reels he used to play were gone and in their place his sad, haunted tunes gave voice to a lost love that he would never find again.

The third picture, while on the same lines, didn't contain a figure, but instead, two bird shapes, one white and one dark red, but their heads were replaced by smudges; the white one resembling Cassie, the other, Hannah. It was the nearest I ever got to abstraction.

One day, Percy knocked on my door and he stood there looking awkward. He pointed past me to my pictures, then raised his eyebrows enquiringly. Did he want to see my paintings? I beckoned him in.

Odd, isn't it, that when someone has to mime to you, you answer in dumbshow, too? He looked at them, nodding, then pointed at them, then at himself. The penny dropped.

"You want me to paint you as well?"

He nodded vigorously. It was the first time I'd ever seen him smile. I thought of him wreathed in the smoke from his oily rags and instantly saw the painting. I sat him down to a cup of tea, wondering why he was so keen on posing naked for me and did a few rapid sketches of his face. He looked at the results and chuckled. We arranged a time for him to come round.

Even when we spent hours together (and he could hold a pose for hours) we never could communicate well enough for me to find out where those rags came from and why he ended up with them each day, or what his story was. He remained an enigma. Painting his face and body half obscured by the smoke seemed to epitomise, not just him, but the whole of the Yard. That picture turned out to be one of the best I'd ever done.

I worked on all four canvases together and what was emerging excited me. The background views of the Yard were worked in more vibrant, yet more subtle colours than I had used before; while the figures were done in ghostly pale tints that seemed to emerge from the stones like vapours.

They excited Penny, too - that pleased me. She kept Ian and Patrick tediously up to date with progress, and our pleasure spilled over into wild, unrestrained sex; so intense that it surprised us both.

By day, she would divide her time between the gallery and the library, for we all still had work to do.

In my case, I would paint or sketch in the Yard, chatting to the other tenants as they came and went. Then I began to take my chair and sketchpad out into the Old Town, sketching views and details of the Grassmarket and the Royal Mile. People got used to seeing me there. That was the whole idea: I became part of the furniture of the Old Town. The steady and quite appreciable stream of income from selling the sketches was an unforeseen bonus.

But in amongst the sketches were plans, notes, and dimensions. I was sure the Oculus headquarters were here, right under our noses. Their rituals fed off Hannah's poor tortured soul and their presence here kept the focus of evil in this place. Somehow I could sense that evil. Not with any of the known senses, but just as vividly. I suppose the visual equivalent might be dark birds flying in the periphery of sight.

I got to know every stone in the locality, noting the irregularities that spoke of centuries of piecemeal addition and alteration in the way they were laid. I worked through the winter days, going out to sketch when the weather allowed and painting in the studio when it didn't. The others were quietly getting on with their assignments.

The dark days of December kept the people in the Yard tucked inside their flats, isolated from the world outside, kept apart from the lights and bustle of the town.

In Princes Street, the Christmas decorations urged on the shoppers in their frenzy of buying. The colour drained from the world, and businessmen went about in sober, expensive overcoats. Flocks of starlings would gather on the city buildings in the dusk, their twitterings almost drowning out the traffic noise.

As presents I painted three small oils of the Grassmarket tenements; one each for Penny, Cissy, and Rosso with a little message on the back of each one. The four of us spent Christmas at Cissy's and by an unspoken agreement, never talked of Oculus. For one day, at least, we could forget all that.

We chatted and sipped wine over dinner and learnt more of each other's past.

Even Rosso opened up his story to us.

As he talked of his service days and his subsequent work as an outdoor instructor, boxing coach, young offender's counsellor and a lot more; I saw a man who didn't care much for his own gain or comfort but who had a huge capacity for caring about others and the world around him.

I've never liked Christmas, but that simple day grew into one of the most special. Penny and I could see the old love between Rosso and Cissy flowering again.

They were both extraordinary people. Cissy had the happy combination of an extraordinary intellect coupled with a sense of adventure and curiosity that had led her to explore regions of the world and the mind that few others would dare and Rosso in his own way was an adventurer.

Hogmanay came and went.

Despite my solitary nature and Penny's normal propriety we joined the revellers in the Royal Mile. On a night when the normal social rules were suspended and strangers would speak and put their arms round each other we found ourselves swept up in the mood. The sweaty noise and warm bright lights kept out the darkness outside and we immersed ourselves in the noise and drunkenness of the night.

Groups of people swirled in and out of the amorphous crowd taking false comfort out of the touch of strangers. A loud woman hitched up her miniskirt and pissed in the gutter while round her in the cobbled street the crowd tumbled and spun in a cavalcade of masks, fancy dress and alcohol-fuelled love.

Penny grew frightened of the increasing physical press of the crowd and wanted to go home. We got her a taxi but I wanted to keep savouring the atmosphere of the wild night.

The sound of bagpipes mixed with the thumping beats of heavy rock and drunken attempts of pub crooners meant anything was possible because everybody had stopped caring. I wanted to drink myself into that state, and I did.

At some point, I met Sadie, at least I think it was she. The next thing I knew, I was with her or whoever in a dark wynd, pressing my groin against hers, while our fingers and mouths brought us to some sort of mucousy satisfaction.

I've no idea how I got home.

Penny and I missed the next day, in common with the rest of the city, whose civic hangover kept the streets deserted and silent. But Hogmanay is a catharsis, a Dionysian re-enactment, a release of all the pent-up shit of the past year. It's a necessary ritual, started in some Greek caves thousands of years ago. They knew what mattered, that lot.

A day or so later, I spotted the final piece of the jigsaw.

There, high up, hidden in the shadows of the surrounding tenements on the wall of the South Bridge itself. A small ball of glass, like a thick lens...an oculus! I could, I fancied, make out the shape of a shallow-carved eye around it. I quickly made a mental note of its position and moved on, not wanting to draw attention to the fact I'd seen it.

I wasted no time in returning to Starlings' Yard and in the privacy of the flat, sketched from memory, the oculus in its position in the wall of the bridge. Then, from under the carpet where I had hidden it, I took the plan. An impressive bit of work, built up over the months, covered in notes and thumbnail sketches surrounding a plan of the whole area.

I'd assumed that the entrance, or one entrance, to the Oculus headquarters must be in Starlings' Yard. O'Hanlon's flat seemed the obvious place. Also, that their headquarters must lie inside the structure of the South Bridge.

It was well known that the Bridge was built over a maze of vaults and caves that had served as storage spaces, workshops and dwelling places. Then sometime in the nineteenth century most of them they were filled in with rubble, deemed unfit for habitation.

I was convinced that quite a few chambers and passage-ways still existed and that was where we would find Oculus. Now I could locate the main chamber, for there must be one for their rituals, and then work out where an inconspicuous air vent I'd spotted must be connected.

I sat, looking at the plan, trying to figure out how it all could fit together.

An hour later, I was none the wiser. I stared at it until the shapes seemed to move and flow, certain that the answer was in front of me, but I could make no sense of it. It was like trying to solve a maze that's hidden in another room.

The next day was bright and frosty. The Yard was as near as it was ever going to get to being picturesque and I went outside to smell the cold.

Rosso was there leaning on the parapet above the tumbling water and together we soaked up the warmth of the winter sun. After chatting about nothing, and making sure the Yard was empty, I told him.

"I've found an oculus."

"What? You've tracked them down?"

"Not the. An oculus. It's a small round window in a wall, but I'm convinced it's where the Oculus must hang out. It's close by, but hard to spot."

"Great!"

"Maybe, but I can't work out the geography. Not yet. How are you getting on?"

"OK. All on schedule. I remember why I fell in love with Cissy, she's doing a grand job."

"You're in touch with her?"

"Only twice. I know the rule."

The rule was limited contact with Rosso and Cissy and only in anonymous places. Penny and I continued to see each other as before. Everything had to seem normal.

Rosso and I chatted about this and that for a while, then as the clouds gathered and the warmth disappeared, we went back to our flats.

By that mysterious subconscious process, the answer came to me in the depths of the night.

I got out of bed quickly and looked at the chart still pinned to the wall. I marked the passages and chambers on the drawings, and it all made sense, every last detail of it! I wanted to ring the others there and then but dare not go to the 'phone box. Instead, I gazed at the drawings, trying to work out how the members of Oculus could get in and out without being noticed.

At the same time, I was racking my brains, trying to work out the enigma that was O'Hanlon.

I was convinced he was on our side but if he was, why was he not helping us? He knew what went on inside Oculus – it would have been so simple if he'd just told us the answers. Or was he the Devil's agent: waiting like a spider for us to enter a trap that Oculus had set up? He was right; either way we couldn't trust him.

Early the next day, I called Penny.

"It's time to meet up," I told her.

At four o'clock the next day the four of us met up at Penny's flat.

I showed them my drawings and ideas about the internal layout of the Oculus headquarters. Starting at the oculus itself, assuming that to be inset into the upper wall of a ritual chamber deep within the very fabric of the South Bridge and assuming this also led to vaults and chambers off and in Starlings' Yard I described the levels and steps that were suggested by the visible stonework. They were impressed and excited.

We made some coffee, then Cicely grinned and took a sheet of paper from a briefcase. She placed it on the table.

"I have some very dear friends who have been rather thrilled to while away their dull widows' days in a little espionage," she chuckled. "I do have some contacts in the commercial world, they were happy to give my little team of spies a window seat in their offices along the Cowgate. There they sat with notebooks and recorded thousands of cars and passers-by. Mainly office workers of course with an astonishing number of illicit liaisons but there were some that didn't fit the pattern of regular commuters. All appeared together on certain days, although the meeting days seem rather random, or came sporadically in between, sometimes in cars and sometimes on foot.

"We'd meet over a sherry or two and collate the results. Out of the thousands of entries we established who came and went regularly and this is the result: a list of the names of the members of Oculus. One way or another, we've been able to identify them – all twelve of them, yes, just twelve! This is the list."

"Twelve?"

"My guess is that O'Hanlon makes up thirteen – a nice witchy number for a secret society. From what you say, Mark, he has his own entrance off his flat. The others have a reserved underground car park in the basement of an office belonging to an outfit called United Chemical Holdings. They are listed at Companies House, but their accounts are out of proportion to the size of the office – one of my dear widow friends is quite an experienced accountant, she tells me the accounts are not genuine."

We all looked at the list of names. It was astounding.

City councillors, at least two police chiefs, a professor, some big business names, a well-known actor, one or two major underworld characters; all people with a lot of power or influence. One name was missing.

"What about this Gerry McCall. He's not on here?" I asked.

Cicely looked at her notes.

"No, but he's been seen going in a few times. He may be a big noise in the underworld but I don't think he's big enough to be one of the initiates. I think there's a second tier that don't get to do the mumbo-jumbo but do get a share of the profits and the power. I've a list others who seem to fit that bill."

"Do we have to track them down and destroy them too?" Penny asked.

"No," said Rosso. "The whole outfit works because of a small but very influential and strong group at the top. Get rid of those and the rest will destroy themselves in the ensuing power struggle. Basic military strategy," he added with a grin.

Cicely looked at my drawings.

"I think that fits in nicely with your hunch: there must be a door from the underground car park with a stair or lift up to the hall. They tend to arrive in dribs and drabs over a couple of hours about once a fortnight, then all leave with other commuters about seven."

Penny was studying the list. "Don't you think we should hand this over to the police now?" she asked.

Rosso snorted.

"What the hell are they going to do with it? Nobody would dare accuse that lot. Anyway, what are we accusing them of? We've no evidence. They'd just hold up their hands to being members of a masonic sort of society and there's no law against that. They keep themselves well apart from any criminal activity. That seems to be handed down to middle-men who'll be well paid for getting their goons to do the dirty work. We've got to stick to Plan A and administer justice ourselves."

"This is beginning to scare me," Penny said.

Rosso put his hand over hers and squeezed it. "And me," he said. "Anyway, let's hear your bit."

Penny had been following up the leads thrown up from digging through newspaper records.

She produced a large dossier of a hundred or so records, drug related deaths from the last five years. All of them seemed insignificant, meagre little entries but on asking around, talking to families, junkies, and prostitutes many were traceable to 'communes'.

Idealistic, naïve girls were introduced to drugs then once addicted, turned onto the streets as prostitutes to line the pockets of their pimps and ultimately the members of Oculus. Girls like Cassie.

The boys like Alan Trapp, presumably became the organisation's thugs. Once trapped in this underworld any attempts to escape to a better life would be rewarded with a violent death.

Penny had uncovered protection rackets, blackmail, gambling rings and money launderers; a vast cancer that was eating away at the city, run by those very people who were entrusted with power.

As she read out her findings, I looked at the others' faces. Revulsion was turning to resolution.

"You're sorted out, Ollie?" Cicely asked.

"Aye, gal," Rosso replied. "I've managed to magic up some explosives and some assault rifles. State of the art, most of it, too."

"What!" Penny looked horrified.

"What do you expect? What are we supposed to do? Go in there and give them a V-sign? This bunch has to be destroyed and I need the tools for the job."

Rosso, I could see was back in his element. All traces of that seemingly ramshackle truculence had disappeared. He was in command, efficient and keen-eyed. My stomach began to churn.

"Isn't this all going to get us life sentences?" I asked. "You can hardly shoot most of the great and the good in the city and get off with a finger-wagging from a judge, can you?"

"Well I for one don't care," Rosso said. Then he looked me in the eye.

"Those bastards killed my daughter and I'll happily swing for them. Maybe it's not the same for you but it burns me inside every minute of the day. I'll take the rap, and you can all be accessories after the fact or whatever."

"Think though, Penny's got a mass of evidence and you are going to get more if you can, lass. It's only circumstantial so far but we'll get more names, connections, and crimes."

"They'll see that their great and good had rubbed shoulders with underworld slime, and maybe they'll have the sense to put two and two together. But who said it was us? I'm not daft in these matters – I'll make it look like an accident, and there'll be very little to tie us in with it." He paused.

"Well?"

"Well, what?" I asked.

"Do we go ahead?"

I looked at Penny at the same time as she looked at me. Cissy looked at Rosso. The silence didn't last long.

"Of course," she said, and Penny nodded.

Images flooded my brain for an instant – a boy in a red hat, Christ on the cross, Cassie posing, Little Robert's face lit with a million colours, Cassie dead, the cankerous woman in the bar, Hannah's face, a drunk Santa who slipped and cried *fuck*...

The Steppenwolf had gone. There was so much to live and die for.

"Yes."

"Right." Rosso was briefing the troops before the battle. He was magnificent.

"Penny – evidence, evidence. As much as you can get. Cissy, get some cameras for your widows and let's have photos. Mark, sorry, pal, you and I get the risky bit. We need to get in there for a recce and O'Hanlon's place is the way in, if you've got it right."

"Oh, I have," I stifled the impulse to say sir.

"We'll have to watch O'Hanlon and see when he goes out and get into his flat. You can see his door best – so give me a wave and we'll break in and have a look."

I remembered something.

"I don't think we'll need to – break in, I mean. I thought it was just him chatting on at the time but he told me specifically his lock was broken. I think that was an invitation to go in."

"That has the nasty whiff of a trap to me," said Cicely.

"Perhaps," I replied. "But I'm sure he's on our side."

Penny looked doubtful. "I don't see how you can be so sure, I don't trust him."

So I told them about the power (no, that sounds silly), the insight I had gained under torture. I had suffered like O'Hanlon suffered and that pain had forged new connections in my head, as it had in his. That last time we had talked, he and I understood that.

"Please. You'll have to trust me on this. He wants me - us - to overcome Oculus. He knows I'm the one. I don't know why. Some sort of destiny thing." They were silent.

"I just know," I added lamely. They were all looking at me.

"Then I'm going to trust your conviction, Mark," Cicely said eventually. "I know what powers the unlocked brain is capable of. I just wish the stakes weren't so high."

"It doesn't make much difference," said Rosso. "We've agreed that's our way in and whether we do it with or without his knowledge, that's what we've got to do. But yes, I'll trust your instinct."

"And me," said Penny.

I stuck my neck out a little further and told them that we should bide our time: O'Hanlon would let us know when to move.

Of course, he did, a week later.

I heard music drifting up from the Yard. I looked out of the window and saw Angus, dressed in unfathomable layers of old coats, sitting on the central block in the middle of the Yard with his concertina.

He was playing a slow, sad tune that filled the place with a wistful peace. It made me think of Robert in his red hat on the swings, it made me hang on to his memory and embrace it for the first time.

I went downstairs and out into the Yard to listen to him. He stopped to greet me but I asked him to keep playing and as the tune spread across the Yard like tendrils of smoke, I knew he was playing for his lost love, his lost life and the might-have-beens we all have to suffer; but I knew he was playing for me too.

It was with a start that I heard O'Hanlon's voice interrupt my thoughts.

"Pretty, isn't it?"

"Mmm"

"Daydreaming music, so I'll not interrupt you, just wanted to say hello. Isn't it a glorious day? Just my luck I've to be out at a meeting. All this nice sun will be gone by the time I get back. Shame."

"That's a pity – perhaps tomorrow will be the same, so you can enjoy it then, eh?"

"Now that's a thing to look forward to."

And he patted my shoulder twice and was off.

I realised what he had just told me. I went into the flat and brought out two cans of beer, and walked nonchalantly over to Rosso's flat, and knocked.

"Fancy a beer?" I said, pushing into his hallway.

Once inside, I told him what O'Hanlon had said and that I was sure it was a deliberate hint to tell us the coast was clear.

Shortly after we walked slowly up the stairs towards the door of his flat, both of us alert for any signs of prying eyes. Rosso tested the handle. As O'Hanlon had promised, the door was unlocked. We looked at one another and went in.

The flat was the same as always but without O'Hanlon's gaunt presence it seemed threatening. It was like being caught up in a web with the spider out of sight.

Despite the heat of the day it seemed cold and gloomy, with the smell of his whisky and cigarettes pervading the whole place. The door opened onto a narrow, dark hall, off it to the left was his living room, the only room I had seen before.

Rosso went in, and looked round with a professional eye. He went to a cupboard beside the blackened fireplace. It was crammed with papers which he quickly sampled, and replaced expertly.

"I don't think we'll find much in that lot," he said, "they're old sermons and research notes. Let's move on."

The room opposite was the bedroom. I began to feel awkward: guilty at prying into a sad, meagre life.

The wardrobes contained a few, musty smelling clothes and on the wall a grimy sepia picture of a young woman in a blouse and gathered hair. His mother? An old lost love?

Rosso was checking under the bed and behind the wardrobe. He shook his head, and we moved on. The kitchen was in a similar sad state, with blackened pans cluttering the work surfaces but nothing to interest us, nothing to lead us toward Oculus.

There was a bathroom and another small room that contained a desk half hidden under more piles of books and papers that revealed nothing. We went back into the hallway.

Rosso's searches had been swift but thorough, his training coming into its own, but he snorted with annoyance.

"Do you get the feeling we've been led up a blind alley?" I asked.

"Maybe, but I don't think so. We've just not seen what's in here, somewhere. Fuck it. Let me think."

I suddenly thought of my sketches and plans. I grabbed his arm.

"I'm being stupid! There's only one room that abuts onto the bridge: it's the only room that can lead into the Oculus headquarters. It has to be in the kitchen!"

We went back there. We tapped the walls, pulled at the cupboards and looked for any signs of a hidden entrance. There was nothing. Again. I shut my eyes, visualising the layout of the flat.

"Got it!" I cried, and went into his small, cluttered study.

The room was dark, as the thin velveteen curtains were drawn over a narrow window, before which his desk and a rickety bentwood chair stood. There was a standard lamp beside it and books strewn everywhere, spilling over from a small bookcase to the other side. Behind the desk in the far corner of the room was a tall bookcase in blackened wood. It was also full of books but around it there were no papers or any of the broken things that O'Hanlon seemed to have everywhere else.

"It's behind there!" I told Rosso. "It has to be! This room is a couple of feet longer than the kitchen; the width of that bookcase, in fact."

Rosso immediately walked over to the bookcase and ran his hands round it, then started pulling books from the shelves, carefully stacking them on the floor in the right order. He soon found what he was looking for: a large chrome lever behind the books. He pulled it down and with a soft clunk, the bookcase cantilevered out on sophisticated steel arms.

Behind it was a dark corridor, hewn out of the sandstone that the house was built into and which led behind the kitchen wall. We replaced the books and jammed open the door. The opening bookcase must have worked a switch, for a fluorescent tube in the roof of the tunnel flickered on, revealing a steel door painted in brown gloss at the end of the corridor. The door sported a dial and a circular handle, like a safe. Rosso cursed under his breath and I found I was talking in a whisper.

"Let's try it. O'Hanlon's been easing our path so far."

Rosso went down to the door, his broad shoulders just fitting the width of the tunnel. He tried the handle and pushed at the door. It wouldn't budge. He turned with difficulty and re-emerged.

"It's a fucking combination lock! We've no chance of cracking that."

I collected my thoughts.

O'Hanlon liked playing cat and mouse; he must have left us a clue. I looked around the study, feeling that he'd have left the answer here for me. Me, because I was somehow his chosen one to destroy Oculus. My brain went into overdrive; it would be something I would see but others wouldn't, something an artist would notice...

It was quite obvious in the end: above the desk were some faded prints in their cheap frames. The *Mona Lisa*, Holman Hunt's *Light of the World*, Botticelli's *Birth of Venus* and a number of depictions of the Blessed Virgin. One of them, I could see, had been recently moved.

There was a patch on the wall where it had come fro, and it now sat awkwardly amongst the others. It was one of those pastel depictions of the Madonna, done on a light blue background littered with petals and showing her radiant and devotional – the sort of cheap icon that made my blood boil. One hand was clasped to her breast, the other pointing. That was why he'd moved it! The hand pointed downwards to an old typewriter on the desktop. In the typewriter was a sheet of paper. I moved over beckoning Rosso to join me. The text was just a collection of what appeared to be bible verses.

"So what's that got to do with anything?" Rosso asked.

"I don't know," I replied. "But I'll bet it's our clue to the combination. He's playing games with me again."

"For God's sake!"

"Exactly."

Beside the typewriter was a conveniently placed bible. We were supposed to look up the verses, which seemed to be rather random.

"How's your bible knowledge?" I asked Rosso, he gave me a look. I read the first verse:

And He was there in the wilderness forty days tempted of Satan, and he was with the wild beasts, and the angels ministered to him.

"It must be the New Testament," said Rosso. "But which book?"

I picked up the bible and flipped through it absently, thinking. Cat and mouse. Teasing me, as ever...

"Mark's gospel," I replied. Rosso snorted and grinned. I went to Mark, chapter one and scanned down the tiny print.

"Here! It's verse 13. I'll bet that's the first number!"

"Maybe, but why he couldn't just write them down, I've nae idea."

"His mind doesn't work like that. Besides, he can't be too careful. Let's see, what's next?"

And the disciples of John and of the Pharisees used to fast and they came and said unto him, Why do the disciples of John and of the Pharisees fast, but thy disciples fast not? And he said unto them, The Sabbath was made for man and not man for the Sabbath.

Rosso grabbed the bible from me and ran his finger down the page.

"I can't see it. No wait! Two - that must mean chapter two. Yes, here we are, verse 18! But there's nothing about the

Sabbath bit. No, hang on, here it is, further down, that's verse 27. Go on."

Verily I say unto you, all sins shall be forgiven unto the sons of men and blasphemies wherewith soever they shall blaspheme. For whoever shall do the will of God, the same is my brother and my sister and mother.

"Chapter three, twenty-eight and wait – ah, thirty five." I took a piece of paper and a pen from the desk and wrote the numbers down.

And he said, So is the kingdom of God, as if a man should cast seed into the ground. And the same day, when the evening was come, He saith unto them, let us pass over unto the other side. And then came a great storm of wind and the water beat into the ship so that it was now full.

Verses twenty-six, thirty-five, and thirty-seven. I wrote them down. Eight numbers. Rosso went down the tunnel to try them, and returned, frowning.

"Doesn't bloody work and anyway, there should be four numbers, not eight."

"Well, there's four lots of verses, so we add the verses in each section together..."

We did so: 13-45-63-98. We both went down to the door and Rosso turned the dial four times. There was a satisfying click. He turned the handle anticlockwise and the heavy door swung open.

"Jesus Christ!" Rosso swore under his breath. I just stood there in amazement

Chapter 13

We were standing in a chamber dimly lit with a blue light, carved into sandstone.

A large metal frame was suspended from the ceiling to our right, on which were fixed six television monitors. In front of them was a desk and two modern office chairs and on the desktop there was a full ashtray and a bottle of whisky.

Thick electrical cables snaked up to the ceiling from the monitors and across the ceiling to a closed door on the far side of the chamber. Other cables led from the monitors to machines on the desk.

"What the hell is this lot?" I asked Rosso.

"This, pal, is televisual monitoring and state of the art stuff, too. They've got cameras mounted in parts of the complex and it must be O'Hanlon's job to watch them for intruders. Those machines are video recorders, so that he can replay them when he's been out."

We looked at the screens, which were glowing with images from the cameras. Our eyes were drawn to the centre top one, and Rosso seized my arm in excitement. We were looking at an Oculus ceremony going on somewhere below us!

The colours were crude and the image slightly fuzzy but it was as plain as day. We were looking at a large circular chamber with the cloaked and hooded members of the inner circle standing in front of wooden chairs spaced around the circumference.

In the centre was an altar block draped in black, on which lay a skeleton. Hannah! It must be! Above the altar, a large wooden cross was suspended, upside down. One of the members stood at the head of the altar, one hand holding a raised chalice, the other on the skull. Briefly the hooded figure looked up. It was O'Hanlon.

The other screens showed Starlings' Yard and the Cowgate entrance. One showed a room which contained an iron cage. It looked like a prison and I momentarily wondered if that was where they'd taken Cassie and pumped her so full of drugs she never really regained consciousness. The other two showed a corridor, and another chamber containing a huge safe, like a bank vault. I felt a chill and turned away. Rosso was staring intently, noting details.

"We ought to go," I said.

"They're busy with their wee games, there's no rush."

"I want to go, please. This is turning my stomach over."

Rosso shrugged, "Just a minute, then." He went over to the door at the far end of the room. He opened it, and peered through, waving me over.

It led to a rough set of spiral stone steps which descended into darkness. He took his cigarette lighter and struck a light while he went quietly down the stairs. He disappeared from sight for a few minutes, before reappearing.

"It goes down about twenty feet, then leads to a curved tunnel. I bottled out of going any further. Come on, let's go."

We went back to the study, closing the steel door and returning the dial to the number it pointed to originally, then closed the bookcase and replaced the books. We looked round to make sure we'd covered our tracks, then left O'Hanlon's flat. It was three o'clock, and getting dark.

Chapter 14

Our foray into the world of Oculus affected me more as the following days wore on.

I became preoccupied and withdrawn.

We were poised on the brink of doing something so reckless and on the face of it, mad, that I wanted to stop it happening there and then.

Their defences were frightening and the feeling that we might have been detected, though irrational, began to take over. I tried to put these thoughts from my mind, tried to talk to Penny about them but she had put her trust in Rosso and knew there was no going back.

I tried to tell her that she'd not been there, that she didn't understand how palpable the air of evil had been. I tried to shake it off but I felt as though I'd been contaminated by some miasma, something of Hannah's influence perhaps. I started drinking again, something I'd not done since New Year. I became argumentative, and my old perverse self re-emerged.

I couldn't talk to Rosso about it, in fact we talked very little. I wondered if he was experiencing something similar, for he too, seemed abstracted and monosyllabic.

I worked on the canvases by day but my elation of previous weeks was replaced by apprehension, not only for what lay ahead, but the opening of the exhibition was looming. And in addition to the dark mood which had rooted itself in me, I began to feel the pangs of anxiety about the reception that my paintings might receive.

Penny tried flattery and encouragement but, in the end lost patience and we would row and sulk and became like strangers.

It came to a head two days before the exhibition. The time had come to hang my six pictures in Patrick's new gallery, so Penny and I drove there in her car. We should have been excited and happy but instead sat in silence like a funeral cortège, both of us staring ahead into the steady rain that had now replaced the sunshine. I was aware that the mood between us was my fault and that I should snap out of it but that just served to stoke the anger that seethed inside me.

The Burn Gallery was an impressive space occupying what had been two ground floor flats in George Street. The wooden floor was gleaming, the walls flat white with some fancy plasterwork picked out in gold and light blue. This was a gallery for serious buyers; the prices were eye-watering and his commission was steep but this was a place which could do you a serious amount of good.

Fliers and catalogues announced the exhibition, which was to run for two months. I had been impressed and flattered by the fellow artists Patrick had chosen, six of us altogether all contemporary.

My damaged canvases had been repaired and looked as though nothing had befallen them and my new ones had arrived from the framers and stood propped against the wall wrapped in sheeting. Some of the other works had already been hung and two other artists were there, supervising the hanging of their works. Patrick came over to us, smiling.

"Penny! Mark! Nice to see you. So what do you think? It's going to look rather excellent; I'm very pleased. I've had so much interest in this show. Very gratifying."

He continued on with these pleasantries and I tried to smile and be effusive back. He introduced us to the two artists there and I was as complimentary about their work as I could be. Then Patrick led us round to an area at the back of the gallery.

"This will be your space Mark, and here's a diagram showing where your pictures are going. Tony over there will lend you a hand."

I looked at the diagram.

"This is all wrong," I complained. "I know which order they should be hung. I'm going to do it the way I see it."

Patrick raised an eyebrow, and Penny looked at the floor. "No, Mark, that's the layout I want. I'd rather you stuck to that."

"It's crap! It won't look right!"

"It'll be fine, Mark, please," Penny said, reddening.

"Shut up!" I cried, "What the fuck do you know?"

Patrick stiffened.

"Mr Kemp, I have devoted a lot of consideration into the look and layout of this exhibition. I am not entirely ignorant of these things. I have to see the overall effect and how your work will blend with the others. You have been very fortunate that I value your work enough to give you this break; now kindly return the compliment and trust my professionalism."

"Oh, so it's professional to hide me away at the back here, is it? Well you can just fuck off!"

"Mark, please, for God's sake!" cried Penny, in tears. "What's got into you? I'm so sorry, Patrick, he's not well, he's been so strange lately –"

"He's been so strange lately," I mimicked, "you can fuck off, too."

"Mr Kemp! I will not allow this behaviour in here, or anywhere else. I insist –"

"Fuck off, fuck off, fuck off!" I shouted, and stormed out of the gallery, aware of Penny's sobs and the shocked silence of the others.

I caught a bus back to Starlings' Yard, thrust a few clothes into a bag, which I threw into the back of the Ford and set off, far too fast.

I drove all afternoon, having no real idea where I was going.

My mind was awash with bad things, so much so I seemed to hear mocking laughter ringing in my head under the noise of the motor.

I drove through Glasgow, past Dumbarton, along Loch Lomond until I reached Inveraray as the evening was settling in. The passion was draining out of me, tiredness getting the upper hand. I booked into a hotel and threw myself onto the bed of a pokey room with drab brown wallpaper patterned with terrifyingly large red flowers and fell asleep.

In the morning, I felt different, peaceful.

I came down to breakfast and treated myself to a pair of Loch Fyne kippers before setting off again. I wandered around Inveraray, remembering the town from happier childhood days. The rain had stopped, and the sun was burning a mist off the loch where fishing boats went about their business while gulls shrieked and wheeled overhead.

This was the eternal, real world.

I passed a 'phone box and remembered with a guilty start that I should ring Penny to apologise and tell her where I was, she must be worried sick by now. My face burned with shame. What had possessed me to behave as I had?

I rang Penny's home number, but there was no answer – she must have set off for work. I got the number of the gallery from directory enquiries and rang it. It was Ian who answered.

"Croesus Gallery."

"Ian, it's Mark Kemp." There was a tiny pause.

"Hello Mark. What's going on? I've had Penny in a real state; she told me about your outburst yesterday. What was all that about?"

"I don't know, Ian, I really don't know. I'm so sorry. Is Penny there? I need to speak to her."

"She's not here, but she should be in later."

"Then tell her I'll ring later, I just had to get away and be on my own. I'm fine, I'm in Inveraray, I'm coming back later; I'll be back for the opening tomorrow. Could you do me a favour and ring Patrick and tell him I'll be there and that I really apologise? And tell Penny..." I paused.

"What?"

"I love her very much."

"Of course. But just get yourself together and come back now. Then you can tell her yourself."

I left the 'phone box happier. It was time to go back and put things to rights with Penny and Patrick. But first I felt a need to go and visit somewhere I visited as a child; a place that had given birth to my fascination with the secret colours and powers of stones.

I drove down to Lochgilphead, then turned right onto the road that led to Kilmartin and on to the head of Loch Craignish. There I found the signpost to my destination: the great standing stone of Kintraw.

I can't understand why this stone holds such a place in my heart; it's a single upright stone some 13 feet high but standing like a solitary giant overlooking the loch. I had touched it as a teenager, on the last holiday that I took with my parents and its hidden colours came alive as I stroked the rough surface. From that day on, I knew my destiny was fixed; I went to Art College despite my parents' doubts, and worked with a passion that even my tutors found alarming.

Now the circle had come round, there it was, standing like some mythical watcher over the loch. As soon as I saw it, I felt its strange pull once again. I walked across to it, yearning to touch it, to tap into the power it held and to see the hidden colours come to life once again. But this time, it was different. The stone seemed to suck the light out from air around it and darkened as I grew near. The pull was intense; I was ten feet away...five...three. Something was wrong, I suddenly felt cold and sick. I should have pulled myself away there and then but there was no way I could. Mesmerised, I reached out my hand.

It seemed like my head had exploded in a blinding flash. I thought I was flung backwards but no, my hand felt glued to the freezing stone which seemed to melt and writhe in agony. A face appeared to grow out of the stone, howling, its gaping mouth as wide as a snake's about to devour its prey - Hannah! Her invisible arms thrust themselves through my ribs and clutched my heart. The monstrous head extended towards me on a pedicle of bloody flesh and I was screaming as loudly as she, while my body was convulsing in painful jerks as my bowels opened.

After that, well, I don't remember.

I don't know why I found myself down by the shore of Craignish, half in the water and half out. My head lay in a pool of vomit and I felt terrible. As the small waves lapped around my body total weariness stopped me from moving.

Eventually, I struggled to my feet and sat on the grass by the shoreline. I felt taken over by something: it was my body but I was looking at the world through different eyes.

I knew Hannah had possessed me.

She had sensed my presence in the Oculus chambers, infected me with her tortured spirit (which must explain my bad mood ever since), tracked me down and by God knows what primordial powers, entered me like a succubus.

Is that what had happened to Cassie? Was I to meet the same fate?

Eventually some walkers found me and I was taken to the hospital in Lochgilphead where an offhand young doctor asked what had got me into this state and plump casualty nurses assumed I was under the influence of some hallucinogen.

What could I tell them? That I was the subject of demonic possession?

So I stuck to an "I don't know what came over me," line, which I knew was a lie and so did they. I was duly tucked up in bed and treated with disapproval.

They tracked Penny down and the next day she came to see me. I felt better, but still knew I was harbouring Hannah in my body. It was like a tingling, buzzing sensation in my guts and my facial muscles would twitch.

Penny didn't know whether she should be concerned, angry, puzzled or happy that I was seemingly all right. Talking in a low urgent voice in case the nurses thought I really was mad, I told Penny what had happened, and why.

To my surprise, she didn't even raise an eyebrow.

"It makes sense," she whispered back. "Since you went into O'Hanlon's you changed and now this. It sounds just like what happened to Cassie. Mark, I'm scared."

"You're scared? You should try being this side of the bed-clothes. I think I know what pregnancy feels like!"

I was trying to joke about it but I didn't feel like laughing, and Penny responded by bursting into tears. She held my hand tightly and leant forward, burying her face in the bedclothes. I stroked her head and talked to her in a soft voice:

"I don't understand it either, but I've been lying here thinking. I know that in some way Hannah's spirit, or

184

whatever, has merged with mine. She entered Cassie too but Cassie was frightened by the feelings she experienced. When that spirit surfaced as that face it was terrifying for both of us and be warned it will almost certainly happen to me. But, however frightening, it didn't kill her: Oculus did.

"Cassie was a sensitive, receptive girl, Hannah sensed that and found a home in her. I wonder how many others her spirit has infected in the past and how many have died in asylums. The big question now though is: why me? From the start, there's been a force that's drawn me into this web, then O'Hanlon going on and on about it being my destiny. Why? How does he know?"

Penny had stopped crying and lifted her mascara streaked face to look at me.

"I've always believed that places have atmospheres," I continued. "But dismissed any idea of spooks and ghosties. What I've experienced changes all that. Some emotions can be so vivid and terrible that they can exist as a separate power outside the body of the sufferer, somehow taking on the physical shape of their originator."

"Kirlian photography!" exclaimed Penny, "I've seen pictures that they can take showing auras round living things! They change with emotion, so it's possible that extreme emotion causes a bit of that aura to flare so much it flies off separately."

"Maybe that's it," I replied. "It must be something like that. I'm no scientist but they do say that matter is energy and exits as vibrations, so some sort of vibration energy can bud off and imprint itself into stones. There's some sort of transmission system too, via standing stones that act as conductors, which is why Hannah's ghost, spirit, vibrations, whatever, found me out here!"

Penny grinned. "Any first year science student would be rolling around laughing if he heard this."

"I know, it's homemade claptrap, but something must explain this. This is real. Hannah is in me, I can feel her. What I don't understand is why I feel OK about it. When I entered the Oculus passage, I picked up something that made me feel so down and negative and behave like a complete bastard. I'm sorry."

"Now I can see what's been happening, I'll forgive you, but yes, you were horrible."

"Hey, I forgot, how did the exhibition opening go?"

"Never mind that. How do you feel now? I'd have thought having this evil tucked right inside you, you'd feel far worse."

"No, I don't. I feel sort of sick and twitchy but mentally, I feel... I don't know how I feel. Like some sort of resolve, like time to face destiny, like she's going to use me, like I'm going to die, but it's OK."

"Don't talk like that, Mark, you don't mean that." Tears were spilling over again.

"No, it's not anything definite, sorry, no I didn't."

I was lying: it did feel just like that. I heard the clock on the wall tick quietly in the silence.

"How did the opening go?" I asked again.

Penny made an effort to keep her emotions under control, and even ventured a smile. "Better than your wildest dreams, honey."

"What?"

"Despite your awful behaviour, I managed to calm Patrick down; I felt I had to be honest with him, so I did tell him about Oculus and the effect it was having on you. I'm sorry, I know I shouldn't but I felt we owed it to him. Anyway, he appreciated being told and understood. He even hung your canvases the way you wanted and offered to help if he could: he's such a good man.

"Anyway, the opening was pretty impressive, it was like a who's who of the art world but with all sorts of celebrities, film stars, and media biggies all there and getting in on the act as well as just the plain stinking rich: you'd have hated it! And, oh darling, your pictures looked fabulous –"

She stood up and kissed me passionately on the lips.

"They were the stars of the whole show! You'll sell the lot, I'm sure. Patrick turned your absence to advantage by saying you were a bit of a recluse and couldn't face crowds. It gave you an air of mystery that made them want your paintings even more! Mark, you're going to make it, big time!"

This time, it was my turn to feel the prick of joyful tears. Despite all my protestations about commercial success and my present troubles, it felt good, very good indeed.

Chapter 15

We were allowed to leave the hospital with a few words of admonition and a short lecture from a chubby little nurse on the dangers of drugs. It was simplest to look contrite and not argue. We drove home in our separate cars. I was listening to Bob Dylan on a tape that kept jamming as I neared Edinburgh. The sun was setting; I saw small clouds hovering over the city which blazed blue and gold against a darkening sky.

Penny had been home a good while when I met her at her flat: her car and her driving abilities both far outstripping mine. We had a makeshift dinner and were about to settle down to some serious foreplay on the couch, when Rosso appeared at the door.

We told him what had happened and to my surprise, he took me seriously.

"So Hannah has got to you, just like she took over and destroyed Cassie," he said.

"I'm not one for spooks, but I saw that other creature too and you've got to believe that. It made her miserable: how do you feel?"

"That's the odd thing," I told him, "I felt so bad after we'd been in the space of Oculus; really down and angry but it got better when I got away, then the feeling when I touched the stone was indescribably awful. Now I feel all right, just – funny.

"I know there's something different inside me, but it's not malevolent to me. Something's curled up in here, waiting. There's just this sense of - what, destiny...purpose? I have to destroy Oculus – it's going to be up to me in the end. I'm sure you will have to do the dirty work but I've been chosen in some way. There must be an end to the evil in that place. It's time, Hannah wants to rest."

We drank a grim toast with my cheap red wine.

The next day was a busy one. I went with Penny to Patrick's gallery to apologise to him and look around. He hurried over when we entered and shook my hand. I started to apologise and explain but he held a hand up.

"Penny explained it all to me, so don't worry! Are you feeling better? Come and have a look. You see, I've even hung yours as you wanted and I admit, I think it looks better. Have a closer look, there, there, and there: three red dots! We've sold three already and only three days in.

"I'm really quite excited, as far as we dealers ever allow ourselves to be. There's quite a bit of interest in the other exhibitors, but they're all quite well known, and – well, have you seen the papers? I thought somehow you wouldn't have. Here's 'The Scotsman' review, go on, read it!"

He handed me the paper, and I read it.

The Scottish art world has been looking forward for some time to the opening of Patrick Burn's new gallery in George Street, Edinburgh. And to say we were not disappointed would be to understate the quite splendid ambience and light in this hymn to Georgian proportion and décor at its finest.

I believe, Mr Burn, being a major player on the world stage, has gone a long way towards achieving his aim of driving Scottish painting forward with an unashamedly contemporary exhibition. Here are works by some of the bright stars of the Scottish scene: Andrew Mathieson, Helen Wheatley, Julian Gilchrist, and Ben Tinsley, all pretty safe bets if you are trying to impress. But Mr Burn's flair lies in placing these alongside some long shots that he has uncovered and it's fair to say that those of us assembled at the opening were drawn to some quite astonishing new talent.

Shona Schofield has been around for a while, but has climbed the hill from craftsperson to fine artist over the last few years. Her seascapes manage to be strikingly original in this rather overworked genre; while Chris Perry's wonderfully playful sculptures in wood and glass demonstrate a mastery of technique that gladdens the heart and impress us with an atmosphere of childish exuberance overshadowed by some of our darker fears.

For me, however, the highlight of the exhibition was a collection of large oil paintings by a complete unknown, Mark Kemp, who for personal reasons wasn't able to be present.

Mr Kemp has turned his back on the abstract and returned to figurative painting. Using all the rich texture and colour of the best abstracts he paints rather pale, waif-like nude portraits, placed against the buildings of the city, making them almost appear to inhabit the stones like ghosts.

His eye for detail and atmosphere is awesome and I can only urge you to go and see for yourselves. Here is someone genuinely new and exciting, who I think, is going to set Scottish art in a new direction. I must congratulate Patrick Burn on finding this extraordinary talent.

"The others are in much the same vein," he smiled. "You're set up, Mark. Keep it up, and you can rate as high as any current artist. Not that you won't do me an awful lot of good as well!"

Then his smile turned to one of concern as he led me by the elbow to a far corner of the gallery and spoke in a low voice:

"Look, I get the feeling all this is running off you like water off a duck's back. This other business is taking you over at the moment; Penny has told me about it. Get back to painting, and forget all the rest of that nonsense."

"She wanted to be honest with you, and I support her in that. We'll say no more, I promise, but I'm not going to let things rest."

"It's driving you mad. Leave it!"

I looked at this man who had my future in his hands.

"No," I said.

Penny and I drove off to Cissy's house to tell her about my experience. We sat on her chintz chairs, drinking tea and while I talked, she listened, staring at the ceiling. I finished, and there was silence until she lowered her eyes and met my gaze.

"What you've just told me is complete nonsense. I'm sorry, Mark, but you know I've made a not insignificant study of such things and your experience doesn't tally with anything I've come across. Shall I tell you what I think happened?"

I felt deflated, and rather cross, but nodded.

"You were so troubled after your incursion into the Oculus, we all noticed how different you had become. I think you had genuinely absorbed the evil atmosphere in there. That is your special gift; it's what makes you such a powerful artist.

"You wanted to escape and drove off but then had an overwhelming compulsion to revisit the Kintraw stone. You expected it to speak to you in some way, and approached it expecting to connect with something. You had been so troubled, I think a lot of negative feeling just welled up at that moment and you had some sort of cathartic moment there. You're not describing anything supernatural, just psychological.

"I'm sorry if that sounds too prosaic, but I've seen people who I believed were genuinely possessed and believe me, they didn't sit around drinking tea in middle aged ladies' front rooms."

"You didn't feel it! You don't know how intense that feeling was."

"I'm sure it was but you are an intense person Mark."

I struggled to control a temper that was welling up. She was making me feel a fool.

"So what about Cassie? Was that just psychological, too?" I blurted. "Because I saw that image of Hannah as clear as daylight. You didn't; I did!"

"I think she was genuinely possessed. She felt desperately haunted by what had taken her over. And there's no need to raise your voice; you'll be a lot more useful if you understand yourself and your own powers rather than believing in the whim of some spirit, wouldn't you say?"

She was wielding a power I hadn't seen before. It was quite frightening. I nodded; it was all I could do.

"Yes?" she demanded.

"Yes!" I felt like a rookie on parade, while she turned to Penny.

"Do you agree with what I'm saying?"

Penny did.

"Good. Now there some things about all this that don't add up and your friend O'Hanlon is at the heart of them. I only saw him at Cassie's funeral but from what you say about your conversations with him, I'd say he was playing with you. All this nonsense with silly clues: it's a tease. He's leading you into a trap. I think you should be paying him a visit – soon."

Penny went back to work, while I drove back to Starlings' Yard. I went straight round to O'Hanlon's and knocked on his door. After some minutes, he came out, smiling.

"Mark! Nice to see you, come in lad, come in! I was expecting you. You're famous now, I see. Oh yes, I saw the write-up in 'The Scotsman', I'm so happy for you."

He kept up this stream of pleasantries until I cut him short.

"We must talk. Now. Would it be more private at my flat?"

"Yours? Hardly, it's bugged. Mind you, there's only really me who listens in. No, here's as private as we'll get. Sit down."

"No more games, O'Hanlon. I need some straight talking. There's not much time left and I need to trust you. Now listen to me."

"Of course, but we'll share a whisky, shall we? While you talk?"

I declined but he poured himself another whisky and listened while I talked.

"I don't know what's going on here but I think you and Oculus are taking me for a lethal ride. It's very quiet, you all must know what we're up to but no thugs or threats. You're sitting quietly as we wander into your trap. I want some truth for once!"

O'Hanlon looked supremely unruffled by this outburst.

"Don't you think I've been honest?"

I knocked the whisky out of his hand and taking him by his worn, grubby lapels, slammed him against the wall and pinned him there by the throat. My face was an inch from his.

"The truth, O'Hanlon! Just for once, stop fucking about and tell me the truth!"

It was the first time I'd seen him look scared. His eyes were wide open as he nodded. I let him go.

"I'm sorry," I said, "but you're just playing cat and mouse with me and I don't like it. I don't know why but I think you're on my side, yet you're the chief rabbit in Oculus. What are you playing at?"

He smoothed his jacket and sat down in his chair. He suddenly seemed an old man.

"I'll tell you, not that I haven't been honest with you all along but perhaps I've not told you everything. But where to begin?"

He begun by refilling his whisky glass.

"My life has not been a good one. Not at all. It's been a battleground between God and the Devil since I was a young man. When I fell out with the Church, no, when the Church fell out with me, that schism grew wider and the pain of trying to reconcile what can't be reconciled turned me. Turned me...strange."

His eyes were closed as he sunk deep into his thoughts.

"The Devil made me do evil things, while God always tried to wrestle me back to him. The guilt and the pain were terrible...terrible. They had to put me in an asylum. Two years in the damned asylum to contain my madness. Then, one day, I had a vision. I saw a burning circle of fire and as I looked at it, I saw within the flames the ouroboros: the ancient symbol of the serpent eating its own tail. It was glorious and I understood what it was saying to me. It was perfection: the purity of the circle formed by the reconciliation of extremes.

"I was to be made whole by accepting I had to embrace those extremes. I felt so happy, as though God had shaken hands with the Devil and agreed I should be the instrument of both. So I am. I do very good things and very terrible things and have no conscience. Oculus exists to glorify evil and I embraced it. I get given a lot of money and that money goes to the Church. All of it. Isn't that a strange tale, now?"

"Yes. This is madness."

"You can't understand; I don't expect you to. I exist on a higher plane, ordinary people like you can never know the higher truth. But I have come to a reckoning and it comes in the shape of Mark Kemp."

"How do you mean?" I asked.

He opened his eyes, took a mouthful of whisky and looked directly at me. It seemed like an hour passed, then he spoke.

"Hannah's full name was Hannah Gowdie; she had two children, her daughter Alice, and a son Davie. Her murderers bricked her near dead body under the foundations of this house and her two unconscious children with her. Alice died, but Davie, who was seven, knew the little maze of passages under the buildings and somehow found his way out onto the street.

"He managed to survive by begging but it wasn't long before a kindly woman spotted him and rescued him. He was put into service in her household and grew up there, further down the Mile. He was a bright lad, became well read and made his own way in life as a cloth merchant. But he never forgot what those murderers had done to him and his family. One by one, they all died by his knife. He was clever and he was never caught."

"Interesting, but what has that to do with us?"

"Ah, well, you see, the family that bought him up didn't know his real name: all he knew was that he was called Davie, so he took their surname and grew up as David Kemp.

"They had no children of their own. You are his direct descendant. Now, I know there are a lot of Kemps, but I've checked. I have your family tree, if you want it. There was even an artist, an engraver, called Matthew.

"I knew that your coming was no coincidence. Something brought you here and it brought you here to finish the job and let your ancestor rest at last. You've seen how we use her bones to channel our powers. You have come to destroy Oculus and all the evil in this place.

"We will try to stop you but I know we are to be destroyed and in those final moments of destruction, I will be judged by both God and the Devil. The ouroboros shall be broken and returned to the flames that forged it."

"So why haven't your thugs done away with me? They were on my tail and now they're obviously leaving me alone."

"Because I told them to. I convinced the members of Oculus that you had taken the hint after the session in the bookshop and were no longer a threat. Luckily, they believed me. No, wrong, not luck. They believe in me, you see.

"Perhaps you've wondered what I'm doing in amongst all these powerful people. What's a scrawny defrocked priest doing in amongst the Great and the Bad, eh? Who let me in? Ah, you see, it's the other way round: I let them join me! I am Oculus!"

He gave a chuckle and poured himself another whisky. He was getting a bit drunk, I suspected, more than usual.

"Have you ever heard of the Order of the Golden Dawn?"

"Yes, Rosso mentioned them. Macgregor Mathers, wasn't it?"

"You've done your homework! Now listen! This is a history lesson, but I want you to hear me out. I want you to know what is unknown except to those of us who are about to die. Yes, you heard me.

"Mathers was the instigator but there was a temple in this city called the Temple of Amen-Ra, the Scottish branch was run by a dear chap called Brodie Innes. However the whole order came crashing down around 1900, after a lot of internal power struggles resulting in it changing to the Alpha and Omega Order. It had quite a number of members but closed down in 1939 fragmenting into many different societies, most of them harmless social clubs which liked a bit of magic mumbo-jumbo, but one, the Order of the Eye of Thoth, was different.

"It was far more interested in the darker side of things and followed the teachings of a self-styled Satanist called Aleister Crowley. He had advocated breaking taboos to liberate the inner self and unleash the dark forces, so they embraced all his sexual teachings and incorporated sexual rituals into their rites. Well you can imagine how the Order grew and one thing led to another. When the women members had been scared off, they would import city prostitutes to aid their practices, and the whole thing became a bit of an occult brothel.

"I admit, I have some strange appetites myself. I too became attracted to the Order and made myself known to them. I was invited to join and it wasn't long before I became the praemonstrator – the top dog in charge of the rituals. I sorted that lot out, Mark, oh, how I sorted them out! I made those rituals into something great. Then I decided there was more to do. We didn't need to pay for the privilege of screwing a few call girls, we could own them and use them. But it had to be secret, very secret. I chose twelve other members: people with power, money and intelligence, oh, and each with his own sick perversions. I chose them to be my Illuminati; my enlightened ones, we took the rituals to a very – refined level and we became Oculus."

"Please, I don't want to –"

"Sex, death and evil! We thirteen Illuminati made this place our home and made it the centre of a web of wickedness. I found out about Hannah and excavated her skeleton, it was under this very flat all along: I find it keeps the focus of evil here. We control most of the crime and rackets in Edinburgh, the other lower orders of Alpha and Omega carry out our wishes. You wanted the truth. There you have it."

He rose unsteadily and went to the kitchen. After a few minutes, he returned with another bottle of whisky, and filled his glass, slopping it as he staggered drunkenly against the wall. I hadn't touched mine. He took a sip, then laid his head back against his chair and to my dismay, started to cry; a high pitched, quavering sound. It was the piping despair of an old man, an old drunk who couldn't even drown his sorrows. I

197

despised him but felt sorry for him at the same time for I knew what he was going to say next.

"I'm sorry, Mark, truly. You must think I'm just a pathetic old man, but when I look at you, I'm looking at my nemesis and I know it has to be so. I could have had you killed but I didn't. I have to let it happen.

"You know, every night I pray to God, not for forgiveness but to thank him. He knows, for did he not send the ouroboros to me? He is the highest plane of all and he, like me, is above the petty rights and wrongs of mortal men. Does he not send death and suffering to us? God understands me! God knows me!"

At this, he fell onto his knees, clasping his hands before him and started to pray. I watched him dispassionately. I wanted to be out of this place. Rather roughly, I raised him up and pushed him back in his chair.

"Two questions O'Hanlon, then I'm going. I've heard enough. First question: did you kill Cassie?"

"She was used in our ritual, so yes."

"Question two: when's the next meeting?"

"Next Monday, five o'clock."

"Are you telling me the truth?"

"I don't lie; I can't."

I marched to the door, and heard him call out behind me. Despite my anger, I had to turn round to him. He came to me, his arms outstretched.

"Embrace me, Mark, I have told you everything and we may not meet again."

Despite everything, I went back to him and held him close to me. Then I watched him go back to his room, like a black spider, banging against the walls of his hallway.

I walked down the staircase and out into the Yard. It was a dark frosty night and a three quarter moon hung in a starry sky. The dark hulks of the buildings rose around me and the air reeked of smoke from the unsavoury embers of Percy's nightly conflagration.

I breathed in deeply, remembering the tune Angus had played sitting in front of his house. The day Cassie was dancing there to the music in her head. Poor Cassie, I thought of how I had loved her and the whole Yard dissolved into a blur of ultramarine, cerulean, and scarlet. I went over to Rosso's flat.

Chapter 16

Rosso answered the door rather grumpily in his pyjamas.

I'd no idea it was that late but as soon as he saw me he ushered me in to his front room. I saw my painting on his wall and thought, for no reason, "That's worth a bit now".

"What the fuck's up? You look terrible! What are you crying for?"

"Am I?"

I told him the gist of my evening with O'Hanlon.

"Fucking perverted loony," he said. "Right, it's time to get going. Have a cup of coffee first, then we're off to visit our twisted friend!"

While I gratefully drank the coffee, he disappeared then returned dressed in combat gear, with a large pack on his back. I felt very much underdressed for whatever we were about to do.

Rosso shushed my questions and together we walked out into the night.

O'Hanlon's front door was unlocked so we just walked in. He was there, slumped in his chair, in a drunken stupor, twitching restlessly. Rosso pointed to the whisky bottle and mimed pouring it down his throat. I shook O'Hanlon into near consciousness and by talking gently to him, managed to get a large amount of whisky down his throat; enough to keep him asleep for some hours.

Rosso, meanwhile had gone into his study and opened up the metal doorway into the Oculus warren. I joined him and together we went into the surveillance room.

He was in his element and magnificent. He looked at the video screens and switched them off and his torch on. We went through the door at the far end, down onto the rough stone steps that led to the tunnel, along the narrow stone passage, his torch lighting up the way a few yards ahead. After another fifty feet or so, we reached a small chamber, just high enough to stand up, carved out of the ancient sandstone many ages ago. At the far end lay the black mouths of two more passages.

"Oh fuck!" Rosso said. "Which way?"

I remembered the map I'd so painstakingly built up.

"The right one. The other one's a ventilation shaft."

We went into the tunnel on the right. My map predicted steps down to a space directly under the North Bridge. There they were! We descended twenty feet or so, then along another short length of passage, only to be met with another steel door: a door of steel slats with no keyhole or any obvious means to get through. I cursed, but Rosso was feeling around it, testing it. He left it and shone his torch around the walls of the passageway until he found what he was looking for. He pulled on a protruding stone that seemed embedded in the wall, but nothing happened. Then he tried pushing it and as he did so, there was a hum of a motor and a quiet rattle as the roller door opened up for us.

A dim blue light filled the passage beyond, coming from a number of safety lights at intervals in the roof of the passages. We were getting close to the main chamber according to my reckoning, and as we walked along the passage which had been enlarged and lined with plaster, we saw symbols painted on the surface. Many of these I recognised as planetary or elemental symbols but reversed like a mirror image. A deep shelf had been carved into the wall, and on this lay the trappings of their ceremonies: a chalice, a scourge, a large shallow silver bowl stained dark inside, a long dagger, and some folded linen cloths. A black robe hung on the wall opposite. A few more steps, and we emerged into the main chamber itself.

I'd predicted its size, but even so, found myself, like Rosso, standing in awe at the scale of the space.

It was circular, some forty feet across and if my plans were right, directly under the North Bridge itself. As if in confirmation, we could hear the muffled noise of traffic overhead. The plastered walls rose vertically some six feet before sloping upwards to form a shallow dome some twenty foot high at the centre. The dome itself was painted in lurid images, rather crudely done, of demonic figures copulating with naked women. Someone had been trying to copy Hieronymus Bosch and failed. The thought gave me comfort.

Rosso raised his eyebrows and smiled.

"Bunch of old perverts!"

From the centre of the dome, suspended on a rope above us, swaying very slightly from the vibrations of the traffic above was the massive inverted wooden cross we had seen on the video screen. It hung from a pulley arrangement and could obviously be lowered if needed.

Under the cross was a stone altar, covered in painted symbols, on which lay the articulated skeletons of an adult and a small child: Hannah and Alice! I walked over and looked closer at the remains. I saw the fractures and dents in Hannah's skull that attested to her horrid fate and like a mist, the feeling of utter depression came over me as it had when we first entered this evil place.

I could hardly move but forced myself to look around at the wooden chairs, like black carved thrones, that were spaced out round the walls, six on each side of the main axis. The thirteenth chair, O'Hanlon's, stood directly in front of the passageway by which we had entered, while a second entrance lay directly opposite.

A shaft of light cut through the dimness and hit the altar, lighting up the skeletons. Looking up, I saw it came from a narrow circular shaft running from halfway up the dome to daylight at the end – the oculus lens!

I hadn't been prepared for this foray and was regretting the lack of a camera or even a sketchpad to record what we were seeing. I was still standing there taking in as much detail as I could, feeling that awful oppression, when Rosso appeared at the opposite entrance. He beckoned me over, and with an effort, I walked over to where he stood.

"Take a look at this!" he whispered and led me into the other passage.

It was filled with the same blue light as the other passage and chamber but in this case, after a few yards it opened into a square chamber where a number of metal lockers stood: functional things such as you'd find in any gym. There were also three washbasins, a kitchen area with a small gas hob and a kettle, fed from two large gas cylinders bracketed to the wall. It all looked rather incongruous. I tried one of the lockers: it was locked.

Rosso led me down the passage that led into this room; it curved round and after a few more yards we came across the barred side chamber that we had seen on the video screen. Behind the bars was a single bed with a bare mattress. The passage continued to bear round until it ended in a steel roller door identical to the one on O'Hanlon's side.

"No point trying to go through this," Rosso said. "We don't know what's on the other side, we might find ourselves in a tricky situation but we've seen everything we need. Give me a hand to set up."

He went back into the changing room, pointed to the gas cylinders and grinned. He put his rucksack on the floor and pulled the top open. After pulling out an old jumper, he produced a plain metal canister about a foot long and eight inches wide. He unscrewed one end of it, revealing a digital time display. My mouth must have dropped open.

"What the hell's that?" I asked.

"Well, it's not my sandwiches, that's for sure!"

"You mean you've been carting round a load of dynamite in that?"

"Aye, it's quite safe – at the moment, don't worry. Now shut up a minute and let me think!"

He looked at his watch and then set the timer: sixty three hours and eight minutes. He then lifted out the timer and set a switch underneath. He replaced the lid, then together we edged the bottom of the gas cylinders out from the wall and parted them slightly. The canister fitted behind them nicely, we pushed them back into place.

We made our way back into the main chamber, where he took a cloth-wrapped packet from his rucksack which when opened revealed a bundle of explosives taped together. I'd never seen explosives before; it was like watching a movie. He rummaged in his sack again and produced a camera.

This man was a genius! He handed it to me and I took what photographs I could in the poor light, while he taped the explosives to the underside of one of the chairs. Our mission accomplished, he tied up his bag and we returned through the passages back into O'Hanlon's flat, closing the steel doors and switching the video recorders back on. O'Hanlon appeared to be as I'd left him. Sprawled in his chair, still asleep.

I went back to my flat and slept badly, my mind too full of images of the chamber and its nightmarish implications. We were about to kill people and that thought made me feel sick.

When morning came, I felt dreadful. Heavy depression smothered me like a blanket of stone and I didn't get out of bed until mid-day. Over a coffee, I rang Penny and arranged to meet her for dinner at the Melrose Bar, I needed to tell her of the latest developments.

I wanted to go round and see Patrick too, for news of how the exhibition was going but decided my mood might well cause another argument so I busied myself doing sketches from memory of the Oculus chamber. I could see the basis for another painting in that place. The sketches just wouldn't gel into anything, though. In the end, I threw the sketchpad down and went out for a walk.

By now, it was late afternoon, overcast but quite warm. The Mile was alive with people: tourists, shoppers, loafers, students, drunks and businessmen, all milling around me, but I felt wrapped in a cocoon, a transparent bubble which held me apart from all this.

I could hear the conversations and the din of the traffic, but it seemed muffled, and unconnected with the life going on around me. Then, through the sound, I heard the tune that Angus had played in the Yard, I felt overcome with sadness. Then I realised the music came not from inside my head, but from a busker playing a melodeon beside the Mercat Cross. I stopped, and stood in front of him. He looked up briefly to smile at me as he played, but seeing my unkempt figure, wrapped in misery, he looked down again. He must have assumed I was drunk but I just stayed there, staring at him. He played another tune and still I stood looking. In reality, I was looking at the scenes in my own head but eventually, he got uncomfortable with my presence and moved on.

A young couple - students by the look of them - were sitting on the step of the Cross, in an intense embrace, his hand on her rather insubstantial breast. They saw me staring and broke off, looking sheepish. Then a tired looking middle aged woman sat down, with her husband beside her arguing. He strode off in a temper, then she hung her head and wept.

A street preacher came up and started to rant. The others moved away but I stood there, still absorbed in myself. Thinking that I was listening to him, he shouted his message of sin and salvation at me and taking my bent head for repentance came down to embrace me, his breath smelling of cigarettes and beer. Another drunk jostled against us and sat heavily down on the step waving a bottle of beer and shouting, "Hallelujah!", the two of them started to argue and push as I walked on.

Ragged crows flew overhead across the reddening sky that was visible between the tall buildings that lined the sides of the Lawnmarket. They took on an ancient significance in my head, like some prophecy of disaster. Finally, I could take it no more and I went quickly home.

I sat on the couch when I got back and fell asleep. I awoke hours later, feeling a good deal better. I looked at my watch; it was late. I was supposed to meet Penny in ten minutes. I washed quickly, changed and drove across the city too fast, remembering her penchant for punctuality.

I arrived only five minutes late and walked in. The bar was beginning to fill up, I looked round but could see no sign of her. I grinned to myself, thinking that I could rib her about being late, then ordered a couple of white wines. I found a table where I could see the door, and waited.

I finished my glass, drank hers, then ordered another and drank that. An hour passed, and I began to get anxious. Penny wouldn't ever be this late without good reason, she would have let me know. I went out and found a 'phone box and rang her flat. There was no answer. I rang Cissy, but she hadn't seen or heard from Penny that day. I drove to her flat, going round by the Croesus Gallery to make sure she wasn't working late. It was shut and dark.

Her car was there, parked outside. I let myself in. The flat too was in darkness and showed no signs of her returning from work. Breakfast plates were still stacked in the kitchen, and her bed was empty. I sat on the settee, trying to think logically. An accident, maybe? They would have informed Cissy, surely.

Had she gone out with Patrick and forgotten our meeting? Hardly. I rang Cissy again. I didn't want to worry her, but I needed someone else to come up with an alternative, or to tell me what to do. For once, Cissy became flustered and unsure and gave voice to a fear I hadn't, daren't contemplate.

"Mark, you don't suppose that the Oculus goons could have got her?"

"Surely not. What have they got against her? It'd be me they were after. No, I don't think that's a possibility."

I knew it was, though. We discussed whether we should inform the police, given our present intentions. In the end, we agreed Cissy would ring them and I would wait where I was in case she turned up.

Half an hour later, Cissy phoned back. I told her there was still no sign of Penny and she in turn told me she had rung the police. They had taken the details but insisted the standard procedure was to let them know in the morning if she was still missing. After all, they had said, two hours is hardly unusual.

We had no option but to wait. I lay in Penny's bed and spent another restless night.

In the morning, Cissy rang again. She'd rung the police to inform them there was still no sign of Penny and a little later, she'd had a call from a police inspector who wanted to come round to Penny's flat to talk to me about her disappearance. He wished to interview me alone, but had reassured Cissy that there was no bad news; no news at all, in fact. The inspector's name was McLeod.

He was round an hour later.

Now sat in front of me while we both drank tea, was the same soft-spoken inspector who had questioned me after Cassie's death. He asked the usual questions: how well did I know her? When had I last heard from her? Did I have any ideas what might have happened to her? This last question I denied but he looked at me and put away his notebook.

"Mr Kemp, or may I call you Mark?" I nodded.

"Thank you, Mark. Now, we're going to talk strictly off the record, as well, friends in a common cause. It may not have struck you, but I wouldn't normally get involved in missing persons cases."

It had struck me, but I said nothing.

"I get hunches, you see. I get feelings about things. I always blame it on my West Highland blood: we're quite often blessed or cursed with a bit of second sight. It makes me a good copper."

"Ever since we first met, after Cassie's tragic death, I had a hunch about you. You don't fit into this place; I couldn't understand why you were here. Then, after I'd spoken to you again, I knew you had some sort of second sight, too. You'd seen the evil spirit that haunts this place. There was a reason for your being here, even though you didn't know it – then. You do now, I think." He paused.

"Mind if I smoke my pipe in here?"

"No, carry on. It's not my flat anyway. What makes you say that?"

"What, about smoking?"

"No, about my knowing why I'm here!"

"I follow my hunches. I've been following your progress with a lot of interest. Oh, and congratulations on your artistic success by the way. They are remarkable paintings. I only wish I could afford one, but on my salary, huh!"

He stood up, chuckling, and went over to the window, pulling aside the lace curtain and looked across the city. Heavy black rainclouds were darkening the day. I thought I heard a distant rumble of thunder.

208

"We've followed you, on and off, all four of you, since Cassie died."

"Not you as well!"

"Aye, us as well, partly to find out what you were up to, and partly to protect you. You and I are on the same side Mark; Oculus is a very dangerous enemy."

"How much do you know about Oculus?"

"Almost as much as you, but my hands are tied. I've been brought up in the Church, and I've some old fashioned Christian values. It's a Sunday morning, and I should be at the kirk, not working, but this is important.

"I may be simple, but I see my job as fighting evil. Oculus represents most of the evil in this city and beyond, and I hate the organisation with what amounts to an obsession.

"Three of my bosses are in it, as I'm sure you know, they spend a lot of time and public money making sure their tracks are covered. Officially, I have to warn you that if you attempt to take the law into your own hands, then you have to face the consequences of any criminal actions. But that's another thing we have in common, lad: we don't let go easily, and I'm sure you'll go ahead anyway.

"I want you to know off the record that if my bosses were to face, shall we say, divine retribution, with you as God's instrument; then I will be in charge. Two can play their game and though it goes against all my principles, the end, in this case, would justify any means.

"What I'm trying to say is: evidence can be...adjusted, if you understand me."

I looked long and hard at him. His face, everything about him, told me he was as straight and honest as he said. I so wanted to confide in him, yet something held me back. We were playing for the highest stakes and I couldn't trust anybody.

"I understand you," I replied. He dropped the curtain and faced me. It was his turn to look me in the eye for some moments.

"Good," he said. "Now, another hunch tells me that things are coming to the boil. I'm sure Miss Bowman's disappearance is connected with them. We'll keep a lookout for her, of course, my men are asking her neighbours if they saw anything. However, I think you need to speak to our friend O'Hanlon to learn more."

"I will. Thank you....McLeod," I answered.

"I know nothing of your plans and don't want to, right? I just want you to know that I'm behind you all." He shook my hand. "Gur math a thèid leat!"

"Pardon?"

"Good luck, it means. I just think it works better in Gaelic! Now remember, we never had this conversation and if you need me, you can get me on this number."

With that, he handed me a card, put his pipe in his pocket, and left.

I rang Cissy and told her about McLeod's visit, but didn't mention our off-record conversation. I tried to be as reassuring as possible, but I could tell she was worried sick. So was I.

I had to confront O'Hanlon again. After our last conversation, he had no reason to lie to me. It had to be Oculus that had taken Penny but there was no ransom note or demand. What were they doing with her?

I got in the car, the black sky seemed to bathe everything in a greenish gold light. Then, with a crash of thunder, the rain started. Torrents swept the streets, and the single wiper on my windscreen was no match for the downpour. I waited for the worst to pass.

Through the curtains of water running down the windows I noticed a cream coloured car parked on the other side of the road, just behind me. I could just make out the shapes of two men sitting in the front. I've no idea why, but some animal instinct took me over and I felt panic taking hold. Perhaps I had seen the car before, I don't know, but I knew something was wrong. I threw myself over to the passenger side, opened the door, and rolled out into a large puddle. I threw myself forward to Penny's car which was parked in front of mine, unlocked the passenger side and crawled in.

As I did so, the cream car moved off and shots rang out. The driver's side window shattered as bullets tore into it. I felt a sharp pain in my left thigh, one of the bullets must have ricocheted off the dashboard. Blood started to soak through my trousers.

A moment later, there was a loud explosion, the remains of the windows of Penny's car shattered in the blast and I saw that my car was a blackened, burning wreck. I must have passed out. The next thing I remembered was a sea of faces as I was lifted into an ambulance and a tight tourniquet being applied around my thigh.

I was taken to the Western General Hospital where there were questions, drips, X-rays and an operation to remove the bullet. Luckily, it was just into muscle and I was soon tucked up in yet another hospital ward. I was becoming quite a feature at various Scottish hospitals.

It wasn't long before the police arrived, in the shape of McLeod. My bed was wheeled into a side ward on his instructions and he sat down beside me.

"I didn't expect that we'd meet again quite so soon," he joked, "how are you feeling?"

"Better than my car."

He smiled; a rather rueful smile.

"That's not all, I'm afraid. They also went after Mr Ross - Rosso, sorry - and were rather more successful. He's been critically injured, poor fellow. He's in the Royal Infirmary at the moment and I'm sorry, Mark, he's struggling."

I felt my stomach turn and wanted to be sick. "What happened?" I asked.

He glanced at the open door and lowered his voice.

"Some thugs from - the organisation - threw a grenade through his window. Quite a blast, I understand: it's blown one wall of his flat out completely."

"He sustained some burns but mainly it was the explosion that did the damage, his ribcage and lungs were very badly injured. He's alive, but on a ventilator and they tell me his oxygen levels are very poor." He paused, "I'm sorry, son."

"*We will try to stop you, of course,*" I remembered O'Hanlon's words.

"I must go and see him!" I cried, "Now."

"I don't think they'll let you out just yet."

"Just spring me out, I must go to him. Please. I'm OK now, honestly."

McLeod got up with a nod and went out to speak to the sister. She in turn went to find the doctor, who turned up fifteen minutes later. He tried to dissuade me, but I wasn't having any of it. He grudgingly produced a form and I signed myself out.

I nearly passed out when I tried to stand, the pain was unbelievable. But I stood my ground and left with McLeod and a walking stick to steady me.

He drove me straight to the Royal Infirmary, in Lauriston Place.

As he did so, he answered my questions. No, there was still no trace of Penny and yes, Cissy was fine, but had two policemen assigned to guard her house, where she was confined for the time being.

212

The rather forbidding Victorian hospital building added to my feelings of hopelessness as I limped in with McLeod. Getting up the stairs made me break into a pale sweat of pain, but we managed.

There, in a side ward, was Rosso, a uniformed policeman sitting beside him.

Poor Rosso; he was unconscious still, looking pale and cyanosed. His face was burnt and blistered. A tube led into a tracheostomy in his throat and was attached to a cumbersome machine beside his bed that made wheezing and clicking noises as it breathed for him. Yet again, I felt my tears on my cheeks.

McLeod went into the ward to seek out a doctor.

I touched his arm, then stroked his head. His eyes opened slowly and his hand came up to his face to grasp mine. The corners of his mouth tried to smile and he gave me a feeble wink before his eyes closed and his hand fell away.

The policeman stood and offered me his seat, which I took gladly. I held Rosso's hand as McLeod reappeared with a doctor.

The doctor explained that the blast had injured his lungs, which were responding by secreting a lot of liquid, filling them up and effectively drowning him. They were giving him big doses of diuretics to squeeze the fluid out, but...a forty per cent chance of survival, the doctor told us, with an expression that told me he was being generous with the chances.

Seeing him lying there, I realised just how much I had grown to love and depend on this man. I felt so alone and vulnerable.

"Please, please," I prayed to whatever God was looking after us. "Please, make it all right."

I stayed there for half an hour, then McLeod drove me back to Cissy's house, where I was to stay the night.

Cissy had been told about Rosso and complained furiously to McLeod that she was being kept prisoner in her own house and wanted to visit him right now. I'd seen her icy before, of course, but never this out of control. McLeod took the force of her outburst.

"I can imagine what torments you are going through, Mrs Bowman, or maybe I can't, but I have to consider your safety and that of my men. In the morning I can have you taken to him under escort but for now you are staying here. There will be an officer in the hall and a further two in a car outside. Mr Ross is a tough character: he'll be all right overnight, I'm sure. If there's any news about him or your daughter, we'll inform you immediately, you have my word."

Cissy sighed and shook her head, deflated and helpless. McLeod left, and, even though it was only eight thirty, there was nothing to do but go to bed.

Cissy showed me to a spare bedroom, ready with linen and towels. She bade me goodnight, her voice sounding hollow and expressionless. She made to go, then turned, and said:

"This was Cassie's room. She grew up in here. The walls were covered with pictures of fairies; I used to listen to her talking to them as though they were real. She always preferred an imaginary, magic world where everything was always going to be all right. When she died, I redecorated it. Goodnight."

That night, it felt as if Cassie was in the room with me. I saw her as a young girl, about seven years old, solemnly showing me her fairy pictures and explaining who they were. I was lying in the bed, while she sat on the bedspread, dressed in a smocked nightdress, with long straight fair hair going half way down her back. It seemed I was talking back to her and we were smiling.

I woke early in the morning, feeling a glow of comfort, still with the vision clear in my head. I got washed and dressed.

Cissy was still asleep. I searched around and found a writing pad and a pen. I drew the scene I'd dreamt in as much detail as I could, then tucked the picture out of sight.

Over breakfast, I told Cissy about my dream, but she was dismissive.

"You have a highly suggestible imagination, don't you? It's what makes you an artist, I suppose, but I'm not really in the mood for reminiscences right now."

"It was so real, though! Cissy, do you have any pictures of her when she was about seven? Please, I'd love to know what she looked like then."

"I don't think it's appropriate. Those are my memories, Mark, not yours."

I fetched my drawing and handed it to her, silently. Her hands looked old as she took it and looked at the picture of the small girl on the bed.

I'd been able to draw the wallpaper, the pattern on the bedspread, the bedhead, even the brace on her teeth. Cissy's breathing became laboured, and she went pale.

"Oh, dear God," she whispered, "What's happening to me? No, she must have described all this to you. Stop trying to spook me!"

"No, she didn't, Cissy, I swear."

"Then what's happening?"

"Who knows? I just know that Cassie's still here. I can sense these things, that's all. I always had a sense of atmosphere, but since that business with my fingernails, it's become clearer, more defined. I can't explain it; no one can, but I can sense these things. Believe me."

Cissy got up and pulled a photograph album from the bookcase. She turned the leaves over, then sat at the table again, staring at a page. I got up and stood looking over her shoulder. I felt a prickling on my neck, for there was a black and white photograph of Cassie in her bedroom nearly identical to my sketch.

"I suppose you think I crept in overnight and found it and copied it," I said. "But I haven't, anyway see, the bedspread is completely different."

"That photograph was taken because she asked me to take one with her new bedspread, with a fairy design on. The one you've drawn is the one she had before."

A tear dropped onto the photo and she wiped it away quickly. I put my hand on her shoulder, and she put her hand over it. I bent and kissed her on the head.

"They never go away," I said.

Her hand squeezed mine. "No, they don't."

Soon after that, McLeod arrived to take us to visit Rosso. He escorted us outside to a waiting car, with a police motorcyclist in front. McLeod sat in the front with the police driver while Cissy and I were in the back.

"This will have the neighbours talking; they'll think we've been done for a robbery." She was trying to make light of things, but her hand was gripping mine, hard.

We arrived at Rosso's bed and I felt a pang of disappointment. I'd half hoped he would be off the ventilator and sitting up; but he was still just lying there, unconscious and pale, with a different policeman by his side, and the same plethora of tubes and machines connected to him. McLeod left us and later, the same young doctor came to speak to us.

"There's not much difference," he explained. "But there are some more hopeful signs. His oxygen saturations have risen to seventy percent from fifty and there's an improvement in his renal function, so..."

"Thank God," said Cissy, "you're a tough old thing, you."

She tousled his hair, but there was no response. We sat there for an hour or so. I could feel the sheer will that she was giving out to him.

Later on, McLeod returned and despite his protestations, Cissy insisted on going out for lunch and paying.

I think she couldn't stand the thought of going back to the armed confinement of her house, so we descended on the Balmoral Hotel. It was a pleasant enough lunch; Cissy had been buoyed up by the doctor's words and was swapping tales with McLeod, but I was feeling anxious and didn't say much.

It was two o'clock on Monday. In three and a half hours, Rosso's bomb was due to go off and without him, I was feeling lost.

We returned to Cissy's house and the mood darkened.

It made a strange, sad scene. Cissy and I sat on her pale leather sofa, McLeod sat back on the armchair opposite and a bored-looking policeman sat apart by the door, a rifle in his hands.

There were long silences, punctuated with attempts at conversation, but what was there to say, other than clichés? Cissy desperately wanted to be with Rosso, I could tell.

I was thinking hard. It was now three-thirty and the bomb was timed to go off in two hours. Did I say nothing, and hope? Something told me I had to be in at the end but I was stuck here, confined to quarters, the others not knowing what was going to happen.

The mantle clocked ticked the time away.

"You have to be somewhere?" McLeod asked, "You keep glancing at the clock."

I made up my mind and I told him about the entrance, the chamber, the meeting, and the explosives. Cissy listened with alarm, but McLeod's eyes glinted and even the policeman at the door raised his eyebrows.

"Don't you think there may be a reception committee waiting for you if you try going back to Starlings' Yard? O'Hanlon could have told them everything."

I admitted this hadn't crossed my mind; but then my mind went back to that last conversation with that unhappy black spider of a man who had gone mad trying to reconcile the irreconcilable.

"No," I said, "O'Hanlon is convinced his nemesis is coming; it's taken on huge religious significance for him. It's his reconciliation with both God and the Devil. He wants it to happen. Why he ordered his thugs to get us, I don't know, but my guess is he wanted to play the game to the end, testing God to see if he would still bring it about."

McLeod cocked his head to one side, as I'd noticed he did when he was thinking hard. His eyes looked into mine. The ticking clock said four o'clock.

"OK, it's your show. We'll take you over there, but allow me to help you. I've been waiting a long time for this. Have you thought about evacuating the flats? Do you know how severe the blast is going to be?"

None of this had occurred to me, either. I'd rather left the details up to Rosso and I had no idea what his intentions were.

McLeod and I left a tearful Cissy who announced she was going to bake some sponge cakes and that she might even break a habit and pray, and we drove off in his car.

On the way he radioed through a stream of instructions to a voice on the other end. He asked me about the amount of explosive that Rosso had used and got some technical answer from an explosives expert. His eyebrows shot up as he received the information.

"Hell's teeth!" he smiled. "Our friend Rosso doesn't do things by halves."

"No," I said, "he doesn't."

We pulled up a few hundred yards from Starlings' Yard and waited. McLeod chatted about his tastes in art, and other things. I wondered how he could be so relaxed while I was shaking inside but I sensed that this was what policemen do in those interminable waits.

At five minutes to five, we drove up nearer to Starlings' Yard. I saw a silent line of armed policemen across the entrance, while others were efficiently calling the other residents into the street. A puzzled uniformed officer approached us and told McLeod that the residents all appeared to have already left the Yard some time before.

My palms were sweaty and my heart pounded. At precisely five o'clock, McLeod and I went up to O'Hanlon's flat, a burning pain in my injured leg. The door had been left unlocked. Inside, the place was unnaturally, almost eerily tidy. The broken things had gone. Papers were stacked neatly; surfaces had been dusted and cleaned.

I thought of O'Hanlon walking from his sitting room to what he knew would be the final meeting of Oculus. Was he pondering the nature of his fate? No, I didn't think he was, for I could see him clearly in my thoughts; purposeful, and with an ecstatic smile on his face, walking into the study, and down into the tunnel…

"Where's this door, then?" McLeod's quiet voice interrupted my thoughts.

I led him towards the study. We both heard the tiniest of clicks but loud enough in that silent space. McLeod stiffened and motioned me into stillness and silence.

There was someone in the study, someone with a gun. I was in a terrified sweat as McLeod pulled a gun out from under his jacket and waited.

Minutes seemed to pass, then a few footsteps. An arm holding a gun appeared at the study door, followed by the fleeting head of a man. There was a deafening noise as he fired the pistol blindly at us, missing us by a good margin but causing a shower of plaster from the wall nearby. I hardly saw McLeod move, but in an instant he had the man's arm in his grip and using it as a lever, swung him round to him. The pistol dropped to the floor and McLeod was holding him from behind, his arm crooked around the man's neck. The man squirmed, and I saw his face. It was Alan Trapp, the young man from the bookshop.

McLeod gave Trapp's arm a wrench and there was a nauseating crack as he dropped heavily to the floor, his head at an impossible angle to the rest of him. McLeod straightened up at the same time that I bent over and was sick on the linoleum floor.

"No time for that now," he said. "Come on."

The door into the video room had been left open and McLeod gave a murmur of admiration for the set-up. The screens were glowing and a cigarette was still burning in the ashtray where Trapp had been sitting. A book lay open on the desk, cover upwards: Bunyan's *Pilgrim's Progress*. The world never did make any sense.

We looked at the screens in front of us and I let out a cry of shock. The ceremony was proceeding. I could see O'Hanlon standing by the altar intoning, the great inverted cross hung above and in front of him. On it a naked woman was bound, upside down in the posture of a crucifixion. Details were hard to make out but from wounds in her neck, rivulets of blood were running down her inverted face, down the long hair and into the silver bowl beneath.

I didn't have to see her face; the shape of her body and the hair told me: it was Penny! If she wasn't already dead, then she was about to be blown apart with the rest of them.

I turned to McLeod in a panic.

"That's Penny. I've got to get her out of there!"

"Don't be an idiot, it's too late!" he barked, then looked at me. "Go on, then, but take the gun, for God's sake."

I did take the gun, and ran down the steps and into the tunnel. My leg should have hurt but it didn't, even when I felt the stitches burst open and there was the wetness of warm blood, I could feel nothing except love and hate. I reached the steel door and pushed at the stone to open it. I had no plan in my head, nothing now but blind anger.

I ducked under the door as it opened, running down the tunnel and through the entrance to the chamber.

What followed is a blur, like trying to piece together a drunken previous night. I shouted something like, "Bastards! Fucking bastards!" and I remember O'Hanlon turning slowly round to me as the other members rose in consternation.

His arms were outstretched to me, as if in greeting and he had a smile on his face.

The other members were advancing towards me now and a guard appeared at the other entrance, with a gun. He couldn't take a shot at me as the other members were in the way, but as soon as he jostled his way to the front of them, I shot him. I saw the blood spurt out of his chest, but felt nothing, not then. The others backed off for a moment, I turned to O'Hanlon shouting, "Let her down – now!"

"The hour is come!" he cried, and unwound the ropes that held the cross from their anchor on the wall. The weight of the wood and the body tied on to it made the rope whip round and caught him by the arm, carrying him upwards as the cross descended.

He screamed as his arm was wrenched out of its socket, then cried "God, forgive me!" as he dropped to the floor. One of the hooded members tried to rush at me, and I shot him, too. The massive cross descended and I flung myself at it, trying to break Penny's fall. The cross landed on the altar,

221

crushing the two skeletons beneath it, and splintering Hannah's skull into fragments.

It could only be a matter of seconds before the explosives went off. I picked up the knife that O'Hanlon had dropped and desperately sawed at the ropes that bound Penny to the cross, trying at the same time to train my gun on the confused crowd around me. Then I saw another knife quickly slicing the ropes; it was McLeod. He must have watched my predicament and fetched a knife from O'Hanlon's kitchen. Together we freed her and pulled her body towards the exit. I had no idea whether she was alive or dead.

We dragged her through the steel door. The dazed Oculus members still in the chamber, too scared of being shot to follow us. I pushed the stone frantically and it started to close behind us as we lifted Penny on to my shoulder and ran blindly towards the study. I heard O'Hanlon's screams as he ducked under the descending door running after us.

We reached the mouth of the ventilation tunnel and McLeod pushed me towards it. We doubled back down it, towards the sound of a large fan in the darkness at the other end, and felt the strong surge of air pushing against us.

I felt a jolt, like an earthquake and McLeod pushed me down onto the floor of the tunnel. A deafening explosion blasted the chamber apart and a shock wave hit us physically as it crashed through the steel door.

A ball of flame and shrapnel tore past us, followed by another. The explosion caught O'Hanlon as he staggered past the entrance to our shaft, then he too burst into flames as the flying metal tore his body apart. He was screaming, "God, oh God!" and then there was nothing but mortuary silence.

The air was cinder hot and difficult to breathe. I picked Penny's limp body up in my arms, stepping over the black and crimson mass that was all that remained of O'Hanlon, and we made our way up the stairs and through the wrecked video room as fast as we could.

We could see O'Hanlon's study through the open doorway. Fierce flames were swiftly devouring his books and papers and a large crack was opening in the outside wall. As we plunged quickly through the blaze, the crack became a large hole as the wall fell into the Yard.

We reached the door and a few moments later reached the Yard. The whole side of the house was falling down in an avalanche of stone and dust. An army of rats fled from the upstairs rooms like a grey flying carpet. I gulped down the sweet air while uniformed arms took Penny from me. The world turned into a swirl of noise and movement and the next thing I knew I was in the back of an ambulance watching the buildings pass by through the smoked glass. Then I was being wheeled down yet another hospital corridor, then a cubicle, the prick of a needle and later the soft face of a nurse and the smell of clean sheets.

As I swam back to consciousness, voices told me what was happening. Penny was going to be all right: she had lost a lot of blood and had been in shock, but her condition had stabilised and she was off the critical list. She had also broken both collar bones but these weren't going to pose any problems. McLeod had suffered from some superficial burns to the face, but was otherwise unscathed and had returned to take control of the mopping-up operation. Rosso seemed to be getting a bit stronger, though still dependent on the respirator.

The next day Cissy came to see me and put her arms round me. She looked exhausted, and I guessed the waiting and not knowing had been very hard for her. She was chatting away now though, and with a nurse, bundled me into a wheelchair to take me to see Penny.

There she was, lying in bed, connected to a half empty bag of blood. Her cleaned-up hair was spread over the white pillow and her face had a waxy hue, like a pre-Raphaelite painting. She turned to me with a puzzled expression on her face, her cheeks wet with tears. She slid her hand along the bed sheets towards me. I took it in my mine, stood up, and kissed her lips. She smiled as I wiped the tears off her cheeks. Cissy too, was weeping and smiling, all at the same time.

Chapter 17

That night, at eleven twenty five, Rosso died. His lungs just couldn't recover from the damage they'd suffered.

McLeod came in and woke me up and broke the news as I lay in my hospital bed. Something just switched off in my head, it all went black. I'd known him just a year, but it seemed like forever.

"I'm sorry," I heard McLeod say. He sat in silence beside me, I could sense he was praying. Eventually he said, "There's a lot more to tell you, but it'll wait. I'll see you tomorrow."

He took my hand in both of his for a few seconds, then left, leaving me to stare up at the ceiling, feeling the scalding tears run down my cheeks and onto the pillow.

In the morning they took me to Penny's bed again, Cissy was there with her, distraught. They pulled the curtains round us. There was nothing to say, so we sat there, each one of us wrapped in grief. Eventually, McLeod appeared. He looked tired. After a few words, he offered to lead us in a prayer for Rosso. Cissy's wet eyes shot him a look.

"You'll forgive me, Mr McLeod, if I don't pray with you. Ollie was the only man I ever really loved. For so many years I lived without him, but every day of those years I missed him. Then your God saw fit to bring him back to me and reawaken those feelings, only to snatch him away so soon. Have you any idea how that hurts? What sort of God could do this to me? Sorry, no, your God and I have fallen out for the time being."

"Aye, He's a funny way of showing His love sometimes, I know. But all this has been the Devil's work and thanks to you, his grip on this city has weakened.

"Forgive me, I shouldn't thrust my old fangled beliefs on you. I knew Rosso quite well, did he tell you? He was my firearms instructor in the force. He was one of those men you have immediate and lasting respect for: one of those special souls you don't meet very often."

"Amen," said Cissy, and she threw a forgiving smile at him.

I shook my head in wonder; here was yet another facet of a special man's life he'd not revealed. That would explain why the police hadn't taken him in after Cassie died.

"Anyway," McLeod continued, "the job's done. Oculus has been destroyed, along with most of Starlings' Yard, I'm afraid. Mind you, it's a blessing; it's time those rat-infested slums were pulled down and now they're going to have to. The other residents are being rehoused, none of them seem too upset about it."

"The blast was enough to do them permanent damage and knowing Rosso, he'd got it all planned to do just that. I gather that he'd been round them all to tell them to get out at the time of the explosion, which explains why it was deserted when we got there."

"So, no other casualties?" I asked.

"Miraculously, no. Well, nothing serious. The explosion blew quite a big hole in South Bridge, so that's had to be closed down and a few cars collided into one another when it did, but nobody else got hurt, thank God."

He turned to Penny. "How are you feeling today?"

"Oh, top-notch. What do you think? I feel horrible; like I'm in a nightmare," she replied.

"I still don't know how I got to be lying in this bed with a couple of holes in my neck, wired up to a bottle of blood, or what happened to Oculus, or why Rosso died or - anything." Her voice was getting almost hysterical. "It's surreal. I hate it!"

So McLeod and I told Penny and Cissy what had happened, quickly and quietly in case we were overheard.

How Rosso and I had been into the chamber and laid the explosives, how Penny had gone missing, the attacks on Rosso and I and what had gone on in the chamber just before it exploded. They listened incredulously, Cissy with her hand to her mouth in mounting disbelief. Penny just shut her eyes, shaking her head. When we'd sketched out the events of the past few days, McLeod asked her what had happened to her.

"I don't know. I just remember coming back from work, getting out of the car, a hand around my mouth and another one twisting my arm behind my back. Two men bundled me into a car: a white one, I think I had the impression of something expensive."

"I was trying to scream for help, but they hit me and put tape round my mouth. Then they rolled up my sleeve and injected me with something. I don't remember much more, only a few flashes where I became aware of being in a cage, like a prison cell, lying on a mattress, then they'd inject me again. Then I woke up here, aching all over and feeling crap."

"You're lucky to be alive," McLeod said, "and it's thanks to Mark here. But I'd better be getting along, I've a bit of a showdown with the Secretary of State first thing tomorrow."

"The news is breaking all over the place and he's not happy at all. There's uproar everywhere out there. It's headline news all over the world. There's a pack of press outside right now, so you're all staying in here for a few more days, even you, Mrs Bowman. I've arranged a room in the private ward for you."

"There's a police guard on each of you and I've assigned a WPC to fetch and carry anything you might need. Sorry, but it's for your own good and I'd also prefer it if the press didn't get anything from you until we've worked out the right angle and got official approval."

Cissy gave a little moan of frustration, but Penny propped herself up on one elbow with an effort.

"If it's any help, Mr McLeod, I have a large dossier that I keep in the safe at work. It's got all the information I've managed to dig up on nearly a hundred young people who had suspicious deaths in the last five years. No doubt you have a similar record, but if it's any help…"

"Help? That's a gift from heaven, Miss Bowman! I keep my own secret files but the official evidence has been altered by my bosses who were part of Oculus. I've not had the opportunity to investigate further because they were watching me, so I'm afraid my gleanings have been rather insubstantial. If I can tie the two together, I'm sure the Secretary will see why it needed to happen."

"If he needs further persuasion," I said, "I've a camera in the flat with pictures of the chamber in it. If you want to get the film developed, it could be useful."

"It certainly will be. I also took the videotape out of the machine in the surveillance room after you had gone down, so luckily we've got proof of what went on there."

A nasty thought struck me.

"If someone's going to my flat for the camera, could they make sure my paintings are all right? They're rather precious to me."

"They're rather precious to everyone," he smiled. "Don't worry, we've been in and rescued them. They were fine, even though you've no windows any more. They've been taken round to Mr Burn's fine new gallery for safekeeping. The rest of your stuff is in a warehouse with the other residents' chattels until we get them rehoused."

"You're very efficient."

"I am."

He left us to it.

We mourned the loss of Rosso and tried to speculate what our legal fate might be. Strangely, we didn't talk about the destruction of Oculus, or even think about it much. It was just too raw, too big, to contemplate. Two days later, we were allowed home under police escort.

We were bundled out into a waiting car, through a crowd of reporters still at the gate.

Questions were being shouted at us but we had been told to say nothing. It was hard to say what the mood of the crowd was. Were we heroes or mass murderers?

I shut my eyes to the world as we sped to Penny's flat. A uniformed police officer was already standing outside, together with a pack of reporters. Flashlights went off as we hurried from the car to the door, I turned to look at the reporters, and bulbs went off everywhere. I felt like an exhausted hunted animal.

For our own protection, we were virtually under house arrest and the three of us started to get on each other's nerves: petty little squabbles about trivial things, even though we all knew what emotional struggles we were going through. We saw little of McLeod and he was sparing in the news he brought us.

Three days later though, he called round and asked me to come with him. We drove in the back of a white leather upholstered Bentley. He seemed rather distracted, almost worried.

"Where are we going?" I asked him, after we'd exchanged some remarks about the weather.

"To the top. We're off to the Scottish Office to see Oor Wullie himself. I've been talking to him over the past few days and he wants to talk to you himself. I warn you, he's not in a very good mood about all this. I've not had too easy a time with him myself. William Ross is not the gentlest of men, but he's astute and pragmatic. Stand up for yourself, and I think he'll listen."

The car drew up outside the Scottish Office; an imposing building in the lee of Carleton Hill. We got out and entered the sober entrance hall. McLeod announced our arrival at the reception desk and I saw the willowy receptionist's eyes glance at me with interest.

She rang someone and a few minutes later a well-dressed young man came down. We followed him up an imposing flight of steps to a door with the Scottish coat of arms above it.

I was feeling very sick and my palms were sweating. We were told to wait in the outer office, while he knocked on the door of the inner office, then escorted us in.

The Secretary of State for Scotland sat behind a large desk. He stood up as we entered and shook our hands. We sat on formal chairs in front of him. There were many files on the desk and I recognised one of them as Penny's dossier.

He must have been a bit over sixty, still with light sandy hair, a cleft chin and frightening grey gaze. His chin rested on his clasped hands as he looked at me in silence. This is just a ploy to intimidate me, I told myself. Eventually he spoke.

"You present me with a difficult dilemma, Mr Kemp. I don't know whether I should have you clapped in jail for life or award you the OBE. Ten years ago you would have been hung for what you have done.

"You have been kept apart and out of the glare of the press since the event and you are probably not aware of the major embarrassment this has caused the country. It has been seen as an act of terrorism perpetrated against a number of Edinburgh notables and an act of vandalism towards some of the historic fabric of the city. There is no question as to your guilt and that of the late Mr Ross, is there?"

"No, we planned and executed it ourselves," I answered, "because –"

He waved me to silence.

"I am aware of the reasons. Detective Chief Inspector McLeod has exhausted himself and me I might add, in explaining the circumstances that led you to do what you did. Mr McLeod has also put his distinguished career on the line by admitting that he was aware of your plans, and nevertheless allowed you to go ahead. That breaks every rule in the book, too."

He looked at us both again, and allowed himself a wry smile.

"You're all completely mad, that goes without saying. But then, so was William Wallace.

"I've read the evidence you have presented and I congratulate Miss Bowman and her mother on doing a very thorough job. McLeod here has convinced me that the facts you have gathered agree with his own records and suspicions. I have also seen the way evidence was rigged by his superiors, quite clumsily too, at times. I know you, McLeod, and you're a good Presbyterian, as I am and I know you to be one of the best and most incorruptible men we have."

"I therefore accept that Oculus was an evil organisation, responsible for a huge number of shocking crimes. I also accept that there were few opportunities of bringing these people to justice by the customary channels and that you had little option but to act as you did and that Colin McLeod had little option but to let you."

"We have talked long and hard over the past few days and we would like to put a proposal to you. Will you explain, Colin? But let's have a coffee, shall we?"

As we waited for the coffee, the Secretary's stern look evaporated as he praised my paintings, which he'd taken the trouble to view at the gallery. I felt matters were going the right way. As we sipped our coffee, McLeod explained their proposal.

"When all this literally blew up, the press had the knee jerk reaction of condemning it as an act of terrorism perpetrated by madmen with a grudge against a harmless men's club."

"Now they're beginning to swing and speaking cynically, the true story will make much spicier reading. We are proposing to let them know the truth of the matter, but with one exception, we want to write you and I out of the story. I need to get on with my job and I'm sure you just want to get on with yours. So I propose that Mr Ross, sorry sir, I'll call him Rosso to save confusion, is cast as the one who perpetrated the deed."

I opened my mouth to protest: Rosso's character was about to be slurred for expedience's sake. The Secretary gave a small snort and got up to stand by the long window, looking out. McLeod cut in before I could speak.

"I know, I know, and your loyalty does you credit. Just think about it, though. There will have to be a large and very public inquest and justice must be seen to be done and the fact remains that you are an accessory to mass murder."

"We have thought about blaming the gas cylinders, but forensics just couldn't buy that. There would be no question that you would face trial and be found guilty and whatever extenuating circumstances we could marshal it wouldn't stop you getting a very long sentence."

"On the other hand, if we put you in the role of the innocent who was just trying to save his girlfriend, then the guilt falls squarely on Rosso's shoulders and without being callous, what can they do about it?"

They were right of course, but it seemed wrong, somehow.

"I'm sorry, I can't do this to someone who I regarded as a friend, a straightforward, honest, caring friend. He paid the price in full, the least I can do is to take my share with him. I can't do with your politics and intrigues! I loved Cassie and

232

I'm prepared to shoulder my part of the blame and suffer the consequences for her sake. Whatever the punishment, I'll take it!"

The Secretary turned his gaze from the window to look at me, wearily.

"Then you are a fool. Are you being deliberately perverse? We are trying to save your skin Mr Kemp, save you from a life sentence. We have been working night and day for you, because we both happen to believe you are worth it."

"Fine, if you want to go down that's up to you, but you'd drag McLeod here down with you and your career would end there and then. Not only that, you'd be doing Mr Ross a great disservice."

"Oh? Why?"

"For God's sake! It's plain enough! You tell him Colin, I'm losing patience."

McLeod's Highland voice was soothing. It was just as well: though this man did wield power, I was ready for a fight, perhaps because he had power.

"Perhaps you're not aware of what's going on out there. We've kept you in the dark, I know. We've held a press conference and presented the press with a dossier of facts – true facts – about what was going on."

"I think it's fair to say that this was one of the most significant press releases ever in Scotland. The Secretary himself was kind enough to attend. Now they've got the facts, they are going to wipe the floor with Oculus. And although he'll be found technically guilty, which let's face it, he was, whether or not you're implicated, he's going to be a hero. Rosso will become an iconic figure; the fighter that died in his fight against evil. You'd deny him that?"

I suddenly felt rather foolish. I remembered his words: "*I'll take the blame, I'm prepared to swing for Cassie if I have to.*"

233

"I hadn't thought of that," I said, "I'm sorry."

The Secretary's face softened.

"If it's further consolation, Oliver Ross will be recommended for a posthumous George Cross, when public opinion has come round. In some ways, Detective Chief Superintendent McLeod and I knew him better than you. There are things I don't believe you know about him."

"Like what?"

"His funeral is next week. Wait and hear."

I looked at the two men and became aware that power did not necessarily mean corruption. Two Churchmen, two very good brains, two very dedicated men.

"Then I completely accept your proposal," I said. "And I'm sorry if I was difficult."

The Secretary chuckled, "McLeod warned me you would be."

McLeod blushed a little at this, but changed the subject quickly.

"You'll also be happy to hear that we're having a field day with the yobs and gangsters that worked for Oculus. We've got evidence by the bucket load; I've just never been able to use it. We're rounding them up like sheep right now and they're all like frightened bairns, shopping each other like there's no tomorrow. I think the police guard on you can be lifted."

"That's a relief."

"There's something else; Rosso was a bit of a loner and the three of you were as close to him as anyone. The funeral has been arranged for Wednesday week at the Warriston Crematorium, that's the nineteenth of February, at three o'clock. Here's a rough order of service, but we'd like it if you could choose the hymns and music – that sort of thing, take it over: put the frills on, so to speak."

"It would be an honour," I said.

I glanced at the paper he had handed me. There were to be eulogies from some high ranking people in the forces and the police. I looked at him, puzzled.

"Just do it," he smiled.

That was the end of the meeting, almost. They briefed me on my storyline and then I was dismissed, McLeod staying behind to talk to the Secretary. As I went, Mr Ross called my name. I stopped and turned.

"You are a remarkable man, Mr Kemp. You have done this country a great service. I shall be watching your progress with interest. Thank you."

He turned away, and I left. The Bentley took me back to Penny's flat and I told them about the meeting.

That night Penny and I made quick, quiet love in her leather patchwork bed, but afterwards, as we lay side by side, we could hear Cissy's stifled sobs coming from the next room. I lay there, open eyed, thinking of Rosso, and Cassie and of so much else as well.

Chapter 18

The funeral arrangements gave the three of us something practical to distract us in the dangling days when there was so little to say to each other.

McLeod had notified the appropriate people, so all we had to do was organise the flowers and discuss details with the undertakers and wait.

The television still ran reports of the explosion and its aftermath. McLeod's face became a familiar one, explaining to reporters the history of Oculus. With stories of evil secret societies, human sacrifices and the communes, the press were having a field day.

I felt curiously detached, as though I were the quiet stillness at the centre of a storm. A private obsession was now a salacious public scandal and I just wanted it to go away.

Penny went back to work, Cissy returned to her flat and I busied myself with a portrait of Rosso to hang over his coffin. Even if there were only a handful of us at his funeral, it was going to be a proper send-off for him.

I painted from memory, quickly and lovingly. He was standing tall and determined, but dressed in his old Afghan coat. Behind him, a stormy sky represented his life and beneath it, the silhouette of the Edinburgh skyline. I was pleased with it; it was my present to him.

One morning, I went round to George Street to see Patrick Burn. Something had been niggling away at me; a chance remark of his, that was all, but it had been worrying me.

He was there and so were my paintings. While he disentangled himself from a telephone conversation, I looked to see which of mine were now on display, and my eyes widened as

I saw the prices he was now charging for them. It was also gratifying to see red dots on some of them.

He came over, all smiles and greeted me warmly. He filled me in on what had been happening with my pictures and who had bought them. Then he winked at me and, steering me by the elbow, took me over to the picture of Murdo, which had another red dot stuck on the frame.

"Guess who's just bought this one!" he said.

I just shook my head; he could hardly contain himself,

"Just Willie Ross, the Secretary of State, that's who! He came in here and seemed particularly interested in your work. Said it was a reminder to everybody in power that there are souls who suffer out there.

"A bit of patronage from the top won't do you or me any harm at all, eh? But I'm going on. It's good to see you at large again. You've been through hell, and all I can do is talk of sales. Come for some lunch with me, and tell me how things are with you; Megan can look after the shop."

He took me to a discreetly understated bistro nearby. While we ate, I told him some of the events of the past weeks; events I was sure he'd already know from the news.

I didn't want to tell him everything, not yet, but was relieved to find I could tell him how I was feeling and of the events in the chamber. He listened, shaking his head in disbelief. It was good to find someone who wasn't directly involved.

We clinked glasses and shook hands. Then he said,

"What happens now?"

"What? To me?"

"Yes. Now Starlings' Yard is gone, what are you going to do next?"

I looked at him. The thought hadn't occurred to me.

"I've no idea."

"Ah. You're staying in Penny's flat just now?"

"Yes, and I've set up my easel there, though it's not ideal. I'm just painting a picture of Rosso for the funeral, but after that…"

It was true: my golden goose was no more. I'd probably squeezed it dry, anyway. I was tired and couldn't think about the future, not yet.

"You're staying in Edinburgh, though?" Patrick asked.

"Yes, for the time being, anyway. I don't know; I may go away for a bit after the funeral. I need to escape the town for a while. "

"Of course, but will you come and see me again after the funeral? I've a suggestion to put to you."

I promised him I would, and then we walked back to the gallery. I was saying goodbye to him, but he stopped me.

"I think you're forgetting something! I've sold a fair few of your paintings, remember? I owe you a bit of cash for them."

He wrote me out a cheque. It came to over five thousand pounds. Perhaps I should be thinking about the future.

I walked back to Penny's flat, lit the fire and drew the curtains. The February dusk was settling over the city, smearing a crimson slash across the dark sky. Down below, the Water of Leith churned on. I put something in the oven for when she returned, then went back to the easel and picked up the paintbrush. On a whim, I painted Cassie's face into one of the clouds.

I'd been thinking about her recently, and it was right that she should be somewhere there in the picture with her father. While I painted, I could hear her voice in my head, and I smiled to myself as I thought about her.

I heard the faintest of thumps against the window and ignored it, but then it came again. Puzzled, I walked over and peered through the curtains, then let out a shriek.

There, hovering in the night through the window, was Cassie. My beautiful Cassie! She was such a ghostly white, with her hair floating around her face, while her wide dark eyes and the red slash of her mouth seemed to beckon me to her.

I put my hand to the window pane and she placed her hand on her breast. I watched hypnotized as she floated silently away like some ghastly parody of Peter Pan, her arms outstretched to me, drifting back into the night and then faded from sight.

I was sweating and convinced myself that it was yet another trick of my imagination. I'd been thinking about her and truth to tell, was feeling close to cracking point these days. I threw the paintbrush down and went to the 'fridge for a beer.

I was still sitting hunched on the sofa with the bottle when Penny returned. After telling me off for dropping the paintbrush and getting paint on the carpet, she went off to get a cloth to mop it up.

I tried to get my thoughts in order and act as if nothing happened. I don't know why, but I just didn't feel I could tell her about what I'd just seen. So, when she asked me what the matter was, I just told her, quite truthfully, that painting Rosso's picture was stirring up too many emotions in me; emotions that were flogged to death and getting me down.

She went over to the painting and saw that I'd just painted Cassie's face in.

"What's this?"

"It's Cassie."

"I can see it's Cassie. What's she doing in there?"

"She was his daughter, his only relative. It just seemed right."

"Hmm. It's your painting; you can put in whoever you like, I suppose."

That's how it was. I didn't even mention the cheque. I knew Penny must be feeling as exhausted as I was, but we seemed to be distant again. It would pass.

Wednesday arrived, the day of Rosso's funeral.

The morning was sunny but windy; one of those matter-of-fact days and interminable; a silent, dangling time.

Cissy arrived and we had some lunch, then carried on waiting until the undertaker's car arrived to escort us behind the hearse to the crematorium.

I could see the coffin in front, laden with wreaths. We arrived at the Lorimer chapel, and I was amazed to see a huge crowd waiting outside. There must have been two hundred people there. Rosso's coffin was carried to the front of the chapel and my picture was hung above it.

We were escorted to the front pew where I kept my eyes on the coffin, images of Rosso floating in front of me. I could hear the rest of the murmuring mourners filling the seats behind us.

A hand tapped my shoulder and I turned round to see McLeod in the pew behind. I shook his hand and exchanged a few words, while I took in some of the others in the congregation. Many were in naval or police uniform, but there, near the back, were the others from Starlings' Yard. Sadie caught my eye and gave a wistful smile and a wave.

A row of men with raincoats and notebooks stood at the back.

Knowing Rosso's feelings, Cissy had insisted on keeping the religion to a minimum. Instead, she had chosen some music that he had liked – Barber's *Adagio*, and Vaughan William's *Sea Symphony*. In between Cissy and I gave some readings that seemed appropriate.

Then a naval captain got up to give his eulogy and I listened with awe. Rosso had joined the Navy as a rating in 1939 and had a meteoric rise through the ranks. He'd seen some of the worst of the fighting in the Baltic, had become a commander and collected a lot of medals on the way.

He received special training with the newly-formed Special Boat Section and became trained in firearms, explosives and hand to hand combat. He had been in Alexandria and Crete. His story was pure James Bond, except the shambling figure I first remembered was as far away from Bond as you could imagine.

Then, after another hymn, McLeod rose and carried on the story.

He left the Navy in 1960, and joined the police. As the need for special armed squads became apparent, he became a firearms and combat instructor for them. He'd taught McLeod and I remembered how McLeod had so efficiently dispatched Alan Trapp.

Later, he'd been given the job he relished. He was one of the first undercover agents: highly trained police officers who were 'cut loose' from the service, given fresh identities and sent to live in and infiltrate the underworld. That was when he'd moved into Starlings' Yard. He had been sending back information on the petty gangsters in the city ever since.

This had been my friend, but I had no idea about any of this. Typical bloody Rosso: he always played his cards close to his chest, but now the whole world was going to know the truth about him. The unassuming soldier who knew he had to die, but did so willingly for his daughter and for the rest of us.

Cissy got up then and in a clear voice said,

"He was my Rosso and the only man I have ever loved. He was also Cassie's father and loved her dearly. I can imagine his feelings when he knew that that evil organisation had murdered her.

"So began his final battle and his greatest victory. Oliver Ross was a hero. One of those rare men who leaves the world a better place than he found it. We had so little time together

241

and now he has been taken away from me. But this I have painfully learnt: time does not matter; whether it's one hour or fifty years, love abides."

The moment came for the committal.

I'd planned that his portrait should go to the flames with him, but Cissy had persuaded me otherwise. I'd decided I'd give it to her as some feeble consolation.

Angus, as I'd arranged, stepped forward with his concertina and played *The Dark Island* as the coffin slid through the doors and into the flames. As it did, Cassie appeared again, walking behind the coffin and through the doors with him. I involuntarily let out a cry, and thank God, it was taken as just a louder outburst of grief among the stifled sobs of the others, although Penny turned and looked at me with a frown.

After the valediction and blessing, we started to file out.

Cissy, Penny and I were to be at the door to shake the hand of all the guests, but, as we were halfway to the door, Angus started playing his concertina again. As he struck up *Will Ye Go, Lassie, Go?* everyone stopped. I couldn't help it; I started singing, and then everyone in the chapel started singing at the top of their voices, just as we had done for Cassie, that day in Starlings' Yard. Every single one of the newsmen joined in too.

We got through the reception; I even enjoyed it. It was the first chance I'd had to speak to my former neighbours since Rosso and I had destroyed their homes. They were in a small group, overawed by the uniformed guests.

I went over to thank Angus for his music. Sadie landed a wet kiss on my cheek and snuggled her breasts against me. My former neighbours tumbled over themselves to tell me what had happened – of the emergency shelter for a week where they had lived and talked and sung. And then, when they had been rehoused in a modern block of flats off Dalry Road, they had stuck together, helping and supporting one another (they still called their little community 'The Yard'). Indeed, they had become celebrities amongst their neighbours since Starlings' Yard had become such a news story.

Released from the evil atmosphere of the place, they looked different; happier, and I was happy for them. The couple who had wheeled the empty pram around were standing quietly in the corner behind them, holding hands, but then the young man came forward.

"Mr Kemp, a word, please?" he said. They, too, looked different. The Victorian clothes had gone, and they looked as though they belonged in this century, almost.

"Elise and I would just like to say a word of thanks." He paused, fidgeting nervously, "Um, thank you. That's right, thank you, yes."

"What for?" I asked.

He took his wife's arm, and drew her towards me. She lifted her eyes to mine. Her voice, when she spoke, was in the lilt of the West Highlands.

"You've taken the sorrow away from us, Mr Kemp. We're grateful."

She turned to go back to the corner, but I wanted to talk to her. I touched her arm and again she looked at me with a disconcerting stare.

"Things will be different now," she said, "for all of us. You have some strange and lonely paths to tread still and I wish you good luck. But you'll find happiness of a sort, as I have now."

She smiled the faintest of smiles and patted her stomach, then moved away, leaving me staring after her.

I went up to McLeod – I even called him Colin – and thanked him. He looked thoughtful, and drew me aside.

"I didn't tell you before," he said, "but Rosso and I were very close, I've known him and looked after him for years. He reported to me directly. I was as upset as you were by his death. He was a wonderful one-off." He raised his glass, I touched it with mine. "On a lighter note, Willie Ross is very grateful to us for what's happened. He's impressed with you, you know."

"So I gather; he's just bought one of my paintings."

"Ah, but what you don't know is that he's given it to me as a thank you."

"I now have an original one of your paintings on the wall of my office that I could never have afforded. Although I am now the new Chief Constable, so perhaps I'll be able to get another in the future. So what are you going to do now?"

"I don't know. I just want to get away and think for a while."

"With Penny?"

"No. On my own. I came here not knowing and I'll go away, not knowing. How's that for progress?"

"Immense, I'd say. There's not knowing and then there's another sort of not knowing."

"Look, if you want to get away for a while, I've a place on Colonsay: it's my old family home. Why don't you stay there for a while? Lord knows, I might even join you, we both need a break. Get all this out of your system. It's not fancy, but it has something about it, a certain magic, you'll find. It's yours if you want it."

"Thank you. I'm inclined to take you up on that. My head's a complete jumble, a bit of Hebridean air might just get it straight."

The day drew to a close.

Penny and I went back to her flat with Cissy, drank too much and did all the talking we should have done the week before.

Chapter 19

It was time to escape.

The reporters were driving me crazy; I'd no home of my own, no studio, no car, no plans, nothing. Less than I'd arrived with, in fact. I'd a lot of money, but that wasn't the point. I needed some direction, something to aim for, but since the explosion and Rosso's death, I was an empty figure in an empty landscape.

Then there was Penny. She was reacting to all the events of the past few weeks with her typical brusqueness, keeping busy to avoid having to think about the nightmare we'd been through and making me feel ashamed of my brooding inertia.

She threw herself into her work, and tried to jolly me out of myself. She would try to tease me into having sex and make light of it when I couldn't respond. Eventually she stopped trying. She'd take me out for a drink or a meal, chat to me about her work, or try to get me to make some plans. I tried to reciprocate, but I was poor company. Our conversations dwindled into single words.

One Sunday, she coaxed me out for a walk. It was a fine clear February day. We climbed Arthur's Seat with a good deal of puffing on my part; the healing wound on my leg hurting with the unaccustomed effort.

Penny seemed preoccupied and kept up a determined pace as we climbed to the summit, passing more leisurely strollers. We looked at the city below in a moment of silence and stillness. The seethe and scramble of the city was reduced to a silent tableau; the purple and white buses gliding silently through the streets like fishes in a still pond.

"Puts it into perspective, doesn't it?" I ventured. I looked for Starlings' Yard, or what was left of it, but it was hidden somewhere in the jumble of tenements that lined the Royal Mile.

Penny just nodded, looking at the view below. A tear rolled down her cheek.

"Whatever happened, it's as though you've throw a stone into a pool," I said. "There's a little splash, the stone sinks, and then – nothing. It's over. I think it's time to put Starlings' Yard behind us."

"Yes," she said, "it's over, Mark." Her words hung in the space between us. "Let's go back."

We climbed back down and got into the car parked by Duddingston Loch.

"OK," I said, "what's the matter? You're away in your own world. It's scaring me."

"You were right," she said, "Starlings' Yard is finished and I think it's time we ended our relationship, too"

I felt my mouth go dry and my stomach contract.

"Look, I know I've been moping about recently, and I'm sorry, but –"

"It's not that," she said, "I know that and that's OK, because that will get better. I'm as bad as you; I just plough on and keep busy and witter on and that must annoy you as much as you moping about annoys me. But that's not it."

"Then what is?"

"Don't you know? Really not know?"

"I'm a man. We're thick like that. So tell me, what's the big problem?"

She looked hard at me and let out a sigh, "You're in love with somebody else."

Had she found out about my night with Sadie?

"That's idiotic," I said, "I don't know anyone else. Who am I supposed to be in love with?"

"You are in love with Cassie."

"Cassie's dead, in case you'd forgotten."

"That doesn't matter to you! In fact it makes you love her more. Mark, you're in love with a ghost!"

"That's just stupid..."

"Is it? Is it? You keep seeing her – no, don't deny it. I can tell when you have, like when you dropped the paintbrush, you'd seen her then, hadn't you? And you saw her in the crematorium, didn't you?"

"I don't choose to see her!"

"Oh, so there really is a ghost, is there? Grow up, will you? You are obsessed with her, and your imagination makes her real to you. There's no room for me in your fantasies!

"I'm a real person, Mark. I pass wind in bed, I have to cut my toenails, I get grumpy when I have a period. I'm real. But that can never be good enough for you, can it? You've found your well-beloved; your ideal woman who is up there with the angels.

"Never mind that she was a real woman and you'd probably be fed up to the back teeth with her now if she was still alive. You're in love with your fantasy and I can't compete with that!"

I couldn't say anything because of course, she was right. My face flushed and sweated, as if I'd been caught with a dirty magazine.

"God knows, I loved you, and you saved my life," she went on, "but I've outlived my purpose, haven't I? You talk of going to Colonsay to sort yourself out. What about me? You wonder where you're going. What about me? I don't figure in your plans, do I? You just want to move on with your fantasy woman and I can't bear to be pushed aside like that. Try telling me it's not true."

I couldn't. She'd got that women's knack of seeing the truth. Why is it we men just can't? Or do we see a different truth? I still don't know, but then, stripped down to inescapable facts, I had nothing to say.

"Say something."

"I can't."

"Look, we're not doing each other any good. We should be supporting each other, but we're not. This mess should have welded us closer together, but it hasn't. Look at me! Here's a woman that loved you, and still wants to love you, but I'm just somewhere in the background of your world, and that's not going to change. I kept thinking it would, but it won't."

I felt a tide of sadness and loneliness wash over me as she went on saying one truth after another.

"You painted her, but it's never occurred to you to paint me; I just don't have that 'thing' you see in other people. It's not going to work, is it? Say something, please."

Then it all made some sort of sense.

"You're right, love. I've been unable to see into the future because I've not seen it as something we do together. OK, my fault, but I just can't see us walking hand in hand into the sunset and I've been too scared to face it."

"I kept telling myself I loved you because it seemed like the one constant thing in a world which was all turned upside down. Now the storm's passed, I don't know any more. That's what I've been moping about, I suppose."

"Thank you, at least you're being honest."

"I have to move on, but I don't know where to and I can't see us sharing any common goals. I loved Cassie, it's not something you can explain, not when you really love somebody so much that you want them to be half your life.

"At least I know what real love is; I know I loved, no, you're right, still love, a real woman who cut her toenails and passed wind, but she's dead and I wish she wasn't. I'll probably never find that again. I like you very much and you like me, but I don't think you know what real passionate love is. It's willingly flinging yourself off the safe ledge you live on and falling into the whirlpool below. I don't think you could ever do that."

She was just looking at me, then the tears came. I felt horrid, but, yes, I'd spoken my truth and it felt like someone had unlocked some heavy iron shackles. But Penny was sitting there, hurting. I leaned over awkwardly and put my arms around her. She put hers around me. Which wasn't easy in the front seats of a car with thick anoraks on.

"Maybe what we have is a sort of love," I went on. "Maybe we should settle for that because probably neither of us will find real passion again, it's just that I did find it once and that makes it hard to be with me. Because once you've tasted it, you have to keep hopelessly searching for it."

We had our arms round each other, but it felt as though we were doing it because that's what we should be doing. She pushed us apart.

"Just drive."

I started the car and we headed back into town.

"You know," she said, as we drove along Princes Street.

"Maybe I'd have settled for that, once. But it can't be like that, can it? I can't live with you, knowing you're always going to be looking for something better. I can't throw myself into the whirlpool; I'm just not that sort, am I? I'll probably never know what passion is. You're the nearest thing I've found to it, though, so I call it love. I've no option, though, have I? I have to let you go."

As she spoke, I knew she was right, but I also saw a waste-land ahead of me. Was this something I was going to hear over and over again as I chased a non-existent ideal? Was Cassie only ideal because I'd printed my idea of perfection onto her? Had she not died, would I have grown tired of her when she didn't fit my blueprint?

I wanted to rush back and bang on the doors of Penny's heart and shout "Let me in!", but it was too late, the door was locked. I had to turn my back and set off on a lonely road again. Elise's words came back to me and I felt a shudder pass through me.

We stopped at a café in Queensferry Street for lunch.

Penny, I could see, was trying hard to be her usual practical self, so we talked of practical things. She would go and stay a few days with Cissy, to give me time to find somewhere else. We'd meet in the evenings for a drink, if I wanted, as she was determined we'd stay friends. She was talking, but I only half heard what she was saying; my head was too full of the prospect of that lonely road.

I drove her round to Cissy's that afternoon. The house had a melancholy air and Cissy herself was looking strained. I could imagine what she was going through. Rosso's portrait hung over the fire in the living room and I noticed two half burnt candles on the mantelpiece below it. The atmosphere wasn't improved by our news, although Cissy seemed to take it in her stride.

"A pity, a real pity," she said. "I'd rather hoped some phoenix would rise from this sorry pile of ashes, some good from all that bad, but perhaps it just has to all come to a close. I'm so sorry, my dears, but I'm sure you both know what's best. Penny, why don't you take your bags upstairs, I'd like a few minutes with Mark."

Penny left us with a quizzical look and I stood, fearing a reproach, mustering a defence, but Cissy just took my hand between hers and smiled.

"I shall play the sympathetic mother, Mark, but I think it is right that you move on. Move on in the spiritual sense, I mean; I'd be distraught if you moved away from Edinburgh. I've come to think of you as a close friend. But you're a restless soul, aren't you? Just like me."

"I've been thinking, perhaps it's time I had another spell in South America. What about you? What are you going to do?"

"I've no bloody idea. I might go to Colonsay for a few weeks to sort myself out."

"Ah, dear Colin McLeod's place! He mentioned it to me, too. I thought about going there to do just the same thing. Well, whatever happens, don't lose touch. You've no idea how much I shall miss you."

I just scooped her up in my arms and hugged her. We were still in each other's arms when Penny came into the room. She raised her eyebrows and snorted.

"Pardon me for interrupting."

Cissy didn't let go of me, nor did I want her to, but she extended an arm to Penny.

"Don't be silly, dear. Come here and give us a hug too. Look at us, we're little lost souls, all of us, we've got nothing but each other to cling to. Come on!"

Penny looked like a little schoolgirl as she ran over to us and joined us. We held on to each other and the sadness of the day gave way to acceptance, forgiveness, then a paradoxical happiness.

Cissy, bless her, whose ability to turn things around like that, produced some very fine whisky and negatives turned to positives and Penny and I became the firm friends we are today.

I don't even remember getting home that night, but I must have done somehow, for I woke up in her bed in her flat, alone.

I washed and dressed, feeling surprisingly clear headed, then took a taxi to Patrick's gallery, and told him of my predicament. He seemed actually pleased at the news that I was sans girlfriend, sans place to live, sans inspiration, sans car, and sans everything. All right for some, I thought.

"I told you though didn't I, that I had a proposition to put to you?" he said.

He called another taxi round and as we drove down Leith Walk, he kept saying not to worry and wait and see. The taxi took us to Leith, which then was a grim place, with grey streets lined with tall buildings which shut out the light and run-down, derelict docklands.

I was beginning to see why Patrick might be taking me here; he must be anxious that I might have run out of subject matter. There was certainly plenty of character here. He directed the taxi to a quay on one of the docks, where we got out and he sniffed at the sea air.

"Come on, Patrick, what are you playing at?" I asked, "Why are we here?"

Patrick just smiled and walked me to a large warehouse. It was deserted, many of the windows were boarded up or broken, but he took out a bunch of keys and we entered the small hallway, where we took the lift to the third floor. A large window looked out over the Firth of Forth, I admired the view while he struggled with another key in an iron doorway that led into a massive empty space.

It must have been a hundred feet long and fifty feet wide. High up, semi-circular windows let in shafts of light that lit up the dusty wooden floor. Metal pillars supported an arched ceiling in an industrialist's answer to ecclesiastical perpendicular style. It was an impressive building and I felt an immediate bond with it. But what was Patrick up to?

"Nice space, isn't it?" he asked.

"It's fantastic, but what are we doing here?"

252

He gave me a look that must have been the nearest that Patrick could get to mischievous.

"Welcome to your new studio, if you want it. It's far too big, of course, but I thought we could have a flat built in one half of it for you to live in and the rest would make quite an airy studio, don't you think? I've an architect friend who's got quite a name for converting these places..."

I was speechless. There was a huge lump in my throat as I looked around. I put my arms around Patrick and hugged him. This hugging thing was getting to be a habit.

"It's fantastic!"

I walked around, while Patrick stood in the centre of the room, lit by a shaft of sunlight.

"Think about it. If you want some characters for models, there's plenty in Leith, believe me. It's obviously not the most genteel of districts, but I didn't think you'd want to live in some well-heeled suburb.

"You can rent this for thirty pounds a week, but if you can afford a bit more and you can, why don't you buy it? It's all run down now, but how long will it stay like that? Cheap rents on the coast near Edinburgh? The developers will be moving in very soon, believe me, and this place will be worth a fortune. But we can talk finances later. What do you say?"

"It's too much to take in."

"Fine. Look, I've got to get back. Why don't you get a feel for the place, see if you've any ideas for an apartment in here. Oh, and just so that you know, the ground floor I intend to make into another gallery, and turn the rest into flats. But this floor – well, I'll leave you to have a think, eh?"

"You haven't got a bit of paper in your case, and a pencil?" I asked.

"I thought you'd need them," he replied, "here's a sketchpad, some pencils, and a tape measure. Oh, and here are the keys. Spend as long as you like; I'll see you back at the gallery."

You had to hand it to him; he was always a jump or two ahead. With a clang of the iron door and the whirr of the lift fading into silence as it descended, he left me alone in the empty space.

I walked round it again, my imagination on fire, half thinking I was in a dream. I took the tape measure and noted the dimensions of the room, then set to work sketching out ideas.

I could enlarge the semi-circular windows, bringing them right down to flood the place with daylight. The far end would be the studio, and the flat – mezzanine floor, open plan, two bedrooms, no, hang it, three…I was sitting cross-legged on the floor, covering sheets of paper with plans, scribbling down dimensions, when I heard her: a girl's quiet voice, singing.

"Girls and boys come out to play

The moon does shine as bright as day…"

I looked up, and there was Cassie again. She was naked, and dancing as she sang. She was lit by a shaft of sunlight at the far end of the room, with her eyes fixed on mine, teasing. I stood up and started to walk towards her, but then she gave a little laugh and disappeared along with the shaft of light. I never saw her again, well, not like that.

I moved to the spot where she'd been dancing. A faint smell of patchouli lingered in the air, I felt overpowered by a sense of loss and of yearning. I hung my head; it was no use. I gathered up the notebook and tape measure, locked up, and took the bus back into town.

Patrick was in the gallery, talking to some prospective clients. He looked over at me as I came in, and smiled. When they had left, he came over.

"Well, have you been hatching a few ideas for the place? You don't have to stint, you know, we can arrange a cheap loan to cover building costs, and –"

"I'm not going to take it, Patrick." There was a silence.

"Why, for God's sake? It would be ideal! I don't understand how –"

"I can't put it into words. I'm so grateful for the opportunity and you're right, it would be ideal. Perhaps that's why... I don't know... I've just got this thing about taking the difficult path all the time. I'm an artist, remember, we don't do logical."

"Dear God, Mark. Life's hard enough without going out of your way to make it harder! Look, just have a think about it. You can go questing on as many rocky roads as you want, but you might as well have somewhere decent to work, at least."

"I know, I just have to go with my feelings. I'm sorry, Patrick. Don't worry; you'll still be my agent and my friend, wherever I end up."

He made a dismissive gesture, obviously disappointed.

"I'm glad to hear it." He turned away. It seemed the conversation was over.

Later, when the sun was fading and the street lights were coming on, I sat in the Melrose Bar in Queensbury Street, eating some tea, trying to make sense of it all.

I needed to find somewhere to live and quite quickly. Well, that was easily sorted – tomorrow.

But why had I turned down Patrick's offer? The answer just came to me there and then: because I am an artist and an artist has to be an outsider, the Steppenwolf who prowls around the edges of society but can't be a part of it.

That means not putting yourself in the clutches of dealers who could manipulate you and make you feel obliged to them. I had to stay apart. I'd tell Patrick that, and he'd understand.

I stepped outside into the street, heading towards Penny's flat. March had just slid into April and there was still a chill in the night air.

I felt a hand clutching to the sleeve of my overcoat, looked round, and saw Robert, still wearing that silly red bobble hat. He smiled up at me, then put his small hand in mine. There was a conscious part of me that knew that this was yet another hallucination, yet...

I felt happy and relieved to see him again. He seemed in a hurry and led me down a side street. We were in a part of town I didn't recognise, suffused with a cast of dark blue light which dimly illuminated dirt streets with no pavements.

Candlelight spilt into the streets from some of the houses, some of which were timber-framed, some built in stone. Some were mean cottages, some towering tenements. It was like wandering through a Doré engraving, but there was no strangeness here. It felt completely normal, wandering with my son pulling me onwards, or skipping ahead, chattering and beckoning.

We walked for hours, it seemed, along the maze of streets; Robert talking of unknown friends and I about the events of the past year. He seemed to know where he was going, as he guided me along roads where wooden carts stood parked for the long night, through yards where wooden stairs and galleries clung to the silent houses and light from the casement windows dimly lit the narrow wynds. Worn stone steps led off through archways to other closes and streets. The city seemed to sprawl into an infinity of shadows.

He led me eventually to a waterfront. Bollards marked the edge of the stone quayside, where I could make out the black shapes of wooden ships moored up, creaking comfortably as they rocked and rubbed in the breeze. The dockside, like the streets, was deserted. Out over the inky blackness of the water, I could hear the cries of gulls, like dead souls in the night.

Two figures appeared from behind a large stone-built warehouse, a bearded man, being led, as I was, by a young child. Rosso! It was him, although younger than when I had known him and the child with him was a young Cassie – I recognised her from the picture I had drawn at Cissy's house.

We met as old friends, the two children skipping around us, singing, until Rosso produced a large silver key, and handed it to me with a nod and a smile. Then all three of them faded as the whole scene darkened and disappeared and strong gusts of wind were buffeting me.

I came to in the dismal public bar of 'The Three Sisters'. The bartender was shaking me, asking, "You all right, pal?" over and over.

I looked up at his frightened face, then around the bar.

Luckily it was deserted except the two of us. In front of me was a half-finished pint of beer and beside it, an untouched glass of orange juice. I rubbed my face with my hands and saw I had the warehouse keys clutched in my right hand, so tightly that my palm was bleeding. I must have forgotten to give them back to Patrick.

"I'm sorry! I'm so sorry," I said. "What happened?"

"You just walked in here on your own and asked me for those drinks. You didn't seem with it, then I thought you must have had some dope, 'cos your eyes were all staring. You just picked up the drinks, went and sat there and started talking to some imaginary friend."

"You scared me, I can tell you. I was just going to get the fuzz to sort you out. You OK? Bad trip, eh?"

"Nothing like that, honestly. I've just been under a bit of strain recently. I think it finally got to me. I'm fine now, again I'm really sorry."

He shrugged and went back to the bar to dry some glasses. He was always drying glasses, which seemed odd, when nobody ever came in.

"Has what's-her-name, Winnie, been in tonight?" I ventured.

"Her? No. They carted her off to a nursing home. Didn't last long. Must have died six months ago."

I wondered if she was with her friend in one of those old houses I'd just walked past, still passing comments about passers-by. I sipped at my beer, the images of that strange dream still fresh. The barman was still wiping the glasses.

"Are you the guy that's been on telly? You are, aren't you? You were mixed up with that Starlings' Yard thing."

I nodded and sighed. He pushed a whisky tumbler up to one of the optics.

"Well, here's a double malt on me. I saw an interview with you on the box. I said to them all, 'That's the guy that used to come in here!' You're a hero round this bit of the Mile, I tell ya. That load of filth were making life miserable for everyone round here, the pubs especially. Christ, pal, 'under a bit of strain'. I'm no' surprised you're going off ye're rocker. No offence."

"None taken. Thanks. I'm glad they've stopped bothering you."

"Bothering! Christ, pal, it was a hundred pounds a week of bother. Couldn't afford to do anything with this place. It's a bloody miserable dump because I was just struggling to keep paying them. Now, here, take a peek at this!"

He produced a blue folder from beneath the counter. In it were the plans an architect had drawn up for 'The Three Sisters'. He was animated and smiling and as he talked, I saw just how deeply the tentacles of Oculus had reached into the city and of the collective misery they had caused. Now here was new hope springing up.

"…and the architects said it just needed me to stop being such a miserable bastard," he was saying, "and, believe me, when this lot's finished this summer, I'm going to be the jolliest fuckin' bastard for miles! Have another, no, on me. And here, have a cigar."

As we puffed away and sipped more Scotch like lords, he asked who I'd been talking to in my trance, and I told him.

"Rosso, eh? He was a big man. Used to come in here a fair bit. I'd give him the lowdown on a few of the goings on. Well, next time you meet him tell him Hamish owes him big style."

"No more owing anyone anything, Hamish."

Chapter 20

The next day, feeling a bit the worse for an unending supply of malt courtesy of Hamish, I went to see Patrick again. He was, as I expected, a little stiff-lipped until I told him that I'd been thinking hard about it and had changed my mind. I wanted to live and work in Leith, after all.

"Oh, thank God," he exclaimed.

"Why does it matter so much to you whether I'm there or not? You'd make more money converting that floor into three separate apartments."

"I would, but money's not the point. Come, let's have some coffee in my office."

So we sipped our coffees and he asked me what had changed my mind. I told him, and also told him why I'd refused the offer yesterday. I even told him about my walk with Robert, Cassie, and Rosso.

"I thought so," he said, "we've talked before about being an outsider and beholden to none."

"Let me assure you no financial arrangement we come to will ever threaten your artistic freedom. You are a great artist, so why should I presume to influence that?"

"In some ways, you're an outsider because of your talent, but in other ways you, dammit, you've so much love and passion in you; no outsider could feel that. You're afraid of being stuck in some comfortable middle class groove. Ha! My friend, you will never be stuck in that rut."

"It doesn't matter whether you're in a mud hut in deepest Brazil, or in a villa in Morningside, you will always find adventure and inspiration. You are that sort of person and you'll be that sort of person wherever you are. I've spent a long time thinking about where you could go to, even if you didn't."

"Why are you taking such an interest in me? I know I can earn you money, but so can your other protégés. What's it about, Patrick?"

"Because we're two of a kind! Don't you see? I don't want to own you – I want us to be friends! We're both the Steppenwolves you talk about. Except we're not."

"Everyone wants to know you and yes, I have a huge circle of acquaintances, two hundred Christmas cards a year! But inside, we're both lonely men, Mark. We can't help being somehow apart and that's very hard."

"I recognise you as a kindred spirit and before you get the wrong idea, I'm not queer. I have women, but never for long. I don't know why. It's just that you are someone who knows me and understands me and I don't want to lose you! I need you!"

He suddenly stopped.

"I've said too much, I'm sorry."

"No, Patrick, you haven't. We understand one other. Now let's just get on with the future, eh?"

We raised our coffee cups to each other and laughed like children. Then Patrick said,

"Wait a minute! That dream–fugue–whatever you had last night, I've an old print somewhere here…"

He went to an old plan chest and opened a drawer. His thin pale hands leafed through a wad of old prints. Eventually, after a deal of rummaging, he produced one, its mount foxed with mould spots.

"Was it something like this?"

It was a mezzotint, in dark blue, showing an old street with a jumble of picturesque but forlorn cottages and tenements.

261

Walking towards the shadowy ships in the background was a little group of two men and two children. The artist had gone so far as to hand tint a red hat on one of the children. I peered at the signature. It was a scrawl, but I could make out the name: Matthew Kemp, 1898.

Epilogue

What happened after I moved into Leith is another tale, but to tie up the loose ends of this episode of my life:

Penny and I remain good friends. I was proud to give her away at her wedding to a civil engineer called Mike two years later. I am godfather to their first child, who they called Robert.

Patrick, after I'd told him about all the hallucinations I was having, virtually frog-marched me along to a psychiatrist friend, who didn't bat an eyelid. Stress – shell-shock – fugue states; he reeled off the words and told me it would pass. Nowadays, it's called post-traumatic stress disorder. He offered me some Nobrium tablets, but I refused, and sure enough, I had no more ghostly visitations. Some things though, remain in the realms of the unexplainable.

Rosso received a posthumous George Cross, not to mention a statue commissioned by Sir William Ross himself, who insisted I execute the commission. I tried to explain that painters are as different from sculptors as plumbers are from joiners, but he brushed that aside. It turned out well in the end, for it was done with love.

Cissy did, in the end, go off to Colonsay to sort herself out, and in the process got to know Colin McLeod a deal better. I was pleased and proud to be his best man when they married on the island the next year.

'The Three Sisters' is now a very popular watering hole with crowds flocking to eat and drink there each night. It is well known for its excellent food and the repartee of its landlord.

What was Starlings' Yard now contains some stylish flats, and a small museum devoted to an occult history of Edinburgh. A plaque marks the spot where Hannah died, and inside you can find her story, luridly told, and a model of the Oculus chamber.

And me? Well, the road winds on, the journey doesn't stop when one tale is told. One thing always leads to another. Should one of those dark, quiet ships take me back to the city of the dead, I will find old friends waiting, and the story will carry on...

Fancy another cracking read?

When Marjorie married George and moved to the country, she never imagined she would be trading her career and independence to spend the next 15 years pandering to his every chauvinist whim. To further add to her discontent, her daughter, on the verge of hormone infested teenagedom has begun to treat her like George does – with contempt. Marjorie has ended up with no friends, no social life and an unhealthy fear of the local village.

Realising that if something doesn't change, she will be swallowed into an abyss of anti-depressants and wine, she decides it's time to venture out into the big wide world again.

This is a story of one woman's search to reclaim her identity. Her antics are: hilarious, erotic, tragic, self-affirming and massively entertaining.

Hartlington Press

Hartlington Press is a new publishing house specialising predominantly, although not exclusively in the rapidly expanding e-book sector. Our first two releases were both from new authors, neither of whom had the confidence or belief in their work to risk the rejection of a mainstream publisher.

So how many other great writers are out there, just needing a bit of a push to make them finish their first masterpiece?

We think quite a few. That's what Hartlington Press is all about - finding talented writers that need encouragement and support.

Do we take unsolicited manuscripts?

Yes!

If you have a completed or partly completed book that you would like us to look at then please fill out the enquiry form on the website or contact us via Facebook.

www.hartlingtonpress.co.uk